Lethal Dose

Lethal Dose

Mike Johnson

99% Press,
an imprint of Lasavia Publishing Ltd.
Auckland, New Zealand

This edition published 2019
First published by Hard Echo Press, 1991

www.lasaviapublishing.com

ISBN: 978-0-9951165-3-5

Also by Mike Johnson

Novels
Zombie in a Spacesuit, 99% Press, Auckland.
Hold My Teeth While I Teach you to Dance, 99% Press, Auckland.
Travesty, Titus Books, Auckland.
Stench, Hazard Press, Christchurch.
Counterpart, Harper Collins, Sydney.
Dumbshow, Hard Echo Press, Auckland (republished by 99% Press, Auckland).
Antibody Positive, Hard Echo Press, Auckland.
Lear: The Shakespeare Company Plays Lear at Babylon. Hard Echo Press, Auckland (republished by 99% Press, Auckland).

Shorter Fiction
Back in the Day: Tales of NZ's Own Paradise Island, 99% Press, Auckland.
Foreigners, Penguin Books, Auckland.

Poetry
Two Lines and a Garden, 99% Press, Auckland.
To Beatrice: Where We Crossed the Line, Pie Press, Auckland.
Vertical Harp: The Selected Poems of Li He, Titus Books, Auckland.
Treasure Hunt, Auckland University Press, Auckland.
Standing Wave, Hard Echo Press, Auckland.
From a Woman in Mt Eden Prison & Drawing Lessons, Hard Echo Press, Auckland.
The Palanquin Ropes. Voice Press, Wellington.

Non-Fiction
Angel of Compassion. TP Press, Auckland.

Children's Fiction
Kenni and the Roof Slide, Illustrated by Jennifer Rackham, Beansprout Press, Auckland.
Taniwha. Illustrated by Jennifer Rackham. Beansprout Press. Auckland.

About the Author

Mike Johnson, fabulist and poet, is recognised as one of New Zealand's leading and innovative writers. He lives on Waiheke Island and teaches creative writing at AUT University in Auckland. His first novel, *Lear: The Shakespeare Company Plays Lear at Babylon*, was shortlisted for the New Zealand Book Awards, his novel *Dumb Show* won the Buckland Memorial Award for Literary Excellence and he won the Frances Kean Award for his short story *Magic Strings*. His first book of poetry, *The Palanquin Ropes*, was co-winner of the John Cowie Reid Memorial Competition. You can find more of his published works at www.lasaviapublishing.com

Preface to the 2018 edition:

Putting the extravagant claims of fictional editor, George Stockman, to one side for a moment (see back-cover blurb), I have never considered *Lethal Dose* to be my finest work. That distinction might belong to *Dumb Show* or *Hold My Teeth While I Teach You to Dance*. There is something scungy, scurrilous and scabulous about *Lethal Dose*, and in that respect, George Stockman was right.

The novel began life as a mystical exploration with the title *The Lament of Rilke's Angel*. 'What's a Rilke?' the real George Stockman (the irascible Warwick Jordan) asked on receiving the manuscript. The surviving passages, after Stockman/Jordan cut out the 'the boring bits' were originally intended to be the hard-bitten, earthly, dirty bits that would counterpoint the mystical triumphs of the prose. Just how those passages might read now, we can't know, as they have long gone the way of wanting words.

These were the last, heady days of Hard Echo Press. Warwick Jordan had already published my first four books, two of poetry and two novels, and *Lethal Dose* was to be our last project together. Warwick Jordan was the most wonderfully mad, or madly wonderful editor a new writer could ask for, and he made it clear when he heard what I was writing that he would have to be included as a character in this, our swansong, if I wanted it to be published by him. That suited me fine, as I was looking for a villain and the newly emergent, freshly saturnine, George Stockman fitted right in to that scurrilous, scabulous world. I had the confidence that any scene that contained Stockman, no matter how rank, would not be left on the cutting room floor. In retrospect, I can see a certain fondness in my portrait of the barefoot publisher even while I was gleefully taking the piss.

The new title was Stockman/Jordan's idea, suggesting the thriller genre, recalling the expression used to measure the deadliness of any pesticide

(LD 50), and a line from a Bob Dylan song about bargaining for salvation and receiving a 'lethal dose'. The term eco-thriller wasn't around then, but fits in retrospect. I've made only the most minor corrections to the Hard Echo Press edition.

Apart from the missing mysticism, the novel seems to try to draw disparate threads together. In the year before writing it, I became involved in the Toxin's Awareness Group on Waiheke Island, and my research, featured in the novel, opened a whole window on the planet's most dirty industry – pesticides. I had to grapple with the issue of how to include factual material into the fiction while keeping the narrative alive. Stockman/Jordan's grand publicity strategy was that Monsanto would sue us for libellous things said about their product, Roundup, we would lose everything, even the shirts off our backs, but become literary causes célèbres and sell zillions of books. Didn't happen. We still have our shirts, and a noir-ish bestseller that never quite was.

At the same time, the eternal conundrums of love and desire, connection, disconnection and friendship were never far away. Love may be a counterweight to evil but infatuation is not. There are some hard lessons in here, pedestals and desecrations. Enough said!

The 'last chance decade' referred to by Stockman was of course the 90s. Almost three decades later, this little brush with evil holds true, and we've probably used up our last chance. Given sea level rise, the final painful scene of this novel (which begs to be turned into a short film) takes on a new dimension.

Mike Johnson, 2018, Waiheke Island.

In a room where people unanimously maintain a conspiracy of silence, one true word of truth sounds like a pistol shot. And, alas, a temptation to denounce it, similar to an acute itching, becomes an obsession which doesn't allow one to think of anything else.

Czeslaw Milosz: Nobel Lecture, 1980.

'All that poetry business, it's a con, isn't it?' Heinz the ad-man spoke with a knowing leer and a red-eyed wink. 'It's just a way of putting out for "It", you can't fool me.' His lips twisted in habitual cynicism while his free hand, the hand not holding the glass, roamed through what was left of his hair, scratching as if searching for phantom lice.

'First the poem, then the bottle of leg-opener. I've watched you guys working, you really know how to soften them up.' Envy had arrived, fortified by three or four jugs of malice. The big man's shirt was undone and his face was starting to go red. A small, delicate spray of hair curled under his Adam's apple. The bar hummed and thrummed to the sound of drinkers.

'You've forgotten about the world of finer feelings, Heinz. The grand passions. That wonderful animation of the heart that runs through a great poem. The invisible element, you know, like electrons zipping through telephone wires.'

Heinz looked at him through one eye as if unsure how serious Clyde was. Clyde Aichen, poet extraordinaire, liked to play the Trickster. Liked to set up his audience to pull a fast one on them. Heinz was not about to be set up.

'Finer feelings? Grand fucking passions? Christ! You're deluding yourself, boyo, child of words. You're a laugh a lap, I'll tell you that.' He nodded to himself, apparently confirming some universal truth and lapped his beer.

'How come I don't have these finer feelings, these grand passions, eh, poet? Poet!' He leaned forward aggressively.

'Because you're a coarse, drunken pig,' Clyde answered amiably, 'incapable of finer feelings of any kind.' He raised his glass. At the bottom there was an amber shadow, as if some living thing moved in the depths.

Heinz Major grinned with something resembling happiness; trading insults was familiar, welcome ground.

13

If the truth be known, he'd picked her out in the first twenty minutes.

Faster than that.

He knew where to look, where she'd be likely to sit, the sort of distance she'd put between herself and others. Passing over the pretty blonde with the red head scarf, he located her midway back, a little off towards one side, marked out by her self-absorbed intensity.

'The morality play is the basis of all literature,' he said. 'The first tales were cautionary by nature.' He laughed. He had a pleasing, baritone laugh he knew was open and spontaneous, boyish and engaging. He had ascribed such a laugh once, in those very terms, to a character in a story, only belatedly recognizing the self portrait. 'At least, that's what folk tales seem to be all about. Animal fables. Children's stories.'

Her look was veiled, apprehending him purely in terms of some inner movement.

'There's always a naughty boy to cry wolf and a naughty girl to stop and talk to one.' A titter of appreciation ran around the class. *Madeleine Farquar.*

He had her attention now. Her face was not at all clear and open, like the woman with the braids, but her eyes were fixed on him from beneath amber curls.

'Isn't all this pretty Jungian?' someone asked. Clyde identified the brash looking young man sitting near the pretty blonde with the red head scarf.

He gave both of them a contrite smile. 'It's hard not to be. They might be the voices of angels or devils for all you know.'

He'd gone too far. The young man had wrinkled up his nose as if some distinctly unpleasant odour had entered the room with the word angel, the three golden oldies in the second row were frozen to their seats by this wild talk, and the clear-faced woman with braids (he'd have to start putting names to faces) was staring down at her empty page, lips pursed together.

Perhaps he was talking directly to her angel, which he suddenly saw, hovering beside her. An angel with abnegating wings. He wasn't prepared for this. He wasn't the kind of person to see visions, and, he figured, nor was the decade he was living through. It looked like someone he knew already but couldn't quite place. He could hear a voice, like a child's, singing a lament. Everything in the room began to undulate, as if he were seeing through moving water.

'These are just metaphors,' he said. 'Ultimately. We can't take our metaphors too literally, can we?' A few students laughed. The woman with the braids smiled. The brash young man looked unimpressed.

Clyde Aichen inhaled deeply. The room smelled of varnish and chalk. And, more faintly, the mossy smell of cemeteries. Perhaps that was the smell of cut grass. A melancholy yellow light shone into the room from Princess Street and the student bustle of Albert Park. A dry ache registered at the back of his throat and he marvelled at how completely she could remove herself from the room leaving only the husk behind; the still, dry shell of herself. Her absence was something palpable. Above her head, her angel hovered, a nimbus through which bars of light passed as they do on a TV screen when the reception is weak and a close-up dissolves into a vaporous skull.

What I really need is a drink, he thought.

Around the sixth or seventh beer, Clyde's doom had lifted, his hangover banished. There was an excitement it took him a moment to identify: a poem behind the foamy nimbus, hard as rock, tart as salt. A genuine Aichen poem to be delivered, by God, in language to fit.

And there was something else, something he didn't want to name lest the name in some way betray him. Something bigger than a poem. Than words. He stared at the still, glazed eye at the bottom of his glass. Here was a riddle for the heart. He smelled the leaves of cemeteries and drew cypress trees in the foam of the bar room table top.

You can't afford to get too pissed, he told himself firmly. For one thing you're driving and you don't want to die in a car. And for another thing you have till Friday to finish the Greenpeace article, for which you have done absolutely no research whatsoever as yet. *Iam proixmus ardet Ucalegon.* Already, neighbour, Ucalegon burns.

'I was very sorry to hear about Jeannette,' Heinz said with such obvious insincerity Clyde knew he must be drunk. Besides, he was several months too late, a year even. 'No man likes to have a woman walk out on him,' he added, smirking. And Clyde had to be drunk, at least a little, to allow the remark to get through to him and remind him of Jeannette, and how empty the house felt when he got home, his hideaway Waitakere Range retreat. Where her presence clung to the rooms the way the smell of a rose clings to a vase, and it was easy enough to be led by the nose, to the memory of how she loved to ride him, woman superior position, galloping him like a horse into orgasm; easy to be led by the treacherous clinging scent, to the dusty room whose walls still resonated to the sound of her straight forward, hearty randiness. Big boned and dark-haired, she'd been a formidable lover.

That was the way he'd met her, and the way he lost her. 'I could fuck anything,' she'd say in her rough voice, grabbing herself between the legs. Could she? Could she have fucked something like Heinz the ad-man, hairy armed and balding, stinking of booze and cigarettes? Probably not, but it was not the kind of thought he wanted to take into the next drink, the drink at which he would stop counting.

'Last time a woman walked out on me I was glad, really fucking glad, you know that.' Heinz closed one eye against the ascending smoke from his cigarette. The other, watery and baleful, fixed on Clyde. 'I went out and got drunk for a week I was so relieved.' He drank, apparently in relief, at the very memory.

Only once did Clyde see Jeannette cry, and that was when she had a miscarriage, spilling clotted blood and tears over the chessboard pattern linoleum of the kitchen. In retrospect, through the prism of a few glasses of beer, that miscarriage was the beginning of the end for them. He had commiserated with her, tried to comfort her, but in reality he had been relieved, relieved enough to get drunk for two nights in a row, leaving her to face the stains which were still there when he got back, a dark faint outline that looked vaguely like Australia, with an extra blob for Tasmania where she'd tried to move.

'Screwed my brains out after she left,' Heinz said in confidential tones, 'whereas when I was with her, I was lucky to score a fuck. How do you like that?'

Clyde didn't like it. He wasn't sure what his friend meant, or if Heinz was a friend at all, or if he cared. No matter how long he stayed here, or how many beers he had, the house would be just as empty when he got home. The dusty room had its own hoard of silence, the sheets an eloquent way of staying unwrinkled, unstained. That emptiness was like gravity, a law of the universe, unassailed by his moods or the fluctuations of his memories. No matter how often he dusted it, the room would retain the odour of its own vacancy. That's why he liked to write about *things* in his poetry: stone, street, mountain, river, wood and water, bird and lizard; they too had a stubborn existence of their own. He never wrote about anything gauzy, like angels, and when he wrote about the emptiness of a room, it was as palpable as a mug of warm beer.

'Listen, brother, my brother,' Heinz said, his voice slurring from confidential to conspiratorial, 'let's get the fuck out of here.' He gestured around the bar. 'This place is giving me the creeps. Let's go and get some fun.' His eyebrows rose like a tide of ants. 'Let's check out some arse.'

'I don't have the money,' Clyde said automatically, looking at his empty glass and touching his chequebook. He was drunk enough to sense something of the mystery of this filling and emptying of glasses. 'Poets are always poor, you should know that.'

The ad-man wrinkled his nose in disgust. 'As poor as they are shameless.' He rattled the money in his pocket. 'Whereas we ad-men have wealth and shame in equal measure.' He made an expansive gesture with his cigarette lighter which, turned up too far, flared with reckless heat. 'I have the largesse for us both.'

At that moment Clyde saw the pretty blonde with the red scarf and brash young man walk in. The brash young man was brashly holding the woman's arm. They went up to the bar, their backs to Clyde and Heinz.

Clyde got up and moved for the door. 'You're quite right, boyo.' He caught the movement of the brass lever in the mirror, the foamy flow of lager. Heinz stumbled after, grinning foolishly.

Outside, Clyde waited in vain for the fresh evening air to sober him up. He'd only had a few beers, the night was salvageable. There were still stars in the sky, like little scars, above the Gulf. Below him, Queen Street tipped down into the bay with precipitous disregard for its mirror-glass cargo. Heinz Major was already forging ahead, wading energetically downstream through chambers of light cast by empty, brightly lit shop windows. This was Clyde's opportunity to turn and walk in the other direction. He could go home, cook himself up a mess of something and do some work, write a few lines before turning in early, he wasn't too drunk and there was a poem to be written. On the other hand he was just drunk enough to have that epic, rudderless sensation that preceded a good binge. Besides, his car was down the hill, in the direction Heinz was walking.

A woman took hold of his arm and smiled into his face. It was just like Moira Andrews to appear from nowhere like that, dark curls awry, a tipsy smile.

'Oh how weary, stale, flat and unprofitable
seem to me the uses of this world,'

she said, with a touch of wistfulness. Perhaps it was the quote itself, recalling the profoundly amateur production of Hamlet that had brought them together two years before in a brief romance behind the hastily painted cardboard walls of Elsinore. Clyde had played Horatio to a befuddled and forgetful Hamlet, while Moira had provided a spirited sleaziness to her mother and Queen role.

When Jeannette left he had turned to Moira again, just as briefly, for the affirmation of touch; and had heard in her plaintive cries of pleasure the same wistfulness that now haunted the corners of her mouth.

'Tis an unweeded garden
That grows to seed...'

He patted his belly and grinned, thinking that this was not the right time to meet Moira Andrews.

'Come and have a quick beer with me,' she said, still holding his arm. 'It's been ages since I last saw you. What's been happening with you?'

'Things rank and gross in nature,' he said, determined to keep it light, glancing down the street to where the Heinz had stalled and was looking back, gesturing with his arm for Clyde to follow. The gesture reminded Clyde of the way Ahab had waved from the back of the white whale just before it sounded forever in the Ray Bradbury film version of *Moby Dick*. That same doomed, heraldic quality.

'I just can't tonight, Moira,' he said, putting his arm lightly around her shoulders. 'I've an article to write for Greenpeace. I'm interviewing someone tomorrow.'

For a fraction of a second he felt her resistance, her subconscious awareness of the lie he was telling by telling her the truth. Her small, perky face turned up to him, illuminated by the hard sodium of the street lamps on Mayoral Drive. With a small shock he realized she was already quite drunk.

'And last time we had a quick beer... Jesus.' He kept his tone light and teasing.

'We tied one on, didn't we?' She grimaced. She didn't want to be reminded of that all-nighter. Nor their foolish, clumsy efforts to make love afterward, lying limp and fatigued in each other's arms, unable to fight off repeated swells of drunkenness and nausea.

'Let's meet sometime,' he said, taking a small step away from her. 'Sometime soon. We'll have lunch and a long talk. A drive somewhere, maybe. Around the bays. A bottle of wine and a picnic lunch.'

'That'd be nice.' Her head fell in a nod but did not lift again. Under her light evening jacket, her body hunched in upon itself. He imagined her stepping up to the bar alone, getting the quick once-over from the brash young man when the blonde glanced the other way.

'Monday. I've got a couple of hours from twelve to two.'

'Monday it is,' he said sincerely, taking another step back.

They stood that way for a moment, with nothing to say, feeling more awkward than they had need to feel.

'Monday it is,' she repeated, attempting to match his lightness of tone, her voice light and shivery.

'And we will take a drive,' he said warmly. 'Around the harbour. We'll go to some bay and watch the tide come in.' Like we used to, he was going to add, when Jeannette left me and all I wanted to do was sit in my shagged old Toyota Corolla and drive, drive, drive. Or stop at a beach somewhere to polish off a bottle and watch the movement of light on the water.

She caught it all as he knew she would, and she lifted her face again. Sitting upon it, as if borrowed from a stranger or from the free floating air, was a curious, tiny, will-o'-the-wisp smile. That smile unhinged

Clyde Aichen, scatter-flattened his every stratagem for getting away from her intact. He recalled, with a half-boozy inappropriateness, one of the great smiles in modern literature, the love-smile in *The French Lieutenant's Woman*, dotingly described over several paragraphs by a connoisseur of smiles. Moira's smile was nothing like its literary predecessor, it was far too tiny, too threaded with cross currents, too fleeting an impression.

He'd seen this smile once before, as their Elsinore Romance neared its end, and she'd told him her theory that in the bulk of relationships, or attempted relationships, one partner feels more intensely, loves more passionately, nurses more hopes and dreams, than the other. It was a sad, tragic picture that emerged amongst the shabby props against the murmured backdrop of the play. Male and female, female and male were like the proverbial ships in the night that pass each other with a few blinkered signals, doomed even in their yearning to mismatched intensities. All but a lucky few.

I fall through the hole in your smile and drown, he thought, briefly considering whether or not he could use a line like that before discarding it in disgust. At times such lines slipped through… there are extenuating circumstances… but this was not one of them. He must be drunk to even consider it.

Clyde rejoined Heinz to find the ad-man had lost his sense of humour. He was breathing heavily and his eyes stuck out from his face in a full, thyroid glare.

'Poets have time to stand around picking up handkerchiefs,' he said contemptuously. 'Who's your lady friend?'

'Teaches pottery. I see her at the college.'

The ad-man seemed a little mollified as they set off walking. He thrust his chest out and breasted the air like a swimmer. 'I thought women who did pottery were tall angular creatures in dungarees and short hair living on brown rice and tofu.'

'That's because you think in clichés, ad-man.'

'Get fucked, poetaster.'

'She might look small but she's strong. She's no frail. I've seen her work fifteen hours at a stretch getting a firing together. But she's so light-boned you could lift her up with one hand.'

'What did she want, she was all over you like tomato sauce on chips.' There was still a trace of belligerence, but now the danger had passed it was shifting into a prurient curiosity.

'She wanted to have a drink with me.'

'Then why aren't you in there right now, nodding in sympathy, filling up her glass.' They were passing the pie cart, through a zone of stewed coffee and fried food smells. The pie cart always looked so seventies, to Clyde. Like a piece of history. Comfortable, familiar. While around them old Auckland was being pulled down and the mirror-glass towers of the corporate rich were rising, like slivers of ice, from the ruins of old warehouses and Georgian office blocks. Clyde wondered how long the pie cart would last here, or if it might be eternal, frozen in time.

'It's funny.' Clyde had a silly urge to explain himself. 'We had an affair which lost its taste. She started to get serious.'

The ad-man shook his head in sympathy. Such incomprehensible female behaviour was not unknown, even to him.

'Even though I like her, I mean we're friends, I sort of avoid her. She knows it too, that's the curse of it.'

Why he should want to explain himself to Heinz was quite beyond him. As usual, when he had such silly urges, he regretted what came out of his mouth. It wasn't anything like what he had wanted to say. It was like listening to somebody else talking.

Heinz, also, was ruminating on the matter and had come to his own conclusions based on what he imagined Clyde was telling him. 'There's no fathoming cunt,' he said gloomily. 'Sometimes it twitches, sometimes it doesn't.'

Heinz found the kind of dive he was looking for, near the waterfront at the back of Fort Street where the massage parlours and fantasy houses lit up after dark like toffee apples.

For Clyde the whole thing was a mistake. His few beers would carry him this far, but not a step further.

'Let's go to a bar,' he said.

'I'm going in,' Heinz announced. His complexion had become choleric, his expression fixed.

'I'll come in and wait for you. I've lost interest. Wasn't interested in the first place, actually.'

'Perhaps you should go back to your potter bird.'

'That mightn't be a bad idea,' Clyde admitted. He followed in the wake of his big companion.

'The trouble with you poets is that you don't live in the real world,' Heinz said over his shoulder. 'If you lived in the real world you wouldn't be poets.'

'What would we be?' He'd written a poem once about burning down his library, inspired by Elias Canetti's *Auto-da-Fé*. In the poem, the inferno of exploding books contrasted with a lazy arc of smoke seen from a distance, by a man, say, walking his dog, or a woman, say, hanging out washing.

'Ad-men, like me, or whores, like this woman.' Heinz gestured to a fat blonde who sat behind a counter chewing on something.

'Any shit from you and you'll be out on your arse,' the woman said without ceasing to chew. She had a trick of not moving her head so that her large, hooped earrings hung still, vibrating only slightly to her speech.

They were in a small, hastily partitioned entrance painted purple and decorated by the covers of x-rated videos. Most portrayed women in various forms of contortion and bondage.

'My friend's a man of discernment, a poet no less,' Heinz said to the woman. 'Do you have any refined women here, or are they all like you?'

A large Samoan man stepped through a curtain hanging behind the woman and glanced at them indifferently.

The woman jerked her thumb. 'Videos that way, raps and fantasies that way. Fifteen dollars to get into the videos but you can stay as long as you like.' She glanced up at the large Samoan. 'Here's one with a lip,' she said to him. Her earrings turned in a lazy arc. The man grunted.

'How much for a woman?'

22

The woman paused. Unsurprisingly, she couldn't fit him up as a cop. 'Twenty dollars for a five minute warm-up,' she said. 'Then fifty to finish, if you want to. You pay your twenty here and give the fifty over in there,' she inclined her head to the 'rap and fantasy' door. She slipped something into her mouth.

'I'll wait for you at the Soldier's Arms,' Clyde said, planning to go straight home. 'You can have a drink through there,' the woman said, smiling pleasantly at Clyde. 'Bar prices, no obligation.'

Clyde opened his mouth.

'Just five dollars entry fee,' she said. Heinz was already paying it, plus his twenty dollars warm-up fee. Crushed and wrinkled, the money dropped out of Heinz's meaty fist, the notes slowly unwrinkling on the counter as if in pain.

A few moments later they found themselves in a larger room lined with settees. Three young women sat chatting quietly. An older man sat in an easy chair near them, his elbows on his knees, his face in his hands. Ornately framed bad taste paintings hung from the walls.

As soon as they entered, the three women turned in their direction. Shamed, Clyde looked away, not before noting one of the women, the stillness of her posture. It's not possible he thought, refusing to confirm his impression. It's just not possible that I should know one of these women.

As they sat down on the nearest settee, one of the young women rose and came over to them. She wore a white blouse and a simple short skirt that offered easy access to the eye. Her calves were well shaped and slick with nylon. She sat down beside Heinz and smiled at them both.

'What can we do for you boys? I'm Betty.'

'I bet you are,' Heinz said handing her the receipt for his twenty dollars. The wind seemed to have gone out of his sails, Clyde noted; the ad-man was suddenly tense and nervous.

'A warm-up? Alright. That'll be fun. What's your name?' Betty had a low, sultry voice, perfectly suitable for warm-ups.

'Charles Atlas.'

She looked inquiringly at Clyde.

'Clyde,' Clyde said. 'And I just want a beer, a cold one, thanks.'

'Sure, Clyde. Do you want to relax and have a beer first too, Charles?'

'I want it now,' Heinz said in a strained voice. 'Sure, Charley.' Her voice lowered. 'What's your fantasy? We have nurses, Amazon Island, schoolgirls, air-hostesses, lion tamers…' She glanced briefly at Clyde, '…girl next door, Victorian maid…'

'That's the one,' Heinz said, breathing heavily, as if in a diver's suit. The other woman was coming across the room with his beer, Clyde knew, although he didn't look up.

'Victorian maid,' Betty said with a giggle. 'You know, Charley, that's one of my favourites.'

Clyde's beer appeared on the low table in front of them. The hand that delivered it was young and gracefully shaped. He glanced up but the light was behind her. How could he know? He hadn't seen her face clearly in class, just a general impression, an ambience for Christ sake, a hovering angel. He was angry now. Angry with Heinz and with himself. And with Moira. And with fucking Jeannette who walked out one day while he was dead to the world sleeping off a hangover. Gone, without so much as a kiss-your-arse. He looked across at the older man who still sat in the same posture, head between his hands.

'Let's go then,' Heinz said.

Betty's eyes widened with anticipated delight.

The woman in front of Clyde was young, maybe nineteen or twenty, although she was made up to look younger. Maybe a student who couldn't pay her fees, he'd heard of that; it was all part of the brave new decade. Why pay for a kid's education when they can whore their way through uni? Ain't the free market wonderful?

She had high cheek-bones and widely spaced eyes that slanted a little, making her look Eurasian or East European. She wore a black Cleopatra wig and a long falling gown loosely tied as far as her waist with lace ribbons. No amber curls. Still he couldn't tell.

'Five minutes,' Heinz said, getting to his feet and giving Clyde a heavy look. He held up five fingers as if Clyde were deaf or had not understood him.

Clyde paid Cleopatra for the beer, noting that the price was a dollar a bottle more than in a bar. Still, with the beer installed on his lap, he felt a little more at ease.

'I'm Cleo,' the young woman said, giving him his change and sitting down beside him. She was attractive, there was no denying that; her hands in particular were slender and finely wrought. He gazed at them, determined to commit them to memory. The ambience was the same. The same veiled feel; that capacity for profound absence. Her voice was light, languid and detached. He tried to remember if she had said anything in class.

'You sure you don't want a warm-up, Clyde, isn't it? Maybe a rap session, some sweet talk.'

'No thanks,' he said, adding feebly, 'I'm warm enough now.' Clyde hesitated. Quickly he said, 'What I would really like is to watch my friend, you know… *watch* him.'

It was her turn to hesitate. 'We don't do that here.'

'I'm sure you do.' Clyde pulled out his chequebook. 'I'll pay. How much?' There was an urgency in his voice. Cleo glanced at the chequebook. 'He knows. He likes someone watching. He'll expect me to tell him how great he looked, what a stud he was and that kind of thing.'

Cleo looked dubious. This kind of thing was above her pay scale. An older woman, dressed in what might have been a black ballgown, joined them. She listened to Clyde, inspected his chequebook and a moment later he was following Cleo into a small cubical, bare but for a plum covered mattress on a low bed. On the wall hung a small painting, depicting a bucolic English rural scene. In the foreground three huntsmen on horseback, in full fox-hunt regalia, confronted a naked woman who knelt on the turf before them, her head bent. Behind her a large, chocolate-box hunting dog was in the act of lowering its nose towards her buttocks.

Cleo pulled the painting aside to reveal a peep-hole. Before putting his eye to it, he stared at her more closely, aware of the quietness of this small room. The bed was more like a wide massage table. The walls were painted a subdued pink.

'Full body massage, thirty dollars,' she said, noting his glance. She was wearing enough make-up to give her face an ashen, mask-like appearance, like the face of a Nu dancer, white against the clean black cut of her wig.

Her eyes, wide and mobile met his with a professional boldness behind which there was a flicker, maybe of nervousness. That was not it either, the flicker was something else; if he took a step sideways, caught her from another angle, he could see it: a strobed undulation of luminous wings. Flame-like, they were, growing out from her shoulders.

How embarrassing. He'd already seen the same thing today, in class. *Madeleine Farquar*. Was Clyde Aichen, whose poems were as rich as dung, full of solid landscapes and recognizable people, going to start writing like William Blake who saw angels in trees where apples should be and heard celestial music where there should only have been wind and mountains? Already Clyde was seeing angels weeping in classrooms and auras in brothels.

The room next door, as seen from the peep-hole, was a replica of the room he was in. The same pink walls and plum coloured mattress. Betty was standing side on to him, dressed in a short black skirt with a frilly white apron and a white, fluffy sleeved blouse. Heinz the ad-man, naked, knelt before her, leaning forward, his cheek resting on her calf. His bulky shoulders were rounded forward, giving him the appearance of a kneeling fish. So still were they both that Clyde immediately imagined they had been that way for a long time. A still life. A pose held for an invisible painter long beyond the point of comfort.

Betty had a hard, neutral look on her face at complete variance to the provocative stance of her body, while Heinz stared out into the middle distance with an abstracted, forlorn expression. Clyde noticed a peculiar mark on his inner arm, like a tattoo. Slowly he drew back, raising his eyes to her face. She immediately assumed a coquettish, simpering reluctance, better intentioned than well-acted. Heinz lifted her dress and put his face between her legs and remained that way for a moment as Betty's face relapsed into a neutral, stony expression. As Heinz urged his body forward against her leg, tucking his buttocks in the way a dog might, Clyde saw the source of the problem. It hung, limp and tired between the ad-man's legs; nothing more than a bent reed.

Heinz suddenly pulled back, anger flashing across his face. He said something and Betty crouched, took the bundle of his genitals in both hands and lowered her mouth to them. Putting his hands on her shoulders, Heinz gazed up at the ceiling as if he were praying. A moment later a tear made a glistening track down his cheek. Betty pulled back, turning her head towards Clyde as if revealing, just for him, the sour taste on her lips.

Her attentions had done nothing for the stricken Heinz whose member still hung glazed, bowed before the abdicated territory of frilly knickers and black garters. As she pulled away he sank from his knees to his buttocks and bent over himself, cradling his flaccid genitals in one hand with a gentle valediction.

Betty stood up and ran her hand through his hair with an unexpectedly tender gesture. The big man hung his head in defeat.

'He can't get it up,' Clyde whispered to Cleo. His voice was conspiratorial, there was a delicious thrill in betraying the ad-man this way. It was this, the humiliation of Heinz, that Clyde had wanted to see with his own eyes. The very reason he'd asked for this little sojourn at the peep-hole.

'That often happens,' Cleo whispered back, fellow conspirator.

In the other room, Heinz reached for his trousers. While standing on one leg to pull on his underpants, he half fell over. Cleo's arms slipped around Clyde's waist as he giggled, her fingers idling across the buckles of his belt.

Gently, Clyde unhooked her arms and moved for the door. He wanted to touch this beautiful girl, he felt sure he could do better than Heinz, but something, maybe fear, held him back. When he left he felt curiously purified, as if he had just received some kind of absolution, or had had a long, cool shower.

By the time Heinz emerged from his room, Clyde was installed on the couch once more, his half drunk beer secured in one hand. Across from him the older man remained bent over. Cleo had risen to attend to a new client and Clyde felt a peculiar and unwarranted pang of regret as she left. At the same time his impression that she was the same woman he'd noticed in class was fading; certainly if she'd recognised him she'd given no indication whatsoever, and he was convinced, as he watched her walk across the room, that she'd forgotten him utterly, her only concern now being the nervous young man who'd just come through the door.

Heinz sauntered over to the couch, a satisfied smirk on his face. He sat down, took Clyde's beer out of his hand and threw it back with a practised, devil-may-care gesture.

'Let's go, brother, my brother.'

'Not staying for the full course?' Clyde retrieved his glass.

'Don't have to, mate.' He clicked his tongue and lifted the corner of his mouth. 'Shot my bolt right into her cake-hole.' He favoured Clyde with a superior smirk. 'Why pay seventy bucks when you can pay twenty? You poets may be into hour-long epic fucks, but you know us ad-men,' he clicked his tongue again and nodded his head as if he had the whole universe sewn up. He wriggled his eyebrows, 'We only get in to get out. Very Hemingway. Like the sound of a shotgun going off in someone's mouth. Thank you, mam. Short and sharp.' He laughed, apparently at the memory of his moment of triumph; 'You should have seen the look on her face.'

Clyde considered the look on his. 'Let's get out of here then.' Heinz was full of easy, satisfied jocularity and bonhomie. 'You mirror my sentiments exactly, Shakes old son.'

As they neared the door, Cleo stood back for them, her hand at the nervous young man's elbow. The young man gave Clyde a brief, hard glance. Clyde contrived to glance at her but she vanished from the corner of his vision leaving a faint phosphorescence, something that sparkled and was gone just like, God help him, the fairy dust that falls from Tinkerbell's wand when the little Darlings fly from their window to join the lost boys on the Island of Neverland.

His apparently upbeat mood carried Heinz out onto the pavement. Then he turned on Clyde, his face sour.

'What the fuck's eating you, word-man? You walk on broken glass or something.'

'I'm going home,' Clyde said. Seemed like he'd been going home most of the night, even before the first beer.

'Christ!' Heinz threw his chest out, 'The night is but a pup.' His voice was hearty. 'Let's put away a couple of beers. We'll go to a Chinese place and have a fry up.'

'I've got to go. I've got an article to write on the chemical issue.'

'Chemical shemical, don't bullshit me. I'm not so fuckin easy to fool.'

'No bullshit. I'm in deadly earnest.'

'Deadly Earnest? Never met him. Does he write?'

'I'm going home.'

'Just because *you* didn't get your rocks off you go all morose. Jesus, you had your chance with Cleo the Clit. Don't get into a huff now because you blew it.' Sneeringly he added, 'I saw the way you looked at her. There was lust written all over your poet's face. You can't fool me.'

'I'm not in a huff, Heinz. I'm just tired. I've had enough of this.' It was more than tiredness of the body, rather a moral weariness that went much deeper.

'Had enough slumming for the night, huh, word-man, hacking about with the hack? Had enough slumming with the bestial Heinz? The bestial Heinz who has his snout in all kinds of filth. Who has just tupped a whore with his rampant woody.'

'Aw, come on Heinz. I've no axe to grind.'

'A poet without an axe to grind is like a donkey without his bray. Like a whore without a honey pot. That's when you hear what comes out the other end. Fuck, I need a drink!'

'I like that. Did you just make it up?'

'You can have it. Come on.' He was pleading. 'Let's have a quick snifter. A little double brandy to finish off the night. I'll even pay with some filthy lucre I got from Moloch for peddling his product.'

'No.' Clyde turned away, thinking of a little nip he had left in a bottle at home. A couple of fingers worth. A nice little nightcap. He could sit in his favourite chair and look out over the city that Moloch built. That god of avarice, the god of Ponzi schemes, the god that neither pardoned nor forgave.

Heinz grabbed his arm. 'Fuck you, poet! You think you're so fucking superior, so fucking aloof, sitting in the whorehouse with your finger up your arse sipping a beer, no doubt pondering the fallen State of Man. Who are you to sit in fuckin judgement? Who are you? You despise me, don't you? Every time you open your mouth you sneer at me. You're so full of hot shit contempt. You see me as an inferior breed. Heinz the ad-man, the dregs of humanity. I know. I'm not stupid. I see the way you look at me, just as I saw the way you looked at that piece of arse.' A cunning note entered his voice. 'Who knows, after a quiet drink you might feel like a bit more, if you can overcome your fucking scruples.' A terrible bitterness entered his voice. 'You'll regret this night, of course, in the morning. You'll make a resolution to stay out of my way. You'll tell yourself you're glad you didn't screw the whore, but underneath you'll wish you had. You'll gloat over that moral triumph while you shake your head in disgust at me. Fuck you! I know you despise me. I know who I am. I'm a bag of shit. I'm Heinz, the ad-man, easy to read as a can of beans. Heinz the Hack who turns out words for the shit-machine for booze money. Shit words for the shit machine. Just call me Heinz the hideous. But what makes you think you're so much fucking better than me? Hypocrisy rules ok? I use words, just the same as you. I gotta get them from somewhere, just the same as you. You gotta fool people with them, just the same as me. Beguile Moloch's multitudes. Make people believe things you've just made up.' He beat his chest with one rhetorical fist. 'I've got to put the words down, haven't I, just the same as you? Don't I work for deadlines, just like you? Don't I sweat over the difference between assonance and asinine, just like you? But you! You use people as leverage in some private game you think you're playing with God. A game only poets get to play, in realms of pure, unpolluted language. Only of course God isn't playing. That's the whole fucking joke.' He shook his head unbelievingly. 'Who'd believe it? What a shemozzle.'

He stepped ceremonially onto his back heel.

'I'm going to smash your smug poet's face in. Taste your words, word-taster.'

He swung wildly.

Clyde dreamed he met the poet Rilke, who'd turned into an angel, and who floated luminous in a starless night.

He woke abruptly, snapping open to the early light. This was the writing hour, and he wasn't going to waste it by lying in bed. Aichen poems were no different from any other in this respect, they had to get written sometime and the morning was the best time. The best poems he'd ever written, or read for that matter, had that quality of seeming to have just emerged, still fresh, from some anterior dream.

It was a short walk from the bed to the writing desk, and the inert eye of his word processor, even for legs that were somewhat shaky. He ignored the inert eye and pulled out some paper, grabbing a pen from a pottery cup Moira had given him when Jeannette had walked out with most of their marriage's accumulated loot. He did a small, meditative practice, imagining himself as gull, soaring high, seeing through its eye the sharp particularity below. This dissolved into a picture of Heinz berating him, swinging at him with his hammy fists. He grinned nervously at the memory, and doodled a grinning face on the margin of his paper. It struck him that something dreadful had happened at that parlour, something wiped from his memory.

He stared down at the blank paper and doubt ate in at the edges of his confidence. As yet there were no words, no act as such, merely the courtship of words and paper. He recalled Heinz's words, 'I gotta get them from somewhere, just the same as you.'

He recalled, also the strange mark on Heinz's arm and wondered where he'd seen it before. He thought of a poem, how words were a way of reclaiming memory. He tried not to think about the article he had to write, and idly looked over some notes, scanning them for likely lines. A starting place. A hook for memory. Among the bits of prose and found language there were a few finished first drafts. All were very conscientiously Aichen-like in their appearance, solid, massed with stanzas of eight or twelve lines each. His typical lines, he noticed, urged towards that same place – a cleft of hills, a wedge of sky, a scribble of bush, a face or a figure; all lit by the same quick, animal light. They were peopled with finely observed beings doing very ordinary things like climbing onto a tractor or taking money from a dispensing machine. They reminded him a little of Bruegel with their comic grotesquery and richness. This was the Aichen trademark, his distinctive voice. 'I know an Aichen poem by the time I'm three lines in,' a critic had written approvingly.

He shaded a cigarette into the mouth of his grinning doodle. Let the doodle smoke and save Aichen his lungs; he had no desire to start with tobacco this early in the day. A settled stubbornness came over him. There was no way he could command words, but he could outwait them, trick them into existence.

When the first lines appeared, they were spare, vulnerable, intensely self-revealing. Three or four groups of two or three thin lines. Four or five pages. Clyde stared at them with amazement, got up and walked into the kitchen to make coffee. He hadn't written like that in years. Fifteen years, to be exact, when he had met Jeannette in Greece and had written her a cycle of love poems. Words, hot and hasty, with no solidity at all.

He shoved the coffee into his perc and ran back to the desk, flipping the switch on his word processor. While its blank eye blinked open, Clyde Aichen looked anxiously over his lines. Not the meaning, just the shape of them on the page, their feel for the white borders, for the spaces they inhabited. Immediately he saw how slender and frail they looked, dwarfed by the blankness around them.

There was a shy, half revealed feel to the shape the line endings made down the page; at the same time there was a certain boldness in the run-on lines, a readiness to leap into the empty space of a verse break at the merest hint of pressure.

The telephone rang on the kitchen table and on the bench the coffee boiled over, but Clyde stared down at the page, running over his words with lips moving, reading like a child, listening to them, not to the meaning, but the sound they made, the way they came up out of silence and went back into it again, like dolphins breaking the surface of a wave. This sound he played back through his ear, testing it for resonance and melodic virtue. There was a certain tensile strength in the sounds, but also a lyrical vulnerability that made him wince. He ignored the phone and ran for the coffee, quickly rinsing a cup. The telephone stopped ringing. He contemplated pulling the plug on it.

There was more yet, much more, but why write like this?

He returned to his desk and quickly put the lines onto the screen, where he could see them in print, pin them down in the no-nonsense

Geneva font with its straight, unadorned lettering.

In terms of content these lines were both particular and elusive, which pleased him, but they could bear no weight, no critical scrutiny, so tense and defenseless were they. Reading them through again he realised what they sounded like. A prelude. That elusiveness, that sense of preparedness and suspension, the tentative reaching forward for the major motif, which has yet to declare itself.

He wrote a few more lines, straight onto the screen, feeling the gentle, sustained movement. Restless, he jumped up and went back to the coffee pot, taking a sideways look at the empty whisky bottle on the table. Was he about to start writing fragile imagist poems, like a beginner, for Christ's sake? Lines with an unresolved centre like a soft chocolate?

That wasn't the Aichen style at all. He glanced up to where he'd pinned on the wall Charles Olsen's statement, *the material determines the form.*

This apparently simple dictum came into his mind suddenly possessed of a gnomic force. What was simple became mysterious – that's all very well, Mr Olsen, but what *is* the material? Do we ever fully know?

The phone rang again and he got up with disgust. Somewhere he'd slipped a cog, reverted; a marble had rolled into some familiar dusty spot.

It could happen to the best of poets.

'Hello Moira,' he said, wishing he had pulled the plug on the phone.

'You still unnerve me, when you do that.'

'I'm a shrewd guesser.'

'So you say. I hope I wasn't too obnoxious last night?'

By obnoxious she meant pissed.

'Not that I remember. I remember somebody taking a swing at me, but that wasn't you. And I remember an angel with fairy-dust on her wings, but that wasn't you either.'

'Fairy-dust? Did you get drunk? Smoke something?'

'Me? Drunk? You must be kidding.'

They both laughed.

'Actually I only had a few beers.'

'So did I,' she said fervently, 'But I've still got a bit of a head this morning.'

'It's the chemicals in the booze.' Trailing the phone, he walked back to his desk, picked up his pen and added cartoon angel wings to the back of his grinning, smoking doodle, penning in little asterisks for the fairy-dust.

Now his doodle looked positively demonic.

'I think it's time for me to knock the booze on the head.' Her voice was hoarse.

'You must have a hangover.'

'Me? Hangover? You must be kidding.'

They both laughed. He reached down into the poem and pulled a couple of lines out, watching them disentangle from the rest. Christ! Pull a line out and the whole thing unravels like a badly knitted jersey, how was he expected to write this way? He put words back in, different words, something to toughen up the feel of the thing. This was the Aichen work-back method, to go over every line scrutinising it, calling it to account, upgrading it, until what was left was as solid, turned and fired as a Moira Andrews clay sculpture.

'I'm serious, Clyde. I've been thinking about it for a long time.'

'So have I. Giving up's easy, I do it every morning.'

'You silly bastard. You're incorrigible. Anyway, you stole that from somebody.'

'Incorruptible, did you say? I deny everything. And steal nothing.' He fattened doodle's cheeks and put heavy rings under his eyes. Now he had a debauched doodle.

'I've got to do something, Clyde. I've been living broke too long. I've got just enough to see me through the day. Just enough energy, just enough time, just enough money, just enough faith, just enough thread. Always on the edge.'

'There is no edge,' Clyde said, quoting, he hoped, some famous postmodernist. Someone who'd never heard of Gerald Manley Hopkins:

"O the mind, mind has mountains; cliffs of fall
Frightful, sheer, no-man-fathomed. Hold them cheap
May who ne'er hung there".

'Famous last words.'

'Cliffs of fall,' Clyde said.

'You can say that again.'

The page still did not look right. The new lines were the problem, they looked patched in, as if they had been stolen from some other work. Rather than buttressing the poem these lines drew attention to its frailty. He put the old words back and the page settled into its old shape. Their unsettling transparency.

'What are you doing this morning?' There was an odd edge to the question.

'Writing. Apparently.' Was there no room to move at all in this house of glass? He was naked. Exposed. There was none of the old Aichen density to clothe him.

'Working on anything special?'

'I'm revisiting my Juvenilia.'

'Rewriting old poems?' She sounded shocked. 'You should never do that. That's one thing about clay, you can never fire the same piece twice.'

'No. I mean in spirit. He mimicked a carping critic's voice, *'shows a persistent, residual weakness for lyrical endings.'*

'No shit? Well I've gone abstract. Totally right brain stuff. I don't even look at what I'm doing, I just let my hands do all the work.'

'Gee Moira, I'm really happy for you.'

They both laughed. Clyde Aichen, twice winner of a Prestigious Poetry Prize, sipped coffee and shaded Dorian Gray eyebrows into his doodle. The first sun scratched in around the curtains and the glass, creasing the opposite wall. The poem sat on the page and the screen, intensely inward, the lines reaching back into themselves for some unseen object, leaving their flanks exposed.

'You're such a bastard, Aichen, how come you always manage to cheer me up?'

'That's twice you've called me that this morning. My ear is starting to hurt.' A note of false hurt entered his voice.

'Christ, Clyde, I just get depressed sometimes. A spiritual person once told me I had a black hole inside me. You know, one of those cosmic things that sucks all the energy into itself.' She made slurping noises down the telephone. 'Apparently you get them on the spiritual plane as well. Whirlpools of hunger. They suck out all your life force and feed on your feelings until there's nothing left.'

'Agents of Entropy.' He said in a dramatic voice. 'They can be zapped with powerful affirmations.' He began to draw a second doodle with the vague intention of providing a companion for the first. The Bride of Doodle. The wings and fairy dust came with practised gestures, the face was done before he saw it, before he had eyes or a mouth for it. He lets his hands do the work.

'You can mock but what the fuck do you know, Clyde Aichen? What the fuck do you care?'

'You humble me. I never did like Science Fiction. None of that trendy stuff ever convinced me.'

'I know,' her voice was indulgent. 'I've read your work too, remember?'

Would she ever read this stuff he was writing now, he wondered, hoping not. He glanced over the page again, making small adjustments to enable the lines to feel more at home in their skin of words, struck again by the illusive, elliptical quality of the movement from line to line. In their very frailty there was a certain quality, an opening to a silence which might yet prove interesting. Suddenly he wrote two more lines, swift and unbidden. More of the same. A whisper of secrets back into the electronic hive of his Mac P.

'...work this morning. The clay seemed dead, like it was made of bones. Or just a lifeless muck hanging in my hands. All I wanted to do was have a drink.'

'Did you have one?' Clyde thought of his own empty whisky bottle.

There was silence from the other end. Clyde gave his Bride of Doodle a Medusa hairstyle and a pair of wide-spaced, carefully almond-shaped eyes.

'Not yet.'

There was an awkward moment between them, as there had been on the footpath outside the Queen's Head. Then have one, Clyde thought, for Christ's sake have one and be done with it.

His last few lines were more sinuous, more wiry even, but they still insisted on their personal, revelatory function. He was secretly embarrassed, which was the way he'd felt when his first work had gone into print. It's a good thing poems can go into the bottom drawer where, for a time at least, their nuisance value is minimal.

'I just rang to ask you about Monday. I mean, you said you'd meet me for lunch and maybe we'd go for a drive sometime.'

'Yeah.'

'Just want to make sure it's what you really want to do. I hope you weren't just being polite?' There was a quiver in her voice.

'I'm never polite. I'm socially inept, remember?' He doodled a fine lacy bow for the Bride of Doodle.

'I just don't want you to do me any favours.' It was an eternal line and a bad one. Hangover language. She'd probably picked it up unconsciously from some 1940s cult move, Bette Davis or somebody. It was the sort of line you deliver with a cigarette dangling out of the side of your mouth. People generally have no idea where their language comes from.

'I'm too much of a bastard to do that,' he said in a Mafioso voice. He remembered Heinz the ad-man, his tirade against Clyde Aichen. Has not an ad-man eyes, a nose, an arsehole? However, looking down at his newly emergent Bride of Doodle, complete with small, sensitive lips, he knew that in one respect at least Heinz had been wrong. He did not tell himself how glad he was to have avoided fucking Cleo. He felt no relief that he'd at least escaped *that*. No gloating moral triumph.

Merely regret.

When the movement finished what remained were not lines of poetry so much as a series of intimations and gaping half-thoughts. He sat staring at the paper for a long time before he could accept that there were no more lines, no more words that day, or at least that hour.

He got up, scored a can of beer from the fridge and wandered out onto his deck wondering where the morning had gone. His immediate view was of his own property, falling away gently into a bush-lined valley. Up against the deck, and tending to tower over it, was his pet flax bush complete with black stem. Behind it, taller still, reared his favourite, an ancient cabbage tree whose rustling dignity and curved grace was a steady source of consolation and delight. In his more superstitious moments he took the tree's virtues as indicative of some great vegetable wisdom for which his poor, volatile human mind was unfit yet sorely in need.

A gentle spring wind was now obligingly rustling the leaves. A quiet meditative sound, like the running of water, lightly disturbing the tree's calm. Clyde sat on the edge of the deck, as near to it as he could get, dealt with the can of beer as cans of beer must be dealt with and allowed his mind to unfocus, to drift sideways out over the deck into the horizontal air where there were no words at all. His mind was full of chaos; he knew that; it would never be any different.

In the quiet, caught up in the rustle of the cabbage tree the way seaweed may be dragged on a rock by the action of a retreating wave, he heard a voice, high and thin. He went very still and listened, unable to decide the real source of it. It sounded like the singing of a child. Like something he'd heard before.

He went inside for another can.

Clyde Aichen, fearless investigative reporter, headed south in his battered old Toyota, sucking on a carton of apple and orange juice. The early afternoon city-bound motorway traffic came up at him on the other side of the median strip like a great exhalation of metal. Overhead, a helicopter banked steeply, broadcasting traffic flow updates to the cars below via local radio.

Clyde wasted no time in pointing his intrepid profile in the direction of Drury and the farms that lay beyond, the rich fruit and vegetable growing region on the sunny side of the Bombay Hills. Out there lay his next story for Greenpeace. A pesticide victim; someone who could prove it. Don Bealter; farmer, war veteran.

He badly needed an angle on this story and hoped the coming interview would give him one. Something quick and easy to write up. Sharp and to the point.

On the other side of the median cars sped towards the fury of Moloch to do their Lord's work; ahead, towards the Bombay Hills, the sky was stripped with asphalt clouds. A good, clean story, four or five thousand words. Grab the cheque and run.

He turned off at Drury and his Toyota bitched its way through the traffic to the open country. Soon he was travelling through fruit farms and market gardens. Coming to a roadside stall, he stopped and bought a bag of early apricots. He munched at these as he drove, trying not to think about Moira or his abortive night with Heinz; trying not to think obvious things like why the apricots of childhood always tasted sweeter. The poem was there too, at the back of his mind, cradled in words but not immune to smells. It made him blush to think about it.

The Bealter farmhouse was situated back off the road down a tree lined drive, poplars with orchards in behind. A cow grazing on a well-tended pasture lifted its head to watch him drive past, munching lugubriously. The farm had a clean, smart look about it, but there were some signs of recent neglect. Sprigs of gorse were springing up in the pasture and the drive needed some shingle fill. Two dogs tied to the side of the barn came rushing out at him as he pulled up to the wooden farmhouse, dancing on the end of their chains and barking hoarsely, their collars biting into their throats.

'Good doggies,' Clyde said to the slavering animals, slamming the car door. The doggies were not convinced.

The house was of the old, Colonial style farmhouse, with a wide veranda. Clyde noticed that it was neat and well-kept. The paintwork looked new.

Lorna Bealter was waiting for him in the shadow of the doorway, regarding him with calm, exhausted eyes. In happier, more prosperous times Lorna would have looked like the stereotypical farmers wife – the happy, heavy duty work horse with her sleeves rolled up and a roast in the oven. Now weariness had marked her face with a grey, hollow beauty.

'I'm trying to run this place on my own, Mr Aichen,' she said to him as they went into the kitchen. 'You should write about that. How am I supposed to run a farm and nurse a sick husband? It all falls on the woman, you know.'

'How ill is he? Can he help at all?'

'Some days he can't get out of bed on his own. Some days I've got to feed him with a spoon.' Her eyes, fixed on him, were a dark-ringed intensity. 'Do you think you can help?'.

Clyde felt a familiar shrug coming into his shoulders. She led him down a hall lit by yellow, forty watt light bulbs to a large, high ceilinged bedroom. Although it contained, in addition to the bed, the standard wardrobe and dresser, the room seemed bare to Clyde, bare and grainy shadowed. There was a dry taste to the room which went to his mouth and he began to regret the morning's beers; there was a deadness in the air which made him feel immediately tired.

'You're the writer?' Don Bealter's eyes turned to Clyde, his head remaining perfectly still.

Clyde couldn't deny it. Except for the stillness and slackness of his body there didn't seem to be much wrong with Don Bealter, a short, robust, barrel-chested man in his middle forties. He didn't look as sick as his wife.

'You're going to write something about me?' But his voice was weak and abstracted. He spoke with great effort, as if he were talking about someone far away.

'That depends on what you tell me.'

'Very simple. One day I was spraying and the next I was lying in bed with all the usual symptoms, a rash,' he glanced at his arms and chest, 'that's gone now. Nausea. Loss of balance. Cold sweats. And the old brain won't work properly.'

There was an old fashioned fireplace, darkly tiled. Above, on the heavy mantelpiece rested a photograph of a young Don Bealter, fresh faced and crisply dressed in military uniform.

'What were you spraying?'

The farmer smiled wryly. 'Just Roundup. Just ordinary old Roundup. I should have known better.'

Clyde took a few steps back from the bed. He could feel the illness in the room. Everything, all strength and hope, flowed into it; nothing flowed out. Despite the spacious stud height, there was a low, pressured eddying, like one idea endlessly circulating in some airless chamber of thought.

'You could let some light in here,' Clyde said, gesturing to the curtained windows at the front of the room.

'Light hurts the eyes. Loud noises hurt the ears. A light touch can set my teeth on edge.' Bealter tried to grin.

'How do you know it was the Roundup? People are using that stuff all the time.'

Don nodded. 'I know. We have to go back to the beginning of this. I used to be a fit man. Then I started to get sick. It would come and it would go, lasting anywhere from two weeks to two months. I kept a diary of times, seasons, circumstances.' He gestured to a bedside table on which sat a large notebook. 'The diary helped me figure it out.'

'Figure what out?'

'That I'd been poisoned. I was in Vietnam, Clyde. Is that your name?'

'Yes.'

'Agent Orange was sprayed everywhere. Used as a defoliant. Those guys used to spray each other just for fun, for something to do.' The voice had a grey, washed, emotionless quality, as if he were merely repeating the words by rote. 'We were told it was safe.'

'After the war a lot of us started to get sick. There was a big army cover-up.'

'Didn't the doctors get onto it?'

'The doctors wouldn't know shit from shingle.'

'Have you been in touch with other Vietnam veterans?'

'Sure. Right now, all over the country, there are Vietnam vets lying around wondering why they can't get up in the morning or why they can't get rid of a bloody headache and why their old mates are popping off with liver cancer and God knows what.'

He'd broken out into a sweat. On the bed beside him was a damp flannel, and he made a weak movement with his hand towards it. He pulled it up to his face as if lifting a great weight.

'How does this tie in with the Roundup?'

'You get weakened. Susceptible. Any poison, especially a pesticide, will set you off. I've got to hide inside when my neighbours spray. Shut all the windows.'

'If you knew all this, why did you use Roundup at all, why use any poison?'

Don Bealter's voice came through as a distant, dry leaf whisper.

'I wanted to keep the bloody weeds down...'

Lorna Bealter took Clyde to the kitchen where he sat down to a cup of tea. Old English Breakfast tea, from a teapot. There was a close, humid feel in the air. She put the diary and a fat envelope down in front of Clyde.

'That's the medical record,' she said, gesturing to the envelope, not trying to hide her bitterness. 'It's all there, in black and white.'

Clyde stirred his tea to give him something to do.

'I told him not to use the spray. He was so bloody determined to get the weeds. He's got a thing about weeds.' She looked out the window towards the barn. 'I can't carry on, on my own.'

'No family?'

The woman was quiet, her eyes fixed on the barn. He could feel the tension in her coiled up and held tight, stretched as thin as skin will stretch over knuckles.

A few moments later she showed him back to the hall and pointed towards the lavatory. Clyde found the tall, narrow cell and peed in the cathedral gloom down into the shining enamel bowl, watching the last of his morning beer wash away. He mistimed the finish, however, and peed a little on the floor. A few drops. Cursing, he pulled some more toilet paper and cleaned the floor. Where he'd wiped, the interlacing black and white diamond lino was perceptibly cleaner.

On his way back to the kitchen he noticed a darkened room and what he took for a flicker of light. Glancing in, he saw that a TV was showing Star Wars to an empty room.

'I've got some biscuits if you'd like them,' Mrs Bealter said behind him. She pointed towards her husband's room. 'He's gone to sleep.' In the gloom her face had an oddly soft, luminous quality. She loves him, Aichen thought with a shiver. Whatever happens, she loves him.

'It's the inactivity that gets him,' she said. 'Having to lie there when it rains and he can't do anything about the weeds growing.'

Clyde glanced in through the open bedroom door. Don Bealter lay propped up as if he were awake, his hands slack at his sides, his head turned away from them.

'When will he come right?' He noted the farmer's powerful wrists and hands.

'He never comes right, not completely.'

They moved quietly back towards the kitchen. Clyde took his empty cup to the sink and rinsed it briefly.

'I'm not sure what I can do, Mrs Bealter.'

'You're a writer, aren't you?'

Again, Clyde could not deny it.

'Then you can write about it.' In her mouth it sounded self-evident. 'People will read it.' She saw words in magical terms; their magic would bring understanding, money, hope. People will read it, therefore something will be done.

'People should know about this,' she said.

His car was stifling hot from having sat in the sun. Clyde wound down the window and nosed the car towards the drive. Behind him the shadow of the house fell away and he breathed deeply. Still munching, the cow looked up at him as he went by.

'Eat the weeds,' Clyde advised it through the open window.

Soon he was back on the road, heading for the motorway, orchards on each side of him. On the seat beside him the apricots he'd bought caught the afternoon sun and glowed as if they were fleshed gold. He picked one out and rubbed it idly against his shirt.

In the distance, across a field of vegetables, he saw a massive machine working in an orchard. It had several revolving wheels that gave off a high, fine spray that reached the very top branches. There was a light wind and he could see the spray straggling off above the orchard as fine as airborne gauze.

He put the apricot back in the bag and wound up his window.

'Some lament that we have still not thrown off the mantle of Romanticism with regard to our poetry. We have to sympathize with them. Romanticism keeps popping up, marring good lines with woolly adjectives, escaping into warm fuzzy similes and maudlin metaphors, mistaking sentiment for passion and passion for the mytho-poetic quest. Playing hell with the swift, clean lines of a poem. We have to remember that beauty is truth, but that truth is only beauty in its most terrible, terrifying aspect, the sense Rilke intended when he penned these lines in the early years of the 20th century.' He recited:

"Who, if I cried, would hear me from the Order
of Angels? And even if one suddenly held me
to his heart: I would dissolve there from
his stronger presence. For beauty is only
the beginning of a terror we can just barely endure,
and what we so admire is its calm
disdaining to destroy us. Every angel brings terror..."'

He broke off, his throat was balled up, his lips were tinder dry. He had always liked this old Garmey and Wilson translation, preferring it to the trendier Mitchell and the folksy Bly. Now he could hardly get the words out.

'Every Angel brings terror...' He could feel her attention upon him, wholly and totally absorbed. Madeleine Farquar. Every angel brings terror. Rilke's lines unravelled as if he had never seen them before, and his throat would not shape the sounds. The words entered him without body, like glass, without voice.

'Umm. Ahh. Every angel...' He remembered Heinz Major, the ad-man, heading off down the street after failing to connect with Aichen's jaw, walking with a peculiar swimming motion. His voice arrived, dry, hard, splintered. He read without pretense directly into her ear, as if the marvelous words were his own.

'So I withhold myself and keep back the lure
of my dark sobbing. Oh, who is there
to prevail upon? Neither Angels nor men,
and already the ingenuous beasts are aware
that we are not reliably at home in our interpreted world
...Um...'

Whatever he'd been going to say was lost in the sweep of Rilke's words. 'Um... with Rilke our categories confound us. The language and

44

form look Romantic but the sentiment points out of Romanticism to something quite different.'

Was this true? The whole edifice of his argument seemed suddenly very shaky to Clyde. He moved hastily on, bewildered as to why he'd trotted the Rilke's passage out in the first place. To prove that Rilke took his understanding of Truth and Beauty one step further than Keats? Or to summon Rilke's angel into the room? Christ, it was time to start making a few notes before these classes.

'The world of the Grecian Urn is timeless. It is therefore a world without death, without process. Nothing is consummated. Nothing dies. But since it has banished death, the equation of Truth and Beauty is compromised. When Rilke restores time to the equation, terror enters, since time implies death. The lure of his 'dark sobbing' becomes the lure of that death.'

That was quite enough. He'd strayed far enough from his topic – The Use and Abuse of Imagery. He looked up for the first time in minutes and considered his audience; they were all watching him, alert and attentive, waiting for him to speak. Like him, they were waiting to see where all this was leading. The brash young man was tapping his pad with the sceptical end of his pencil. The woman with braids was making notes. The three Golden Oldies were suspended in their own Keatsian timelessness, waiting for him to release them. He noticed a shy woman with glasses giving him the once-over twice. And *she* had gone very still. Rilke's lines had drawn her forth out of her body to hover beside him, pressing in on him with a disturbing intimacy and hunger. He thought of the yearning that laces Rilke's poetry like a thin golden thread, drawing the spirits of others, particularly women, towards him.

She would be such a woman, he guessed. One who would feel the sensuous shape of the man beneath the lines, hear the cry for love through the verbal music; and her soul would be drawn out like this towards it. It was another woman of this kind, the Princess Marie von Thurn und Taxis Hohenlohe, who provided Rilke with the place, the Castle of Duino, in which the very lines Clyde had quoted were written.

Clyde remembered the letter in which Princess Marie described how Rilke had come upon these lines. It was morning; he'd climbed out on some rocks overlooking the sea, a sheer drop, two hundred feet down.

Then he'd heard a voice calling out of the roaring wind, *'Wer, wenn ich schriee, hörte mich denn aus der Engel Ordnungen?'*

Now she was there standing in front of her, what was he to say to her?

'Shall we have a cup of coffee? We could look at your story there.' It was as good an idea as any. Madeleine Farquar nodded. He was a little disappointed that she was not Marie, or Mary even. If he was going to start calling forth spirits from the Order of Angels, why not signs, mysterious conjunctions, synchronicities, the voodoo of names, the works?

Madeleine was not quite right for her, a little too polished and well dressed, more fit for high heels than sandals; Marie would have been more fitting to the grace and the beauty of her movements than the vaguely grand and somewhat inflated Madeleine. Of course, not half as grand as the Princess Marie von Thurn und Taxis Hohenlohe.

'I just about lost it in there today,' he said. 'I did lose it, in fact. Blame Rilke.'

'It didn't show.' Her eyes rested on him, light and cool.

'I don't see how.'

'Sometimes you stop talking at just the right moments.'

'Sure, it's all planned down to the last breath.'

She smiled, eyed a cake and passed on. For the cake it was a near thing, but the cake was used to that by now. It had suffered hundreds of eyes already and had developed something of a crumbling fatalism; a stale pessimistic outlook that served to ward off assessing glances.

'I'm enjoying your classes, doing lots of writing.' After careful deliberation, she placed a salad roll on her plate.

'That's the whole idea.'

Their coffees came in for a mutual landing, not a drop spilled. Clyde took it as a good omen.

'I've always written. Since I was thirteen. I've got a notebook for every year since then.' Her voice was clear, her diction firm and uncluttered.

'I'll pay,' Clyde said, feeling the weight of coins in his pocket.

'I'll pay for mine,' she said quickly.

'That's ok.' His voice was light. 'Today I have money, tomorrow I'll be broke.'

'No. There's no reason for you to. I'll pay for mine.'

He paid for his and thought about it.

'It *is* important,' he said sitting down.

'Yes,' she said picking up his thought. 'I know it seems like a silly gesture. But it isn't.'

With the veil drawn back from her face, the hair from her eyes, there was nothing murky or misty about Madeleine Farquar. Her capacity for self-absorption was evident in her every movement, but it was not allied to any vagueness or indecisiveness. The initial impression was of cool self-possession.

'I can understand it,' he said quietly, 'given the history of the whole thing. Money equals power, power equals patriarchy.' He was uncomfortably aware of how close the money in his trouser pocked nestled to that other instrument of masculine power. Randomly, he remembered how Rilke's mother, who had wanted a daughter, would then dress him up as a girl.

She was quiet as she considered this, sipping her coffee. 'There's that. For me, I've learned that I have a certain effect on men. I get put in this *femme fatale* role. I have to deal with possessing a face that could be on the cover of Vogue magazine.'

Mildly surprised, he studied her face, at first hesitantly, then openly. Her good looks were of the classic kind; she had high cheekbones and a finely shaped chin, suggestive of inner strength. Her nose was small and arched, with a clear sweep of forehead above. Clean, even lines implied will and intelligence; the effect was aristocratic without the suggestion of snobbery. It was a face that opened out from small, sensitive lips and nose, to widely spaced, arched eyes, framed by long, sloping cheek bones. The eyes themselves were deep-set, clear and steady, meeting Clyde's scrutiny without flinching or embarrassment. And returning it.

Nor did he feel it rude, or too forward, to stare at her for so long so openly. She not only expected to be looked at, she invited it, perhaps to get it over with.

He hadn't seen her without her veil, and it was taking him time to understand what she was saying and what accounted for her beauty.

It was not so much the elements he had noticed, although these in themselves would have made for a striking appearance, but the way they were lit from the golden amber hue of her eyes, pigmenting her skin with the same subtle bronze. This colour was reflected again in her hair which rose back off her high forehead in a rich, tawny wave. Someone had once expounded to Clyde the theory that each human being has an animal spirit in residence, a dominant animal. You can learn to identify people, the friend said, pick the rhinos from the giraffes, the deer from the hedgehogs. Clyde had laughed but here was Madeleine Farquar in front of him, clearly a young lioness, her posture erect and still, her body long and lean, her gaze amber and hypnotic.

'Yes, I see,' Clyde said in a subdued voice, surprised at his sober tone. He did indeed see. This woman would have a 'certain effect' on men all right. Struck by that calm, golden gaze their own souls would turn to amber, and from amber to transparency.

'All sorts of games get tried on,' she said, still scrutinizing him as intently as he had her. One thing for sure, his face was in no danger of ending up on the cover of Vogue magazine.

'I'm sure they do,' he said without mockery. He looked down at his coffee cup and the evil brew it contained. He thought of Don Bealter lying on his bed unable to move; Lorna Bealter, staring out towards the barn.

There was a catch in Madeleine's tone that told him she had been hurt in some way, and why should he be surprised at that? Where did beauty exist in the world that was not besieged and abused, incarcerated or maimed? Where was the purity that had not been poisoned? The alarm bells were ringing but he ignored them. He knew if he wanted to meet this young woman again, and he did very much want to do that, it would be on these terms.

'I've seen some amazing manoeuvres.'

He put up his hands in a gesture of surrender. 'No manoeuvres.'

She was quiet as she considered this. He noticed, with pleasure, her capacity to return to an inner stillness between utterances; not closed and preoccupied but open and receptive. Her alert, receptive pose reminded him of another Rilke poem he'd track down later.

'And I'll try to not put myself in a position to invite manoeuvering,' she said evenly. She picked up the roll, glanced at it briefly, and took a bite.

Clyde Aichen returned his attention to his coffee. Too much golden gazing was getting to him. The ground rules of some sort of relationship were being hammered out here, they both sensed it.

'That might help,' he said feebly, trying to smile, trying to regain something of his old flippancy. At the same time he felt increasingly less able to be the object of her intense observation. He was acutely aware of his age, his bent nose, the veins on the back of his hands, the lines of living on his face. The suggestion of suffering around his eyes. His boozing. His mortality.

'How old are you?'

'Twenty four. And you?'

'Forty two.' Her simplicity and directness invited, required, the same; yet the simple admission of his age was unsettling. It had always seemed right and natural to him to be forty-two.

'Really? I wouldn't have thought so.'

She was not flattering him. For the first time he felt her composure shifting. She had not figured him to be this old. Mid-thirties perhaps, she'd figured. Clyde took refuge in his coffee.

All around them students manoeuvred into chairs and around tables, talking and laughing with animation. Sitting with Madeleine, he felt disassociated from them all in an unsettling way, as if the two of them formed an island around which this restless tide of people moved.

She put her cup down, picked up her bag and took out a sheaf of A4 paper. There was a deft economy and precision in her movements, her hands slender and finely wrought. 'Could you look at the story now?'

'Sure.' It was the last thing he wanted to do. He looked at her hands. Her story was the occasion for this coffee, he'd forgotten that. He took it and read it, trying to concentrate on the words and not her close scrutiny of his reactions. It was a short piece about a girl's sexual awakening at school, being punished by a teacher for touching a boy, her guilt when her mother arrived. It was written simply, in honest, straightforward language.

'It's ok as far as it goes,' he said, frowning over his coffee, desperately trying to think of something useful to say. 'But it doesn't go all that far.

It's a sketch, more than anything, nothing's – ah – fleshed out. We don't see the teacher or the mother, or even the children. It depends on the purpose of the passage, really. Context is all.'

She laughed. 'You mean the context of me showing you this story now?'

Absurdly, he was colouring, losing his cool like some hapless teenager. 'Ah... no. I mean, whether you'd intend this to be a stand-alone story or part of a larger work, like a novel, or just to stay as it is, a recollective piece.'

What an utter shambles he was making of this, the story spread between his hands, looking dumbly back up at him from the flimsy page. 'It's just a beginning, really,' he murmured, something he often said, for it was so often true. 'Sometimes we write something just to clarify or crystallize an inner movement.'

'Do you think that's what I've done here?' She was, at each moment, disturbingly direct. He was trying to choose his words with great care.

'Partly. It's half-way between being written for yourself and written for other people.'

Again she considered what he was saying, her posture alert and concentrated. Again he had the sense of her returning to some point of stillness within herself. In this event, she was not so much absent, as he had felt in class, but present within herself, as if hovering over a very still lake.

'But isn't that true of everything you write. Unless it's just for money?'

Couldn't she see he didn't know what the hell he was saying? Just opening his mouth and letting any old blah-blah come out.

'Perhaps. But the best writing never shows that. Good writing seems to be written for the very reader who is holding the book at that moment. It is the reader who sneaks away for a little feely with the boys, or the girls, it is she or he who faces teacher and mother.'

She nodded, apparently satisfied, but he knew she was not. Beneath her meditative calm he detected a fury of activity. He knew, with almost a grim glee, she would find no satisfaction until she had written something that fully honoured itself. A piece of writing that really faced the music. Her agitation was no more than a flicker of activity playing across her calm like an electrical charge. Clyde finally wondered if this self-possessed young lioness was also Cleo of the red-light district. The shit of it was, he still could not tell. Not a hundred percent. He could remember deciding to commit Cleo's face to memory, but all he could see was the Nu mask, the wide spaced eyes which could have been Madeleine's, well disguised with paint and eye-liner. And a flicker of something.

He was annoyed at the persistence of the association. Madeleine gave the impression of being more angular, taut and alert, but then, she was wearing black jeans and a tight jacket, clothes that accentuated her leanness; and she wore no makeup, highlighting the acetic, almost severe lines of her face.

'Yes,' she said finally, putting the roll aside, 'when I write in my journal it's just for me. What you're talking about is a sense of surrender, so that the writer can be at one with her material…'

'…so the same happens to the reader.' Clyde felt the opening of a sense of discovery within himself. He'd never considered the role of surrender in the creative process. His concentration now matched hers; their minds were moving in swift accord.

'Then when you talk of a necessary distance between the writer and her material, you're not so much talking of detachment as this sense of suspension in which you can be a character and…'

'…return to a wild country,' he said softly, feeling exhilarated, drunk. He wanted to abduct this remarkable young woman immediately, take her home and talk and make love and make love and talk and talk and make love until hell froze over or heaven drowned in a great flood.

He looked up and saw her eyes were fixed over his shoulder. She vanished, forgot him entirely. When she returned, it was as from her own wild country. She pushed her fingers into the upright wave of her hair and shook her head. It was a gesture so full of unconscious sexual power he had to look away, an intruder upon a moment that was entirely and intimately her own.

'I'm sorry,' she said. 'I've forgotten I was supposed to meet someone.' She took her story from his hands and put it back into her bag.

'I'm sorry too.' Then he noticed a young man hesitating at the door of the cafe. He easily recognised the species of nervous young man, he'd been one himself, once. He felt like one right now. He watched her cross the cafe, marvelling again at her capacity to forget him. Her hand hovered at the young man's elbow. The young man gave him a brief, hard glance. As she passed through the door she left a momentary after-image behind her, the now familiar sparkle of luminosity.

He looked at his watch. An hour had passed since they had sat down. He couldn't believe it. He'd missed his lunch with Moira.

Sue Hyde of Greenpeace drew closely-knit circles on the page while Clyde spoke. The effect was not unlike chain mail.

'He's not the only one,' she said, when Clyde had stopped talking. Behind her, in a cage on a stand, her white parrot gave a low wolf whistle. 'You cut that out now, Peres,' she said to the bird. The bird whistled again, low and appreciative.

'You mean other Vietnam vets?'

'I mean ordinary people. People whose resistance has been lowered. People with degraded immune systems. These people are called chemical sensitives. I know some who can't stand the smell of disinfectant; even perfume makes them ill.'

'How many?'

Sue leaned back and grabbed hold of some files. 'I don't know of any statistics. More than you think.'

A shadowy underworld of sick people, a subculture of illness, sub-clinical symptoms that never went away. People dragging themselves through the day, wondering what the hell was wrong with them, breaking into a sweat every time they tried to move like a dreary hangover that never went away. Invisible people.

Sue dropped the fat envelope Lorna Bealter had given him on her desk. Her broad face sagged as she looked at it. Her look suggested, even as she opened the file, that there was not much hope to be found within its covers. The Greenpeace campaigner had short cropped hair and a practical, no-nonsense face, now looking weary and overworked.

'It sounds to me like your Mr Bealter has got M.E. or something very like it. Chronic Fatigue Syndrome, they call it, among other things, Yuppies Disease, Tapanui Flu.' Idly tapping the envelope, she gave a fatigued smile.

'Sometimes I think half of us here have got it.' She gestured out her office window to where a row of people sat bug-eyed at computer screens.

'Could he have chemical poisoning?'

'Does mother's milk have DDT? Proving it is another matter. To some extent we all have chemical poisoning. A threshold is reached and suddenly you react to the slightest whiff of any toxic substance. These sensitives can react to even a few molecules of poison.' She tapped her pencil up and down on the envelope. Clyde noted how remote her voice sounded. Strong as it was, there was an odd similarity to Lorna Bealter in the dark, grey shaded rings under her eyes. She rubbed her forehead as if to generate some heat in her brain. 'I'm sorry, Clyde, I've got other things on my mind.'

'I've got some stuff on Monsanto here. This pesticide business must be the dirtiest on the planet, next to the nuclear industry, that is. And we've gotta watch what we print.' She gestured cynically to the envelope. 'It gets very murky, Clyde, you can't prove a fucking thing. Pretty soon you get down to talking about LD-50 levels and you've lost the argument before you start.'

'What are LD-50 levels?'

'Lethal Dose. The amount of any particular substance required to kill half of any given sample group, usually rats, or rabbits.'

'Christ.'

'You said it, brother.' She gave him a ghoulish grin. 'And there are plenty like your farmer. We've got files full of them. The problem is that the particular can't prove the general case, that's a scientific principle, you know. Anecdotal evidence is worse than no evidence at all.' There was barely a hint of sarcasm in her voice. 'Human testimony is held in lower regard than the LD-50 levels of rats and rabbits, because these are scientific, you see. They are objective while human testimony is subjective. Anecdotal.'

Clyde thought of Don Bealter's powerful hands lying inert and useless on the sheets.

'A farmer dies aged fifty-four from cancer of the liver. He's been using sprays all his life, but he's also been brushing his teeth all his life too, and putting away a few beers on a Friday night. Who or what killed him? Or would he have died anyway, like the story of the bloke who stays in bed to avoid disaster and has the roof fall in on him. Choose your poison: fate or circumstance, hereditary or environment. Take this farmer of yours, maybe he's getting sick from the amalgam in his teeth, heavy metal poisoning.'

'Hello, Hello,' the parrot, Peres, said to Clyde. Fuck it, Clyde thought. The Bealters had pinned some hopes on him and now he was carrying them, hauling them about with him up and down stairs.

'So there's no story in it.'

Sue grinned and through the tiredness her face glowed with warmth. She's too young to be carrying all that she's carrying, he thought. There was a haunted look about her, and it was that that reminded him of Lorna Bealter. Both women had looked upon something they had never wished to see, and kept going. They hadn't given up, even in the face of monstrous odds.

'I didn't say that, Clyde; don't get temperamental. A medical record like Bealter's is valuable because it's very hard to prove even the existence of chemical sensitivity, since the symptoms tend to be amorphous and open to different diagnoses. Add to that a confusion over what is a symptom and what is a cause and you've got a right old mess. It takes a brave doctor to admit to that, of course. A breakdown between theory and practice is what they're faced with.'

'So?'

'So here's your story angle. If you can get Bealter to put his name on this material and stand witness to his medical record, we will be able to push harder for an investigation into official denial. Look at the struggle those firemen had over the ICI fire a few years back. The government hates to admit a connection between these firemen's cancers and their toxic exposure. All that stuff's on public record and it's a bloody disgrace.'

'Bloody disgrace,' Peres chirruped.

Sue grinned. 'Whenever I hit certain notes, he repeats what I say.'

'He's agreeing with you.'

Clyde picked up Bealter's medical record.

'Stick to the facts, huh?'

The campaigner refused to acknowledge Clyde's sarcasm.

'Right, with the conclusion that we need a public inquiry into the medical treatment of toxic victims. But you've got to use real names, and the doctors' names too, none of this protection of the innocent business. Doctors are accountable, use their real names. Nobody's innocent.'

There was a twist of anger in her voice that had its source, it seemed to Clyde, somewhere outside the terms of this conversation. He must ring Moira!

'They're not likely to give their permission.'

She shrugged and gave a suitably crooked grin, 'A medical record is a statement of public fact. It is a secret because of the compact between the patient and his doctor. If the patient wants to break that compact, that's his business. You're only relating the facts.'

'Tricky.'

'It's thin ice anyway.' She rubbed her eyes and stroked the sinus lines over her cheekbones. 'There's a lot of fear around,' she said, half to herself.

'Could I use your phone for a moment?'

'For a moment, yes.' The friendliness had gone out of her voice. She struggled up in her seat as if strong hands were pushing down on her shoulders. Then, abruptly, that did not seem like a metaphor anymore; he saw, in a milky, marble like form, a figure standing behind her chair, bearing down on her shoulders. He closed his eyes and opened them again on the parrot. Peres was watching him with a nimble alertness in the quick of its eye.

'A moment,' it said in a bleak voice.

Dial tone rang down the empty wire.

'You write poetry too, don't you?'

'Yeah.' He heard the circuit connect with her house. The phone began to ring.

'I'd like to write poetry, but I'm too busy writing reports. If you wanna get burned out, come and work at Greenpeace.'

'Jesus, is it that bad?' The phone rang. It rang and rang down an infinity of wires.

'Nah,' she gave her roughhouse grin. 'There's just a war on.' She was trying to make a joke of it but the guts had gone out of her; she held herself upright but inside she was slumped over.

Clyde put the phone down. His heart went into heavy labour as if something viscous had entered his blood. A tightness came into his chest. He'd had waves of such a sensation before and had done his best to ignore them, ignore the fear that one day it would turn into a heart attack. He drank too fucking much, that was the simple truth.

'Thanks,' Clyde said, standing up. 'The intrepid investigative reporter must move on,' he swept up Bealter's medical record.

'I'm sorry if I'm a bit weird today,' she passed her hand in front of her eyes, and furiously massaged her elbow joint. 'I've got something on my mind.'

'Tell Uncle Clyde.'

'I don't know if I should tell you?' Her eyes became hooded.

'Be a devil.'

'I'll leave that to the experts.' She bit her nails. Peres, feeling left out of the action, wolf whistled.

'I won't breathe a word to a soul, cross my heart and hope to die.'

Sue grinned with appreciation. 'You're a born liar. I'd never tell a writer any kind of secret. Writers are on the lookout for secrets.'

'You bet.'

Peres tried to say 'you bet', but ended up saying 'hello' again.

'Well, I suppose you can't do any harm. You know Greenpeace sent a ship to Moruroa.'

'Yeah.'

'Well, they took water samples a hundred miles out from the island and guess what they found? No don't bother,' she went on hastily, seeing the look on Clyde's face, 'I'll tell you. They found Uranium 238.'

'What does it mean?'

'OK. Uranium 238 is not produced by test explosions like they're having at Moruroa, right? Those blasts produce Cesium 134 and Cobalt 60. They have a half-life ranging from several weeks to fifty years or so.'

'I'll believe you.'

'Uranium 238 is a different can of worms, or kettle of fish if you prefer. It's a by-product of the nuclear process. They call it depleted uranium. It occurs in nature, you see. It's supposed to be of low toxicity, like your Roundup. There's an international agency which is supposed to account for this stuff and know where every kilo of it is stored. I see they're trying to store some in Arizona right now. They want assurances from scientists that nothing's going to blow there for the next ten thousand years. How the hell could anyone give them an assurance like that? It'll be fun to watch someone try. There are no sealed compartments in nature, the only sealed compartments are up here.' Angrily she tapped her forehead.

'Go on.'

'Nobody's sure what the French do with their Uranium 238. Now we have an idea. We've discovered Uranium 238 hotspots in the Pacific. These hotspots are assumed to be natural occurrences. But let's imagine for a minute you are the French Government and you want to hide considerable quantities of depleted uranium, where would you put it?'

'Um.' Clyde pretended to think. 'Where there was already a hot spot?'

'Ah! Signs of intelligent life!'

'Go on.'

'Well, I've actually told it, what there is of it, except one final detail. You see Uranium 238, as I said, is assumed to be of low toxicity. It's not as fissionable as Uranium 235 because it's had most of its fissionable material burned up,' she rubbed her eyes, 'but as with all radioactive material, there's no safe minimum dose.'

'But I thought all countries set minimum levels.'

'These are meaningless. There's no minimum levels that scientists can guarantee are harmless to humans. Their safety standards are hopeful guesswork. But you haven't come to the punch line.'

'I don't think I'm going to like it.'

'It's the persistency of the stuff, its half-life.'

'What is it?' The expression had a strange appeal to him beyond its scientific meaning. It made him think of some half realized, ghostly place where nothing properly existed. Half a life.

She didn't blink, 'Two and a half billion years.'

There was a short pause during which eternity ran its course.

'Why aren't you going to town on this?'

'The good old scientific method. We have to duplicate our results. One result is not enough. Our one result has little more validity than your stricken farmer. Remember, Uranium 238 can occur in nature. We'd only bring suspicion onto *us*.' She laughed.

Peres laughed too. Not a pleasant sound.

Gloomily, Clyde said, 'I can see why you can't get excited about one farmer.' It's Virgil's monstrum horrendum, he thought, in another of its disguises; fearful and hideous, vast and eyeless. It takes courage to rise in the morning into the world the beast built, to lift up against the hands pressing down.

Sue said, 'It's a fucking nightmare. How much have they stored there? If it's leaking into the sea it's already too late.' She looked up at him with hollow eyes. 'The further up the chain you go, the more it will concentrate. There's no way of neutralizing it or stopping it unless we learn to live under lead domes and distil all our own water. The bastards are crazy to ever have thought they could produce the stuff at all.'

'The French will deny it, of course.'

Her eyes flared, 'Fuck the French!'

The parrot caught it and passed it on.

Clyde Aichen bought a bottle of goodwill to assuage his own guilt, if not Moira's anger, for missing his lunch date. Quality brandy. A sipping, conversational brandy to go down with coffee. His apology for missing the date was neatly packaged in the bottle, along with an appropriate gesture of penitence, the brandy itself. She could abuse him as she drank it, and by degrees mellow to its warmth and his contrition.

It was spring, the kowhai was in blossom, a trap for a thousand neophyte poets all over the city. Perhaps one of them might be a Tu Fu or a Li Po and spring the trap of the kowhai bloom, perhaps not – this business of writing owes no favours. But at least Moira could not keep a grudge on an evening like this, when there was a sense of tropical quickening in the air, the flash of a bright lava-lava, a brief warm gust of rain. Moira's beloved Ponsonby looked rinsed and bright. There was no sign of any Uranium 238 anywhere.

He arrived unannounced, figuring it the better course. With a little luck her pleasure at seeing him would snuff her resentment fast and they could get on with the brandy and enjoying themselves. And when the brandy ran out, he could do the same before the question of sleeping together arose.

Before the question of deeper resentments arose. Before she started quoting Hamlet. Well before that. A clean getaway.

'What the fuck are you looking so happy about?' He saw immediately that she regretted what had just come out of her mouth, even though he might fucking well deserve it. It was one of her corner of the mouth jobs from the Bogart era.

'Certainly not standing you up for lunch,' he said, following her from the door to the kitchen. Her house was colonial in shape with the inner walls ripped out to dispose of the hall. It seemed to Clyde that everybody in Ponsonby was doing that. They sat around the semi-circular sideboard that connected the living room and kitchen as if they were sitting at some tasteful, homely bar.

There was someone else seated there. A woman with short, spiky hair and an army shirt. She had a broad face and a wide, expressive mouth. Her eyes, a soft grey, fixed on Clyde for an instant before focusing somewhere over his left shoulder. There were the makings of a smile around her lips.

'Yeah,' Moira said carelessly, 'there was that, yeah. I only waited an hour, drank bottomless coffees and had to fend off some punk who claimed I'd met him at a party.'

'And had you?'

'How the fuck should I know, or care? Punks at parties come and go.'

There was a false toughness in her voice. This was not the sentimental forties she usually preferred. This was a fifties James Dean style tough.

'I didn't think you were the punks-at-parties type,' Clyde said. He'd intended lightness, which was not much of an excuse for saying the wrong thing.

'Oh yes? What *type* do you think I am? You're an expert on me now, is that it? After fucking me a few times and crying on my shoulder when Jeannette walked out, you know what *type* I am.'

'That's the way it is,' the woman in the army shirt said, intimating that perhaps there were creatures worse than punks at parties, and that they didn't have far to look to see one.

'This is Snake, by the way,' Moira said. 'A friend of mine.' There was just the slightest stress on the word.

Snake nodded and quirked the corner of her mouth.

'And this is Clyde Aichen, the famous poet. And lover extraordinaire.'

'Hi, famous poet and lover extraordinaire,' Snake said.

Clyde muttered something, unable to meet the woman's easy stare.

Snake was clearly enjoying not being the least bit intimidated. It was starting to look worse than Clyde's worst-case scenario. All he'd done was stand Moira up for lunch, there might be a thousand good reasons for that; he hadn't anticipated the ironically smiling Snake. Hurriedly he produced the bottle and presented it to Moira.

'Allow me to present this peace offering,' he said in his most disarming, charming style, holding the bottle out to her, label first. She glanced at the bottle, opened her mouth, took a second look and closed it again.

'The best laid plans of mice and men,' he said meekly. The bloody brandy alone had cost him half a week's work at the College.

'Which are you?' Moira asked, but the heat had gone out of her voice. 'I suppose you do have an excuse?'

Clyde was prepared for this one. He did have an excuse ready, one of the thousand available, but instead he told the truth. It was some devil twisting his tongue.

'I got caught up after class with a student.'

She could have let it go but she didn't, even though she was half moving to get the glasses. She had special little embossed cognac glasses for liquor like this. Nervously Clyde stuck his fingers into a bowl of potato chips.

'A female, I presume.'

She instantly regretted her words. After all, she had no claim on him, no case for jealousy, no mandate to put him through the third degree. He'd never made any promises to her, not Clyde Aichen. He was free to come and go, put his diddle here or there so long as he didn't get aids or genital warts. Something like that.

'Well…' Amazingly, he coloured, blushed to the roots of his hair. As his face filled up with blood, Moira's emptied. She swayed a little. Snake looked embarrassed on Clyde's behalf. It was a long time since she had a man place himself so neatly in the shit.

'Young, astonishing and beautiful, of course.' Moira had to press on, into this territory, where even she did not want to go, and again she was flabbergasted at his response. He gave a silly, nervous smile and put the bottle on the bench. How, at this stage, could he tell her the truth: that she was absolutely right. He tried to meet her eye and immediately she saw the panic in them. And something else.

'Jesus Christ,' she said faintly. 'No wonder you bought a bottle of,' she glanced at the label, 'Waterloo Brandy, which must have cost you a packet of crisps or two.' For a moment she looked as if she were drowning. She put her hand out to steady herself on the bench and he stared blankly at the bottle. 'Love knows no loyalties,' she said to herself.

'No compunction, more like it,' Snake said to no one in particular, picking up the bottle and looking casually at the label. There was an easy, assured grace in her movements.

Clyde said nothing. Let them run with it. He couldn't believe what had just happened, how he'd just fallen to pieces like that. He was good at not falling to pieces; it was his forte. He munched compulsively on the chips.

And should he try to tell them about Don Bealter, Roundup, or the dastardly French and their nuclear waste. Somehow he couldn't see it going down, not yet. A few more drinks and he might be able to divert the conversation that way.

Mechanically, Moira knelt and drew three glasses out from a lower cupboard, cradling them in one palm. Looking down at her dark, lush hair he remembered her slim, light body, her breasts with what he had called her 'African aureoles', so dark they were, set in fine, silky dark hair; remembered her thighs pale against the black luxuriance of her pubic hair.

'We may as well have a drink,' she said in a toneless voice, as if having a drink was what one did when one was doing nothing else.

'I just got my times fucked up,' he said, wincing at how lame he sounded. The damage was already done, he could only make matters worse.

'The hours fly by like minutes,' Moira said, still far away, back in the forties again. He was further embarrassed by how accurately she had read him. You're absolutely right, he wanted to say to her; that's exactly how it felt. He unscrewed the cap off the bottle and put it down on the bench. Moira did the honours. The three glasses were quickly filled.

Clyde's hopes that the pouring ceremony would be a healing focus were not quite realised.

'Well,' Moira said, holding up her glass, trying to get the false bravado back into her voice. 'Let's drink to love shall we. Love, love…'

'…oh careless love,' Snake sang, tossing hers back with a practised gesture.

Moira spluttered as if Snake had made some compulsively funny joke. Expensive brandy squirted from between her lips and dribbled down her chin.

Clyde didn't get the joke, but he did get his brandy down. Never in the history of brandy had a drink been more welcome and less deserved.

Half the bottle was gone before Clyde Aichen began to feel half-way back to his old self again. Ultimately, there's no arguing with good quality brandy. Under its auspices the three of them got along, sort of. Snake thawed to Clyde sufficiently to accept a second brandy, and a third. For all three, the day they were living through was pushed back into that dim time before the first glass. Clyde's meeting with Madeleine Farquar assumed a surreal quality, like a Man Ray painting. A world of bright, sharp colours and fantastic impressions. Every word spoken and movement made, stood out in fantastic detail. Angels coming out of poems, young lionesses with golden eyes sitting in cafes eating salad rolls. Beauty and terror. He giggled about it.

He retreated into the lavatory. The back wall was dominated by a large facsimile of the Declaration of Human Rights. *All human beings are born free and equal in dignity and rights. They are endowed with reason and conscience and should act towards one another in a spirit of brotherhood.* 'Amen to that,' he said out loud as he relieved himself. In the mirror was a man with a brandified smile. *No one shall be subjected to arbitrary arrest, detention or exile. Amen to that too.*

Well, well, in love are we?

He returned, wanting to tell Moira all about it, the Vogue girl face, the golden gazing, the heady meeting of minds, the rush of blood to the face. All three of them could enjoy the whole story at the famous poet's expense, and all three could happily despise him, despise the image of him goofing on the girl while Moira sat alone in Dominos watching the trendy vegetarians coming and going. With a little luck Clyde himself might escape scot-free. Later he'd been up to Greenpeace and heard about the uranium apocalypse from Sue Hyde. That would shock them. The three pitiful humans would cluster around the bottle like survivors around a fire. Moira would go hysterical and laugh until the tears came into her eyes, tell him what an arsehole he was and fill his empty glass, shaking her head in despair. Snake's wide grey eyes would soften. A jolly time could be had by all.

Except he didn't do it; he wouldn't dream of doing it. To offer himself up for sacrificial mockery was going too far. Not even if he had another bottle he wouldn't. Everything that had happened to him since meeting Madeleine had a sacred, eternal quality to it. This was something he could not share and, at least so far, he wasn't too drunk to realize that.

'I dreamed about death last night,' Moira said solemnly. Clyde checked the level of the bottle. Three quarters empty, time for dreams of death. There is always something melancholy about the final quarter of a bottle. Especially when the first three quarters have gone so fast.

'I'm throwing a pot. A huge clay pot, very simple, Japanese Osaka style. That wonderful fusion of form and function the commentators love to notice. Anyway, I fall into the pot where it's dark. There's just a single circle of light above me. I hammer at the walls of the pot but I've made it too well, it's too strong, too well-fired. I know there are no weak points or fault lines in it. Then I feel death. I don't see any fancy skull or hear any rattling bones, I just feel it all around me coming out of the clay, soaking me away. There is nothing to fight. No monster, no clanking horror. I just feel myself getting sucked away into the baked clay. It is almost nice, like when you slip into sleep, you know, there is a little moment of ecstasy as you pass over. Most people don't notice it.'

'That's scary,' Snake said.

'I had to wake up. I knew at a certain point that if I didn't wake up I really would die, and that's true because when I woke up I'd stopped breathing, I had to force myself to breathe. If I'd died I'd have spent an eternity inside that fucking clay pot, that's what terrifies me.'

'I never dream,' Snake said, helping herself to another glass. It was a race for the bottom. 'When I was a kid, yes, but I gave it up, knocked it on the head. She raised her glass and drank, perhaps to illustrate.

'I do all my dreaming with words, dreaming's a full time job for me.' Clyde infused his words with what he hoped was the proper boozy profundity, at the same time holding himself in contempt for falsity. There was nothing dreamlike about an Aichen poem. An Aichen poem, goddamn it, was a tough, tense verbal structure, bunched-out with the concrete nouns of the world, as solid and as clay-fired as one of Moira's pots, if he hadn't already voiced that to somebody before. And how solid, really, were Moira's pots? As solid as the vacillations in a brandy glass.

Moira got out some cheese and a packet of crackers. 'That's the second time this week I've dreamed of death,' she said, making a point of offering the cheese crackers to Snake before Clyde. Snake got offered everything first. Clyde got the picture.

'Death is a symbol of rebirth too,' he said, putting on a hearty tone.

'Not this death,' Moira said in a submerged voice. 'Have you ever read *The Story of O*? A truly vile book, supposed to be written by a woman into slavery and masochism. There's a portrait of a whole big, rich estate where women are kept as slaves. Anyway there's one horrifying scene in which the woman is taken to an utterly dark room and chained naked to the floor where she remains for days, weeks, being constantly fucked and beaten by men she never sees.'

'It's a fake, that book,' Snake said. 'I know about it. No woman would have written that crap. It's moral sleaze. Only a man can see a woman that way.' She glanced at Clyde.

'I believe a woman did,' Moira said. 'In my dream, I am that woman. I am O. Her dark room is my clay pot. I am naked and kneeling. I can feel the flagstones, damp and thick with moss beneath my knees. Death is approaching the room. Death is a man. He knows how to get into the pot. He knows the secret door. When he opens that door and comes into the dark room, I will die. He is nothing but hard muscle and sinew. There is no softness or compassion in him. There is only the drive for complete possession. It is not even desire that drives him. Desire is hot and salty. This man is driven by something far colder, far more indifferent. Pleasure is not his purpose. It is beyond cruelty even. It distains to destroy me. I dissolve into a puddle of piss and shit. When I orgasm, I die. My clay pot now becomes my urn. It holds my ashes. It locks in my orgasm. I am buried deep underground…'

None of them said anything. The story had taken them way further than the brandy had been designed for. Alcohol was like a leaky craft. It would take them to the middle of the lake, the deepest part, and sink. None of the quasi-flip, drunkenly appropriate comments that came to Clyde's lips seemed the least bit appropriate, and he had enough sobriety left to bite them back. Sobriety seemed to be coming in the back door, cold and godless. There was a stripped down look to everything he saw. He knew though that this was not true sobriety but rather a new stage of drunkenness.

'Heavy shit,' Snake said, picking up the bottle to find it empty.

'I think I was raped to death in a previous lifetime,' Moira said with the true solemnity of the properly drunk.

'Even heavier shit,' Snake said. 'I reckon,' she spoke ponderously. 'That at one time in everybody's life they meet their death. They just don't necessarily recognise it.'

The shit had got too heavy for Clyde, who set off with carefully correct steps for the lavatory. "What if the whole earth is conscious?" the sticker on the cistern beamed at him.

We'd be in the shit, Clyde beamed back, aiming his stream for the rear of the bowl, just above the water, where someone's shit had crud the enamel. The earth thinks therefore I am, he thought, trying to reformulate Descartes for the New Age. *I think therefore the world is.* If the earth was conscious, why not the stars, the galaxies? Perhaps the galaxies were huge jellyfish-like creatures swimming in the murky void; great plasmid consciousnesses wrapped around bunches of stars, swimming together in immense clusters, super-clusters. Super clusters of super plasmids. And what would such beings be doing, clustering and swimming together through the eons? Reciting a poem, of course; a vast, symphonic exchange of information that was all at once their song and their history.

His stream dribbled to a halt and the best of the brandy with it. He steered back into the kitchen. Moira was sure to have something tucked away. She wouldn't be caught short. Nor was she, although at first he thought both the kitchen and the lounge were empty. Their old seats were vacated, the defeated bottle of Waterloo Brandy was a lone sentinel on the clean sweep of the bench. Then he saw it, sitting on the low coffee table at the darkened end of the lounge with the two women sitting on the couch behind it; three-quarters of a bottle of Metaxa cognac. A gut warmer Moira would have stashed for a cold winter night. Snake had a full glass in one hand, the other arm around Moira's shoulders. Moira was staring blankly at the bottle, her head on Snake's breast. Clyde got the picture. He swept his glass off the bench and headed for the table, keeping the bottle in sight, keeping the two women in a background blur.

He knelt at the table to pour, partly so as not to loom in masculine bulk over the two women, partly to ensure he didn't spill any of the precious amber fluid supposedly made from a herbal blend. As he watched the glass fill, he tried to think where he would sit, the politics of it. As soon as his glass was full Moira muttered something, heaved herself with a great sigh off Snake's breast, got up and walked for the door. Clyde stayed where he was, on his knees on front of the bottle.

'Are you really a famous poet?' Snake asked, settling into the couch with a comfortable sense of possession. 'I've never heard of you.'

'There you go,' Clyde said pleasantly. 'A poet is only ever famous in a very limited sense. Even Noble Prize winners. Have you heard of Holub?'

Snake considered this at length, her eyes moving from her hand resting monumentally on the back of the couch to the door and back again. Her jaw unhinged in his direction, 'How come a poet, a famous poet, can act like an arsehole? Towards a woman? Towards anyone, for fuck's sake?' She put her glass on the table, across from Clyde's.

Despite her drunken heaviness, there was a firmness and grace in her movements. In some other situation, Clyde decided, they might have liked each other. Suddenly he saw himself as she saw him and didn't like the picture. This had already happened once that day, sitting with Madeleine, the fact of their eighteen years difference sitting between them. He'd seen the veins on his hands and the lines around his eyes as through her eyes. Now, through Snake's eyes, he saw something similar but worse; a smug, self-satisfied bastard; nay, a drunk, smug, self-satisfied bastard who treated women like shit for the pleasure of it, feeding on their affections and despising them for it, in a grip of a massive masculine conceit that made him ignorant of the feelings of others.

But she's prejudiced, he thought. She's doesn't like men for a start, and she has the hots for Moira; the manacles of a double judgement on Clyde. At the same time he foundered, struggling to incorporate how she saw him with how he saw himself. A hopeless task.

'Because they're poets, not saints.' His own voice sounded terribly feeble in his ears. Again Snake considered deeply, ponderously. She seemed ill-inclined to concede any possible agreement. 'Could you recite me one, right now. A poem I mean.'

Clyde had an Aichen poem he'd memorized for occasions just like this. A showpiece early poem, much praised and anthologized for its 'boldness and muscularity.' It was the only piece of his work that he could remember off by heart no matter how out of it he might be.

So he began, ploughing into the first few lines, relying on memory and automatic pilot to carry him through. That didn't happen. About the fourth or fifth line he began to falter, casting about for the tone. The words were there but the tone to deliver them was gone. No way of shaping them sounded right. Then the words started sounding wrong; the so called muscularity was strained, tense; the boldness was a posture. Rhythmically it was too cluttered, too aimed at, too boastful. He gave a hopeless, discombobulated version of the poem.

When it had finished Snake again went into pondering mode. 'Do you know why women like me?' she said at length.

Clyde shook his head. The room slid from one side to the other. Snake tipped back her head, opened her mouth and out slithered a huge mobile tongue. She waggled it back and forth. There was a gold coloured stud in it. He was surprised he hadn't noticed it before.

The ruins of the poem, its shattered architecture, shone through the gloom and gleam of the coffee table like some exploded relic. Horribly mortal, like all poems, it had long since had its time and time had been cruel to it. It had not aged well. Now, with Snake's tongue waggling in front of him, he saw through the pretence and falsity of it. Its naive assumption that its petulance was its profundity. He was mortified to think of how often he had stood in front of audiences and delivered it, his chin up, full of authority.

Clyde Aichen filled his glass and got down to some serious drinking.

Moira Andrews stood in front of her workbench, her sleeves rolled back, her arms covered to her elbows with wet clay, her lower arms like two foreign appendages that had been sewn there. Between her hands she held a lump of wet clay close to her stomach, just below her breast. Tears fell from her cheeks onto the clay, a sight Clyde didn't know whether to savour or savage for its symbolism. He hated these maudlin scenes, the melodrama, but they were all part and parcel of knowing Moira Andrews, and being her friend.

There was a mortuary cold in her clay room.

Moira had reached the weepy stage. She had put on her work-smock which hung limp, as her head hung limp from her body. He noticed how pouchy and pale her pretty dark face had become, and felt a surge of affection. Perhaps he should sleep with her tonight, just to cuddle, just for the shared warmth; nothing to accuse each other of in the morning but their hangovers. It was an attractive thought.

'It's cold,' Moira said in a slow, half hypnotised voice, pulling her fingers in and out of the clay. 'Cold as death – and as intractable.'

'Not in your hands. Alive is the word they use for your work, Moira.' Clyde shivered and rubbed his hands. Her workroom was large and draughty, the result of knocking out the wall between two high ceilinged rooms. The cold exhaled from the walls and the racks of stacked pots around them. Not only pots but baked design, art pieces.

She gave a sad laugh. 'Come on, Clyde, you know as well as I do that I haven't done anything interesting for five years. Just industry standards, pots and trendy cups. Thirty dollars apiece in Artware. I teach at the College and pay my mortgage.'

Aichen felt the cold settling on his skin, a mask of cold on his face.

'You do yourself an injustice.'

'Come on, Clyde. You look like a fucking mummy standing there opening and shutting your mouth.'

There's no way I can plug a hole like this, Aichen thought, looking at her. A hole like this goes on bleeding until there is nothing left of a person. He could feel it: the sucking, the draining away, the exhaustion and the darkness. And if I'm not careful, she'll pull me down her black hole with her, into her private Plutonium Apocalypse, just the way Don Bealter would do with his chemical wasting or Sue Hyde with her nuclear-waste terror or even Lorna Bealter with her endless dull corridors of work. All children of these times are orphans, he thought, looking at Moira.

'I'm not just saying my present work is crud to dump on myself. I'm saying it because it's true.' Her voice had gone slow and ritual again. 'And don't try to tell me that truth is beauty. You of all people don't try to tell me that.'

'What is truth?' He rolled his eyes rhetorically up to the stucco ceiling with the scroll-like trimmings so trendy in the early 1900s. Seeing it made him realize that this room must once have been a bedroom. 'I can't be as sure of things as you are, this illusion that we do our best work in our youth.' Clyde lost that illusion around the age of thirty.

She had ceased to hear him, her eyes were focused inward upon dreadful, unpalatable truths. Truths not the least beautiful. Clyde remembered Madeleine Farquar's luminous inwardness. He moved around the bench and put his arm around her shoulders, noticing a dry, half eaten piece of toasted cheese sitting up on a plastic bag full of clay, looking like bait on the top of some unlikely trap.

'We all have moments like these, we don't want to indulge them,' he said indulgently. 'You certainly can't work now – you're too pissed. So you might as well put the clay down and come and have a drink.' He spoke with re-assuring logic and squeezed her shoulder. More than anything else her black hole, her emotional sink, frightened him. Should he try to plug it, he would end up like the little Dutch hero, Peter, with his finger in the dike, to be swept away in her tide of terrors.

She pulled away from him. 'Buddy, my buddy,' she said in a cold, clay voice. She held the lump of sticky material up and inspected it. There was nothing in it but a density, the chaos of inertia. It had no plasticity, no inwardness of its own. It was mute and unyielding; a simple coagulation of wet dust. She began to hum one of Ophelia's mad songs from her last scene.

'We'll still go for that drive,' Clyde said quickly. 'To Westlake or Bethells Beach or somewhere.' He saw it. They'd be old friends again. They wouldn't get drunk, just a few cold beers to have with sandwiches and chicken. They could watch the sun go down or the moon come up or whatever the hell was going on. They would talk in quiet voices about familiar things. When he dropped her off afterwards they would touch each other's hands and smile.

Moira looked down at her arms. Perhaps she hadn't heard him. The dry clay was falling off her like an old skin.

Snake had taken possession of the bottle. Now its undisputed master, she poured them all the final glass, to the brim. Clyde planned to nurse this one.

'You're not going to drive way-to-fuck this pissed,' Moira said, barely able to get the words out.

'You're right, I'm not.'

'Good.' Moira nodded as if some transaction of great mutual benefit had just taken place. Her right eye was beginning to descend, making her look sinister.

'There's a nice comfy couch,' Snake said.

Clyde screwed up one eye and stared her. Her face was broad and her mouth was wide and curved, like that of a fish. The muscles of her throat pulsed softly, where gills would have been.

'Let's hear some music,' Moira said in an empty voice.

Clyde polished his glass off with a gulp. 'Not me. I'm ready to crash.' I'll sleep right here, he thought, in the ruin of words. Then crossed the thought out.

Moira sat up, her face flushed. 'The night is young,' she said, her eyes shining. 'I want to dance. To dance and dance. Let's hear some good ol' rock n' roll.'

Snake rose and motored for the stereo. There was an urgent fluidity in her hips. Clyde took the vacant couch and pulled a cushion under his head. He watched while they danced clumsy rock n' roll and a hilariously obscene twist. Their motions became elongated, as if they were moving underwater. Bands of light rolled over them as if they had their own private light show. Their shadows seemed intent on devouring each other.

Aichen opted out.

Clyde Aichen's nest in the Waitakeres had all the primitive grace of a home-made house without Clyde ever having had to raise a hammer. He'd bought it like that from a home handyman lock, stock and barrel, complete with wood-stove and creaking plumbing. When Jeannette had been with him it had always been too small, the rooms designed more around the arbitrary length of sheets of ply rather than for human comfort, but now he was alone it was too big. A workroom for him. An extra bedroom keeping vigil. A room under the house waiting for children. Our nation's writers, someone had told him, like to live on the margins; to be of the city but not in it.

Aichen didn't care about any of that. He just liked the quiet for writing. His first two novels had given him the deposit on this house, and he was grateful to them. When he saw them in his bookcase he greeted them like old friends, with the pride and familiarity of a long and fruitful association. They were not his best fiction but there was plenty of spring in their step, and he could not deny their ongoing popularity.

The nest was also an ideal place to live through a hangover. Aichen's method was to shower first and then lie naked in the sun on his deck, a pitcher of clear cold rainwater by his side, a South American novel in hand, the tall, calm cabbage tree in full view, and a plate of no nonsense cheese and tomato sandwiches by his side. The cabbage tree, he believed on such occasions, was a benevolent force, sending out healing rays all around the valley, channelling good vibes his way. Channelling good vibes into his bruised brain cells. That's how he visualized it. The cabbage tree pouring out its healing light, his grateful brain cells soaking it up.

The South American novel was not necessarily to be read, as the sandwiches were not necessarily to be eaten, but to be on hand as an intellectual comforter of some sort, something upon which he could rest his head, metaphorically and sometimes literally. It is a matter of some doubt whether South American novels are intended to be read at all, being best apprehended snug up against the naked cheek of a half sleeping face belonging to a naked, half sleeping body of a person (a man in this case) living through a hangover. That way it felt as if his whole body were the book while the decking planks beneath became an extension of its pages. If he placed the book beside him, at eye level, he could see the column of ants that climbed up from between the planks and onto the book, along the spine, and raced across the open pages in rhythm to the print, each bearing a letter, having ferreted them out of the dead leaves and the earth and the feathers of rotting birds, and the innards of half-gutted rats, to place them carefully in line, one after the other. These ants were busy constructing the words, letter by letter, but there were others that seemed determined to remove the words, letter by letter, scurrying off them, out of sight under the planking.

He didn't have to read the novel to understand it, only see the ants in motion, their run from touch to touch, their staccato scurrying, their aimless wars and revolutions. He could lie and stare at it all close up, and when he closed one eye and opened the other, ants and book fell through an invisible dimension to land unscathed back on the deck as if nothing had happened. When he closed both eyes, ants and book were still there, in negative, going about their respective business, the words doing their work, the ants doing theirs.

At the same time the book provided a certain intellectual ballast to an otherwise wasted morning. It was a loophole through which he could step to avoid the fact that the poem started the day before was still there to be written and was not being written. The article likewise. Deadlines were moving in on him like contracting horizons. Having the novel by him, absorbing it through his sweating skin, tracking its lines by osmosis, he had something to weigh against the guilt and the emptiness of hangover territory. Sometimes he had to vomit, not over the book but over the decking that supported it, sending its thousand strong supporting cast of ants adrift on a sea of froth and bile. But with the book by his side, its pages compliant, he could feel, against all odds, that something had been done.

At the nest he could pull the plug on the phone and suffer no interruptions to his suffering. In such a silence a headache is possessed of a certain purity, an essential form, and the light hits the trees in a particularly bright, glossy fashion. Clyde could stroll from the shower to the deck and back with confidence that he would not be interrupted. He could allow his body to become sexually aroused without the fear of any more embarrassment than any naked person might feel before the promiscuously open air. It was a puzzle, this sexual response of his body to a hangover. It was like a patch of heat passing through and out his body, returning and passing again. Being alone, he did nothing about these passing flushes of blood. It was not that he was hostile to solitary pleasures, rather he had learned that this post-alcohol arousal was a deceptive and illusive heat, liable to suddenly desert him in the middle of his squirming act.

Alongside the jug of cool, clear rainwater, collected in his own corrugated iron tank, was a jar of ascorbic acid and a teaspoon. He had great belief in the magical properties of ascorbic acid, the wonderful boost it could give the immune system after the battering it had taken from the finest of brandies. Sodium ascorbate would complement nicely the healing influence of the cabbage tree. He was almost superstitiously convinced that vitamin C could undo all the damage he had done the night before. He visualized it restoring the liver, flushing the kidneys, visiting a sharp spice to his brain and messages of love to his benighted genitals which, on this occasion, were flowering like a greenhouse cabbage. And as he stirred the powder in, waiting for it to be totally absorbed into the clear grain of the water, the impossible happened. The phone rang.

Clyde cursed.

The ringing phone was evidence enough of the true treachery of a hangover. He had forgotten to pull the plug on it, there was no other possibility, no one else he could blame. He could let it ring of course, but its shrill insistence cut out across the morning with the effect of a chainsaw starting up, or a motor mower. He tossed the vitamin C down with a grimace and lumbered to answer it, reflecting morosely that there were two kinds of people in the world, those who can happily let a phone ring and those who would bust a gut to answer one. Take your pick. As he strode across the deck, his engorged cock flapping against his stomach, he reflected that he could just as easy reach down and pull the plug now as answer the phone, the caller wouldn't know. But of course it is not just the irritation of the ringing that compels the bust-a-gut phone answerer, or causes the curse and the curious twist of disappointment when the phone falls silent as the hand touches it, he thought as his hand went for the phone. It's just that you never know. Even with a hangover. There are phone calls that can change your life.

The voice on the line was cool and silvery. He sat down when he heard it, his cock nibbling against his belly button.

It was Madeleine Farquar.

At 4 p.m. that afternoon, when the heat had left the deck, Clyde Aichen had a cautious beer and went to work. He started with Don Bealter's diary, not expecting too much, and discovered a meticulously kept record, written in a neat hand, covering from the 1st of June 1974 right up to 1991. These precise, factual entries revealed recurring seasonal bouts of illness covering a wide variety of symptoms from mild lassitude to coma, periods in which he was bedridden from a day to two to three or four months.

And always this tied in with spraying.

22/10/85 – Felt ok in the morning. By 2pm severe muscle aches, asthma much worse, a bit of a skin rash. Neighbour spraying organochlorines on peaches....

4/10/86 – Spray drift so bad we had to shut windows. I had immediate breathing problems. Later I got angry and shouted at Lorna. She cried and got upset. I don't know why I did that. Later on, I got the shits, and now I haven't any strength left to keep writing.

Not all the entries aimed for such objectivity, but became a record of the subjective mental state of his mysterious illness.

12/3/88 – The sprayers are at work, getting the weeds that spring up with the autumn rain. I suspect they're using 245T. I can smell that stuff miles away. I feel like I'm in a prison with no air. I tried to do some simple addition this morning to help Lorna with the accounts and ended up staring at the figures like a Neanderthal. It's taken me half an hour to write these few sentences. I get half way through and forget what I was going to write.

9/7/88 – Suddenly I'm terrified for myself and Lorna. What if this is permanent? What if I just get sicker and sicker? Yesterday I couldn't get to the lavatory. I was too weak to even crawl properly and I lost my bowels half way down the hall. I couldn't lift myself up off the floor let alone clean it up. Lorna had to clean it up. This has never happened before. How are we going to cope on a sickness benefit? My thoughts go round and round like they are being hauled by big rumbling boulders. I'm helpless. What if Lorna ran out on me? Sometimes she looks so tired. I catch her looking at me in a resigned kind of way. I am responsible for taking all the joy and dreams out of her life. I don't know if I have the strength to live with that.

4/12/88 – I get so frustrated and shitty when I'm ill. Every sound scratches across my brain. Human voices sound like chalk squeaking on a blackboard. Every small disturbance infuriates me. A fly buzzing in the room fills me with murderous rage. Lorna takes the brunt of it. Sometimes I've tried to beat her, but I'm usually too weak. I blame her for trapping me here on the farm after 'nam. It seems like she's responsible for closing my life right down. I lash out at her even though she is my only support. It's crazy to think she is responsible for my condition, but when I'm in it, I am crazy. My head doesn't feel right and my emotions are all over the place. All Lorna would have to do is ring the boys in the white coats and I'd be finished. She could lease the farm and do quite well for herself, without me. And now, writing this, I want to start blubbering. I blame the army, I truly do blame the bloody army.

The most recent entry concerned his current bout, and Aichen himself appeared.

I'm back in bed unable to move. This time I poisoned myself with Roundup, because I'm a fool and didn't believe my own history. A writer bloke is coming up to see us and do an article about me. This is very important. People need to know, but it's more than that to me. It's my cry for help. A cry for help here goes no further than my soundless room. Maybe this Aichen can carry my cry for help out into the world. If people knew what was happening, they wouldn't let it go on, I'm sure of that.

I'm not so sure of that, Clyde said silently, picking up Bealter's medical record. Underneath it all, people do know what's going on. Placed alongside the diary, which of course would never stand up as evidence, the medical record made a devastating picture of medical bungling and dishonesty. Consisting of doctors' letters and reports going back to 1974 the record revealed that medical authorities had consistently under-read and misread Don Bealter's illness. The first reports from army doctors, with their references to post war stress, implied that the symptoms were psychological in origin and of a temporary nature.

Tranquilizers were prescribed. Ritalin.

Besides the one reference to 'chronic flu like symptoms and diarrhoea,' the first real effort at a diagnosis wasn't made until the late 1970s by a Dr Alan Temple of Auckland, who suggested angina as the origin of his chest pains, and put him on heart tablets. Apparently Bealter half accepted the diagnosis, but later turned up with rashes and extreme lethargy. A puzzled Dr Temple abandoned his diagnosis but clung to his belief that the heart was the source of the problem. There was an odd, isolated mention of 'mood swings.'

In the early 1980s another Doctor, a Dr Philip James, identified impaired liver function. This organ, which has the job of processing the body's toxins, showed signs of scarring and was performing sluggishly in what Dr James described as 'a manner consistent with a chronic hepatic condition.' He described the liver as being in a 'pre-cancerous' condition and took a blood sample to test for Aids. He suspected his kidneys might also be damaged. He took Bealter off the heart pills and prescribed a tonic for 'on-going tiredness'. Later the same Dr James diagnosed 'moderately severe' candida and put him on a course of antibiotics.

No real progress was made until Bealter went to a young doctor who had just moved into the district. On the 10th of September 1986, Dr Adam Poole identified a blood infection and confirms the weak liver function diagnosis. Antibiotics are prescribed.

On the 12th of September Dr Poole diagnoses gastroenteritis and changes the antibiotic. On the 19th he discovers an arm and stomach rash and takes Bealter off the antibiotics fearing the rash to be an allergic reaction to them. Puzzled by the continuing gastroenteritis symptoms, he suggests bleeding stomach ulcers and tests for stomach cancer. On the 19th he identifies corneal erosion and increased temperature, suggests a low-grade viral infection and takes blood tests for glandular fever.

Poole identified what he called 'irritability and aggression, free-floating anxiety and disproportionate effect.' He wrote: 'Much of the fear and aggression comes from not being able to handle the world.' On the 21st of October of the same year, he treated a migraine with codeine sulphate, and suggested a general 'depression of the immune system.' He noted that the chronic fatigue invites a diagnoses for ME, but held back from making that diagnoses, apparently confused by the amorphous nature of ME symptoms. On the 23rd of October, he made a house visit for 'aggravated asthma and breathing difficulties.' He noted that the patient had no history of asthma. On the 27th he is back with 'itchy dermatitis,' and a tentative diagnoses of shingles. He noted that these rashes are not a common symptom of M.E. On the 30th he made another house call, noting that the patient is too weak to move and seems to have complete 'muscular atrophy.' He noted also a clouded iris and 'mental depression,' random fevers and putrid breath.

On the fourth of November he wrote an official letter to Bealter to take to social welfare. In it he listed most of the symptoms he and those who had come before him had found and concluded that Bealter had chemical poisoning due to Agent Orange exposure and declared him to be 'chemically sensitive to poisons, particularly pesticides.'

Unfortunately, this letter was only in photocopy, and Clyde shortly found out why. The original had gone to the Department of Social Welfare in a bid to win a sickness benefit on the grounds of chemical poisoning. The Social Welfare Department, after doing nothing for a long time, wrote to him and announced that they have lost his letter but have granted him a benefit on the ground of having a 'weak heart.' Attached was a note from the army disclaiming any knowledge of Don Bealter.

Clyde had a second, less cautious beer and walked around the room. His hangover was beginning to disperse. He had to turn on the light to keep reading when he ran out of daytime. When the light came on, the shadows sprang back and the room stepped forward in such relief, he felt a familiar twist of loneliness. At its heart lay the great loneliness of sentience. Is there anybody out there?

What a desperate, unforgiving age we live in, he thought. An age at war. Not the cold war, with its flag-waving and sword rattling, but a deeper, darker war hardly identified. A war that saw the steady destruction of everything, and the rise of the greedy monster whose mirror glass towers fractured the sky. The 1980s! What could be said about it? That the music was good. That the best B grade horror movies were made. That The Terminator arrived. That greed and fear were finally enshrined in the markets. The decade this little country dropped its egalitarian façade and corporates choppered away to $500 lunches while beggars appeared on Queen Street. And a person like Don Bealter was left to rot away on his farm, and to watch his farm and family go under, while the chemical companies responsible were laughing all the way to the bank. Greed works! That was the great catch cry of the age. Greed works! Far from being a deadly sin, it was greed that made the world go around. And it was fair, because everybody had a fair chance to be as greedy as everybody else, if not greedier. The greedier the better. And all the while the invisible war went on, and the darkness grew like the shadows in an Italian horror movie.

He'd heard that the country's jovial and popular prime minister, had had the rug pulled out from under him by the money men who threatened to pull the plug on New Zealand if we didn't start moving some of that public money into corporate hands. It was an ugly, sinister story, and Clyde was sure that it was true.

The file on Monsanto and its popular product, Roundup, said it all. First up on the file was a letter from the Davenport Toxins Action Group to the Davenport Community Board. The letter quoted a medical practitioner detailing reactions to Roundup including fever, muscle aches, skin disorders, behavioural problems, immune system depression, with an exacerbation of pre-existing illnesses such as multiple sclerosis, motor neuron disease, migraine attacks and diabetes. Roundup showed up as a contributing cause of miscarriages – and cancers.

Quoting further from a U.S. magazine, Roundup was cited as being involved with paralysis, severe chemical burns, blindness and bleeding ulcers.

He discovered that most of the original toxicological data on Roundup provided by Monsanto to the U.S. Environmental Protection Agency in the 1970s was faked. The company had not faked its own data, of course, but had used fraudulent data from an 'independent' research lab, Industrial Bio Test. Seventeen of the twenty-six studies undertaken by IBT were found invalid by the EPA. The fraudulent studies related to cancer and birth defects.

He further discovered, in a photocopied article in Progressive Magazine, that Monsanto was IBT's largest customer, 'and was one of the four companies that knew of IBT's fraudulent practices but failed to report them.' According to the article, one of IBT's executives, a Paul L Wright, was employed by Monsanto before and after his job with IBT. It was during his time at IBT that the fake Roundup data was produced. The fake data related to Roundup's connections with mutations in mice and tumours in rabbits. In 1983 a U.S. court convicted him of fraudulent testing. Over two hundred other pesticides were involved.

Since all this had happened more than ten years ago, and Roundup was still happily being sold over the counter, Clyde guessed that these fraudulent tests were old news and that Monsanto had managed to weather the storm. Further reading showed that they had, and claimed to have supplied the EPA with all the missing and relevant data, this time supplied by their own tests and carried out by their own people. Even then they would not release the information or subject it to peer review. Indeed, it was a matter of public record that Monsanto sued the EPA to prevent them from releasing registration data to the public. While this new data was being collected, Roundup continued to be sold with a 'provisional registration' from the EPA, and Monsanto continued to use the old Bio Test results in the process of marketing its product.

The whole product was submerged in an atmosphere of murky secrecy, such as the existence of a 'secret ingredient,' a surfactant, described by the company as 'inert,' therefore not listed as an active ingredient. Not listed at all. The company refused to provide the chemical name for the substance whose job it is to maximise the poison's adherence to the plant, citing, 'industrial secrets.' The formula is an important commercial secret, and no competitors could weasel it out of them! Furthermore, there is no requirement for them to provide toxicological data on the mysterious substance since it is not toxic! *Voila!* It is inert. Except suspicion clung to it the way it does at the door to any mystery, asking questions and hazarding speculations. Is substance X a greater environmental threat than Roundup's active substance, glyphosate, which the company claims is little more than a simple salt? Watch this space.

Clyde's image of the EPA as a vigilant force for ecological security crumbled when he discovered that pesticides could be marketed without registration, and only ten percent of all registered pesticides and their ingredients had complete hazard assessments with available data.

Over ninety percent lacked proper mutation studies with similar gaps in cancer and birth defect studies. None of the required tests examined the cumulative effects of long-term exposure or delayed effects such as nervous system damage or immune suppression. The whole thing was as leaky as a sieve, the safeguards were a laugh if you had that kind of sense of humour.

In the process of reading, something had happened to Clyde's sense of humour. He wasn't laughing. A story like this had to have a cut-off point somewhere.

He felt tainted. He got up and had a shower in clean rainwater.

At least, he hoped it was clean.

After his shower, and to clear his mind of all that nasty stuff, he lingered at his bookcase, thinking of a Rilke poem he'd made a mental note to look up. It was to do with Madeleine Farquar, and the unravelling of his own poem somewhere inside him.

The bookshelves were silent. All their culture was closed away between covers, covers which faced themselves through crowded, silent pages. Collectively, leaning into their accustomed spaces, they had nothing to say to the brutal, documentary realism of the medical file and the Roundup stuff. Their great collective culture fell silent.

When Clyde opened his Rilke and began flicking through the sonnets, he found himself in the presence of a great Innocent celebrating his passion; and his innocence was possible because there was no fucking Roundup or Uranium 238 about to undermine the foundations of the world. He had to go back before Rilke, back to Blake to find a poet who might have understood. 'Little Rose thou art sick.' One hundred and sixty years would not have changed his diagnosis.

It was as if the pesticide had polluted all his books and their strong hard words, undermining them, mocking them, insidiously working its way into the ground soil of the poem seeding inside him, bringing a canker to the rose.

He went to the fridge and uneasily took out another can of beer, even though he was due to go to bed. He was on the edge of some revelation he hoped would not be long delayed.

He returned to the Rilke and began reading, *muscle of infinite reception/ tautened in the quiet starry blossom…*

There was another world sitting inside his skin.

On Sunday afternoon Clyde went to visit his mother, as he usually did, stopping off along the way to buy some flowers to refresh her vase and a packet of her favourite chocolate wheaten biscuits, as he usually did, reflecting, as he usually did, upon the bleak prospects for old age in a declining prosperity. Approaching the 'attractive' modern units of the Westmere Rest Home, with their bright anonymity and cheerful facelessness, he thought of the tribes who'd thrived on this very site with its easy access to the harbour, huddling together in the winter for warmth, old with young, body against body.

A well-tended flower garden skirted the well-trimmed path; the lawn had the scrupulously shaven look of a public park or crematorium grounds. He noted that the edges, where grass met the footpath, had been neatly sprayed. Roundup, no doubt. He'd often vowed that if it came to this for him, he'd rather die, take the clean way out with an overdose of analgesics or a walk into the ocean. It boiled down to a question of aesthetics. He would never be able to bear the neat garden or the scrupulously shaven lawns. He would die with dreams of a tribe pressing their warm bodies in around his, not in a charnel house dressed up to look like a motel.

His mother had been here for two years, since the day she closed her mouth into a thin tight line and refused to speak or acknowledge being spoken to. The doctors were frankly puzzled. Her symptoms matched no known aetiology. She could look after herself, clean up, cook a little, carry on as normal in a minimal way, it was just as if for her the whole human race, and the memory of it ever having existed, had vanished from her mind. Only the artifacts were left, the running water, the boiling jug, chocolate wheaten biscuits – these things went on existing. Clyde marvelled at the great clamped silence her mind must have become. To neither read nor write nor speak nor even, perhaps, hear! To have abandoned words so utterly! He might have believed this silence to be an autumnal calm but for the tightness of mouth, and the emphatic rigidity with which she sat on her chair.

The inside of her unit matched the exterior in tactless good cheer. There was a small kitchen with a faux-Formica unit and sideboard, a small faux-Formica table where two might sit with some discomfort. The other room contained her bed and couch, and an easy chair on which she sat, upright, fixed silent, staring towards the window, not acknowledging his entry.

There was a dry, dustless feel to the room as if it were not occupied at all. The skin of her forehead, where he kissed her, had the same warm, dry feel. He went into the kitchen, threw out the wilting flowers from the previous week, and placed the fresh flowers in the vase. As he put on the jug and squirted the chocolate wheaten out of the packet onto a plate, he chatted to her as if they were having a normal conversation.

'Car's going well, Mum, even if she's full of rust.'

As he placed the tea and biscuits in front of her he wondered, as he usually did, if she lived in a magical world in which such things as tea and biscuits simply appeared from time to time out of thin air, wafted there by genies and spirits; a world of animated things moved by mysterious external agencies she could only guess at. Sitting with her, talking into her frozen silence he didn't believe it for one minute, unless she had come to make it true by sheer effort of will.

It was more likely that her silence was a kind of rage, a tantrum from which she had not been able to shake loose. He believed she saw and heard and understood everything, he had told her as much, and that her silence was the Great Refusal. The Universal Nay. It was not that hard to figure. He had told her this, hoping to catch some acknowledgement, some gleam of conspiracy, but there had been nothing. A nothing so absolute he doubted the awareness he was assuming; and the thought that he (and the doctors) might be wrong, that he was saying these things to a vast and mute deafness, taking soundings in a soundless room, awoke in him ancient childhood terrors of loss and abandonment. At the age of three or four he had woken to the hollow sound an empty house makes, and screamed until his mother had returned from the neighbours. The memory of that occasion had never left him, and was re-awoken in echo every time he sat with her and watched the mechanical movement of her jaws on the chocolate wheaten.

He spoke lightly and casually of his work, saying everything and nothing, answering the questions he imagined she would ask. He described to her in humorous detail the trials and tribulations, imaginary or real, his shagged old Toyota put him through. He spoke of putting a bullet through its head as if it were a diseased dog, a comment that might have amused her in the days when she was still amused at the human world. In fact when he thought about it, her silence had followed hard upon the disappearance of her sense of humour.

There must be some intimate connection, he thought, between laughter and speech. He tried the idea on her in the hope of catching her out but her eyes remained blank.

He didn't mention Jeannette, or Moira, or any other part of his personal life. Once he had brought Moira here, and she swore afterwards that the old lady had followed her with her eyes, but hadn't been able to catch her at it; whenever she had looked the old woman had been facing the window with the same frozen silence, her eyes as hard as polished stones.

Unexpectedly, he longed for Jeannette who was expert at bright and chatty conversation and who always knew how to put his mother at ease. In the days before the old woman's long, elected silence, the two would sit at a window not unlike this and exchange pleasantries with an easy facility Clyde envied. And in the days before the long, strained silences between them, he and Jeannette had been able to talk too; extended supple conversations that were wide ranging rather than deep. Sitting in his mother's silence, he suffered the larger silence of his life.

He got up and went back into the kitchenette, finding what he was looking for among the detergents and polishes under the sink. A half full bottle of Gordon's Gin. This bottle was something of a mystery, since it was always there, always half full. He splashed a little into a glass and topped it up with water. The only logical explanation was that his mother drank the same amount each week, a bottle a week, Clyde's Sunday visits coinciding with the half-way point. This was the logical explanation but he didn't feel it was the true one. Perhaps his mother simply added water to the bottle after he left from some obscure obsession to keep the level at half.

'She was drowned,' his mother said distinctly, as he walked back to join her. Since she was faced away from him in her easy chair, he didn't see her say it, but he heard it plain as day.

'Who was drowned, Mum?' he asked casually, as if they were resuming a conversation momentarily broken off.

But his mother's face was the same frozen mask. Clyde was suddenly frightened. This mask was not his mother at all; another entity entirely lay behind it. Her voice had issued from her mouth, some spooky oracle of the dead. He drank half the gin and tossed the fear away. There is no fear without thought, he thought. It was more likely he'd heard the voice in his head; being with his mother had sparked a memory of something she had said. As with the bottle of gin, there was a logical explanation that didn't sound right, and it brought home to him the mystery of his mother's condition. She could see. She could see wheaten biscuits. She could move her hand out, pick one up and convey it to her mouth. She could hide a bottle of gin among the detergents where he was sure to find it. Of course she could see and hear him. If that were the case, then how to account for her utterly blank features, that carved mask that allowed nothing, no shred of feeling, to leak through? How could she screen out an echo of amusement, a predatory glint? It was not humanly possible.

'Who was drowned?' he repeated, watching her closely, but the game was lost. Out the window, three or four old people had gathered on a bench. They looked like people waiting, for a bus perhaps. The cargo-cult of the aged, he thought.

He finished his gin and prepared to leave, catching a glimpse of a photograph of his mother as a girl placed carefully on the small dressing table by the bed. The little girl was laughing, her mouth wide open, sunlight turning her hair into bright aureoles.

They met in the park, sat on the park bench near a marble statue of a soldier from the Boer War and a mothballed cannon. The soldier had lost his head, and the cannon was aiming its stoppered mouth somewhere in the direction of the gleaming mirror-glass towers of downtown. The day was clear and fine with lots of warm sunlight splashing down. Sparrows and doves were flipping about.

Madeleine said, 'What do you think of my story?' She sat beside him at a suitable distance. Enough to place a paper bag brought from the café. She opened the paper bag and pulled out a salad roll. A sparrow landed on the other side of her and eyed it up.

After a moment, she gestured to the salad roll, saying, 'What do you say before you eat a piece of lettuce?'

He shrugged.

'This is the *crunch*.' She put the roll into her mouth.

'If I debated with food, it might talk me out of eating it,' he said, imagining long, philosophic discussions with garlic and cheese, chicken and chips. 'There are a lot of eggs around with some pretty hard-boiled attitudes.'

She tried not to choke. 'Then you'd starve. But what about my story?'

He wondered what a salad roll and a mince pie would say to each other, how they would get along, what differences in approach they might have as they faced the grinding maw awaiting them. Would the mince pie crack hardy and make jokes? Would the salad roll meditate? Would their discussion reflect national concerns?

'You write with ease and fluency, which is a great start.'

'Maybe so. What's the *but*? There's always a *but*.'

'There's no such thing as a perfect story.'

She grimaced. 'There's no such thing as a perfect love affair.'

There were lots of things Clyde could have said. He didn't say them.

'It's all so painfully overt.' Like I feel now, he thought.

'Is it that bad?'

Idly he moved his feet in the direction of encroaching birds. Doves were scooting around, under the park bench, alert for crumbs. The sparrows were up on the bench, after the main supply.

He had to watch carefully what came out of his mouth. 'Michael's attraction to Mary is done very well. The passage in which he looks at her while she cradles the wounded bird is one of the best in the story.'

Saying that brought home to him just how bad the story really was. A tender moment over a wounded bird? Spare me! He wasn't going to say that. He wasn't going to spoil a good salad roll. And even one of these little sparrows was more robust than the fragile psyches of young writers.

'Did I get Michael right? Is that how a man might feel? His sudden attraction to her? I wasn't sure. Writing from a male point of view is hard.'

'For me, too.'

She laughed. 'But you might understand more about male attraction.'

'I prefer women myself.'

'Ha! Young and beautiful, of course.'

He blushed and gestured quickly to the page, 'I suppose for Mary we can read Madeleine?'

'Is it that obvious? It really did happen, I mean it's objectively true. I found a wounded bird. I've always had this thing about birds, so quick and yet so helpless. Ever since I was young I've had an attachment to them. I must identify with them in some way.' Her hands dipped and swivelled to the rhythm of her words.

'Unfortunately, the fact that something actually happened doesn't automatically make a good story. It's sure as hell no guarantee that you'll write well.'

'That passage where Michael falls for Mary while she held the bird was the hardest to write. I had to think and react as a man would, feel as a man would.' She laughed at the memory of what it was like to try and feel attracted to herself through the agency of a man.

'Maybe that's why it's successful. You had to get at one remove from yourself.'

'Is my self-involvement with the story so appallingly obvious?'

'No.'

Neither was quite sure where that left them and Madeleine retreated into herself, her now familiar vanishing act. He noted how long and curved her eyelashes were, and the faint, trembling muscular movement along her jaw. The fact is, he thought, I am open to her. Incomprehensibly open. So open she could come right into him and wreak all kinds of havoc. What was holding her back?

'Writing is important to me now,' she said. 'I've just emerged from a relationship with a man that became destructive. You can get addicted to people, you know, and to sex. Sex can be very addictive.' She took a thoughtful bite on her filled roll. The roll's screams of fear and ecstasy were cut off by her descending teeth.

'For the addict it can be,' Clyde said cautiously, thinking of Heinz on his knees before Betty, the Victorian Maid, the sad, hanging angle of his genitals.

'I have a tendency towards melodramatic, destructive relationships,' she said.

'*I fall upon the thorns, I bleed,*' he said, clutching his chest, wondering if she'd recognise the Shelley. He thought also of how good Shakespeare was at holding melodrama at bay by the sheer intensity of his language; as if it were up to language to rescue emotion from its fallen condition.

She laughed delightedly. 'That's it!'

'A halo has a very short distance to slip before it becomes a noose.' He was on a roll now! Get 'em laughing, get 'em crying.

'Tell me about it!'

'I'm too bruised.'

Quietly she said, 'I don't ever want that again. That destructive part.'

'Who would?'

A cloud crossed the sun, racing a diffused coastline across the park. A fresh flock of sparrows skipped through the trees above where they sat. Madeleine lifted her head to watch them. Meanwhile, one of the sparrows on the bench beside her made a play for the filled roll which lay half eaten in her lap.

Clyde quoted:

'*…muscle of infinite reception*
tautened in the quiet starry blossom,
sometimes overpowered by such fullness
that the sunset's call to rest
scarcely can return to you
rims of petal sprung wide open
you resolve and strength of many worlds!
We, the violent, last longer.
But when, in which of all lives, when at last

are we open and receptive?'

He hadn't intended to quote it all, but once he had begun it unravelled from his mouth like a silver thread. He suddenly felt the poem was an incantation that might pull Rilke's angel right out of the air. Perhaps offer some practical assistance in this hopeless situation.

'That's something to do with what's wrong with my story, isn't it?' She was watching him intently as if to hypnotise him and get at the truth that way. I'll go under easy, he thought, and caught a vision of himself slipping down between the waves and under blissful water. It's very simple, he thought. She wants to know the truth and I can tell her. She wants to know with the avidity of a lover, because she's a writer and can't resist the truth.

'It's a closed story,' he confessed. 'It's predictable. The moral is predictable. The bird is too easily a symbol for Mary's wounded psyche...' *Clunk* goes the symbol.

'But that's the way it happened,' she said passionately.

'Must your art be as corny and as obvious as your life?' He offered a crooked grin. A little sugar coating for the bitter pill.

It took a while for her grin to come.

'It's an ok story. But that's not enough. An ok story is not really ok. It doesn't risk anything. It doesn't venture anything. It doesn't put you on the line. It comes from a totally rehearsed position.'

Her body went intensely still. There was a quiver beneath the still lake. The cheekiest of the sparrows had a peck at her forgotten filled roll.

'It's a very safe story. Far too safe. It's a ho-hum story. There's no irony in it, no backwash. No backlash. So the language can't rise above a certain level of operation. It's trapped inside a closed structure. It's not naked enough.'

He knew he was destroying the story right in front of her eyes. He remembered a recent drunken moment in which a poem of his own had deconstructed like this right in front of his eyes. No one was immune, no matter how much they'd written.

The recognition of what he was saying ran through her like the touch of a lover. He'd touched her in a very intimate place. Since he couldn't touch her physically, he had done it this way, psychically.

A strain appeared around her eyes and mouth; her skin looked suddenly stretched hard over the bones of her face as if, beneath, her skull was pushing outward. The severity of her facial lines turned to a skeletal gauntness, and there was, behind her wide, beautiful golden eyes, the starving anorexic teenager of a few years before. This girl took her head in her hands and howled. There was a room in his own skull where she sat upon a bed screaming.

He placed both his hands in his lap and stared out across the park. It didn't make any difference where he looked or what he noticed, he was inside her, swimming around in her psyche. It was embarrassing to be inside her this way, to know her so well yet not know her at all.

'You're absolutely right,' she said. She had the look of one accustomed to facing inner demons.

'It's not just a literary matter,' he said.

'I had anorexia bulimia for two years,' she said, hardly seeing him, belatedly sawing at the last of her salad roll. 'But I kept writing all the way through.'

She writes with her teeth clenched, he thought. He'd just seen it in the clamped tension in her face. The death's-head. The passion for control. For self mutilation.

'You went to the doctors?'

'They made it worse.'

'How did you get out of it?'

'I woke up one day and realized that I didn't have to attach myself to any particular thought or desire.'

'Nice trick, if you can do it.'

She threw the remains of her filled roll onto the grass and the sparrows and doves went in for the kill.

They walked back across the park to the College. He waited outside the bookshop while she went in to collect something. The student quadrangle was a holocaust of newspaper pages, lunch wraps, pieces of crumpled tinsel and fallen red-white Coca Cola cups. Students slumped about over their coffees. Music thundered out from the student radio station upstairs. It was Steppenwolf doing their Easy Rider classic, 'The Pusher,' from the sixties, the long lost sixties. Clyde remembered the song from his own youth, when he was Madeleine Farquar's age or younger. The age of closed rooms and sweet smoky smells.

A sudden rush of cool wind stirred the debris, whisked some lighter scraps around in a burst of brief, frenetic animation. The temptation to sentiment was like a taste in his mouth; memory, the deception of spring.

'I've seen a lotta people walking round
with tombstones in their eyes...'

She was back beside him.

'It must be strange for you to be standing here, listening to this kind of music,' she said, reading him accurately. Her comment opened the floodgates within him, however, and he was slammed by the door of time, stricken to the spot. Like Saul on his way to Damascus he was nailed by a hard light. He was glad that she could not see what was happening to him, glad that he had at least that much privacy from her. Why couldn't I have met her in another time, another place, another world? When I was a different person, he wondered.

The music went through its now predictable sixties' riffs.

She was looking at him, smiling. Everything about her smiled.

'The pusher is a monster...'

They walked back down towards the city which was lit by a hazed, curiously beautiful polluted sunset. He felt he had to tread carefully, as if the ground beneath him would break. He had no urge to speak. They walked with quiet accord down towards Queen Street and the bombastic sound of heavy traffic.

'I have to go,' she said quietly.

'Yes.'

They stepped over the space between them and hugged. He closed his eyes and felt the imprint of her on his body.

In the middle of the night the phone rang. Clyde was in the middle of a dream. He was swimming. Moira was sitting on a beach waiting for him.

She'd been waiting so long one of her legs had turned into a twisted, bony piece of driftwood. Grief had just taken hold of his heart. A grand and final grief. This was a great secret he shared with Rilke. Like brothers in complicity, they wrote it down in a poem which Clyde had lost.

Clyde reached across the bed. 'Hello?' The pain was still in his voice.

'Er, is that Mr Clyde Aichen?' A girl, he imagined, about thirteen or fourteen.

'Yes.'

'Sorry to ring you so late. This is the only time I get I can really talk freely.'

'Thaz alright.'

'Have you got a pen and paper handy?'

'Who are you? Does your mother know you're ringing me?'

'My name is Geraldine Parkinson, Mr Aichen, and I did my degree in physics rather than chemistry. But I've worked for the DSIR and the ISF.'

'ISF?' The DSIR, he knew, was the Department of Scientific and Industrial Research.

'International Science Foundation. Tell me, is your phone line safe?'

'It's never done me any harm.'

'I mean, is it likely to be bugged?'

'If they have to start bugging people like me, they're in real trouble.'

'I have some information. Perhaps you have a postal address or something I can send it to.'

Maybe even younger, he thought, eleven or twelve. This was some kind of cute call.

'What kind of information?' That seemed like the line of the moment. It reminded him of Moira's corner of the mouth movie lines.

'Toxicology data on glyphosate. Some info relating to the surfactant. Bits and damning pieces.'

He groped for his pencil and pulled a pad out from underneath the phone, upsetting it onto the floor.

'Are you still there?' Gingerly, he retrieved the phone.

'What's happening to your phone?'

'I dropped it getting a pad. Why can't we meet and talk about this in civilized hours?'

'There are no civilized hours, and I'm a married woman, Mr Aichen.'

Her childlike tones were full of mock reprove. 'Have you heard about canaries?'

'Those are the ones that sing?' He sighed. Canaries were only the beginning of it, he could see that much, blurred as he was.

'If they're alive, they sing. The miners used to use them to test for toxic gases, remember? If the bird stopped singing the miners would go no further.'

'Yes, I remember.'

'Well people like your Mr Bealter are the canaries of our society. Their illness is our warning, if you follow me.'

'Yes I do. Look, who the hell are you? I mean, how do you know about Bealter? Why the cloak and dagger stuff.'

'I told you who I am. I don't have to get involved with this personally. I don't have the time. All you need to do is give me your box number or whatever and I post you the info. I couldn't tell you all this stuff over the phone anyway.' Her manner implied that it would hardly be decent.

'I appreciate that, I'll give you my box number.' But even as he said it. he didn't want to do it. Although his box number was hardly a public secret. She could have found it without ringing up in the middle of the night, playing spooks.

'It doesn't photodegrade.'

'What?'

'Break down in sunlight. All that happens is that the water vapour burns off.'

'Off what?'

'Molecules of glyphosate.'

Her tone was heavy with implication. Clyde gathered that he'd been missing most of the conversation. He wrote the phrase down on his pad. *Molecules of glyphosate.*

'Have you ever done any housework, Mr Aichen? You're a writer, aren't you? I don't know that I've ever meet a real writer before.' Her voice reverted to ten year old awe-struck.

'You only met the unreal ones?'

'Ones that don't do housework.' Her laugh was quite innocent of any malice. 'I don't know about some of the stuff written nowadays. I'm old fashioned in my tastes. I like a drama with a good solid plot.'

'You sound like my publisher.'

'He knows which side his bread is buttered on.'

'Maybe, but he eats both sides anyway.'

She had a way of not laughing when she should.

'Have you noticed, after doing a bit of dusting around the house, how the dust motes just float around in any old shaft of sunlight. Strictly speaking of course they are floating everywhere, it's just that you can see them in the sunlight.' Her voice became wistful.

'I wish I knew what we were talking about.'

'Spray drift,' her little girl tone was wounded. 'If you're going to suggest that people are getting poisoned by chemicals, you have to have a point of entry. Into the body. Ingested, inhaled, absorbed through the skin. I thought you'd know that. Inhalation is a major risk with Roundup for reasons I've outlined.'

Clyde was starting to wake up. He could see it. In any spraying operation so much went into the air in vapour. With the water component burnt off in the sun, the free glyphosate molecule, maybe even bonded to its mysterious surfactant, could bounce about on the air lighter than dust, staying up for hours buoyed up by tiny currents, waiting to land on someone's skin or be drawn into their lungs. Point of entry.

'That's right,' she said, speaking into the silence as if she could read his mind. 'You're a quick learner. We know that spray drift can travel sixty miles in the right weather conditions, but what I'm talking about is something beyond spray drift. I'm talking about residual atmospheric vapour content. Chemical degradation of the air we breathe.'

Clyde wrote down spray drift and drew an arrow to 'molecules of glyphosate.'

'What do you think about this substance X, the surfactant. You know Coca Cola used to have a secret ingredient too. Cocaine.'

'Ah, that creepy surfactant...' the phone began to crackle as if someone were resting a Guy Fawkes night sparkler on the wire. '... little information... but I'll leave you with one thought. The company claims that substance X is inert. Well, truly inert substances are very rare in nature. Everything interacts with something. Even gold, which is as about inert as you can get, still wears away, turns to gold dust. An inert chemical is almost a contradiction in terms, but if it's *that* inert then it's a worry for the environment because how does it break down? By their very nature inert substances tend to hang around, get into food chains and that sort of sneaky business. Like plastic.' She sounded like a child telling her mother off for some infraction of the rules.

'I see your point.'

'I thought you would. As I said, you're a quick learner. I had a boyfriend once who, I found out, was an inert substance. Whether by nature or inclination only he would know. He tended to hang around, get his fingers into my food chain, among other things. No refrigerator was safe. He was a slow learner.'

Clyde laughed politely.

'Who did you say you worked for?'

'I didn't. That's commercially sensitive information. I've given you my name. That's silly enough.'

'You don't have more than one name, then?'

'That's an odd question.'

'I'm not sure how cloak and dagger this is.'

'There may be more than one secret ingredient to Roundup, a substance Y, is that cloak and dagger enough.'

'You like to be mysterious?'

'Look, I know these people, these chemical executives. I dine with them, I flirt with them, I flirt with their wives. I can be very naughty, you know. You've got no idea the silly things people tell me, things they don't think I understand.'

'You meet these people through your husband?'

Her reply was snaky charm mixed with the exasperation of a twelve year old explaining something very obvious to an adult. 'No, you sexist pig, Mr Aichen. I meet these people through my own professional contacts. Colleages and their contacts.'

'Of course.'

'Like the rats.'

'What rats?'

'Used in poisons research. Every company that trots along to the EPA with its latest little poison in tow has a bunch of toxicity studies to establish LD levels.'

'Lethal Dose.'

'You're keeping up,' she said encouragingly, as if she were teaching him to skateboard. 'Well these toxicity studies are usually performed on rats. Your good old rat study. Well it's a sham for a number of reasons, but one is because they breed them.'

'I'm not keeping up again.'

'Yes you are,' she said patiently. 'You're just not perfidious enough. You're not corrupt enough to see corruption. You sound like a nice person. Underneath.'

'Thanks, but what's that got to do with the rats?'

'They breed the rats to specification, with very high resistances to chemicals. You can breed resistant strains pretty fast. A successful resistant strain is worth a good fast kickback.'

'Can you prove any of this?'

'Prove? Don't be too naive. I'm talking about the rumour mill. I'm talking about what might make a good story over champers. Proof is a metaphysical concept. Can you finally prove anything?'

'No, but finality is a metaphysical concept too. In the human world it is sometimes possible to prove or disprove something.'

'Bravo! It's amazing what you can prove, but it's also amazing what you can't prove. It depends on how hard-arsed and reductionist you're going to be. Take Roundup for example. In order to 'prove' that Roundup did damage to, let's say, the chromosomes, you'd have to track a molecule or atom of the stuff as it passed into the body, follow it through the body and actually see it take a nibble at a chromosome. You can't do that. It's technologically and practically unfeasible.'

'Where does that leave us?'

'With statistics. The way they made the tobacco-cancer link. Circumstantial evidence, but there is a point, statistically, at which circumstantial evidence becomes overwhelming, unless you're an idiot or paid not to see it. If you are neither of those things you can see the writing on the wall long before it gets to the overwhelming stage. If enough people smoke and get cancer, you don't have to follow a molecule of nicotine into the body and watch it spark a tumour.'

'I see it.'

'Top of the class. Statistics can be subversive. But here's one to think about before I go. And I am going to, very soon. Look at the amazingly shameless rear guard action put up by the tobacco industry, and they are only peddling *one* poison. Once we'd got the drop on nicotine the jig was virtually up for the tobacco crowd, but look how long they've hung on, look how dirty they fight, trying to get the young people hooked.'

'Nasty stuff.'

'The tip of the iceberg. Now with the pesticide industry, it's a whole other ball game. You haven't just got one poison you're peddling, you have thousands, literally tens of thousands. I don't know exactly, but with mixtures and sizzling cocktails there are endless possible formulations. You spend five years getting the drop on substance 342 when suddenly substance 342 is taken off the market and five new products appear. It's the sorcerer's apprentice all over again. New ones are coming out with soft, user-friendly names like Escort and Network. Network sounds like some kind of support group. An escort is a high class whore, is she not? Meanwhile your old 342 reappears in a new formulation under another name.'

'And they fight every one.'

'Right. Every formulation. They're still fighting 245T even though we've had the dope on that for years. Dow Chemicals. Did you know Dow Chemicals is not even listed on the New Zealand stock exchange?'

'What does that mean?'

'It means it has dubious claims to being a proper company. But I have to go now, it's past my bedtime.'

'I've enjoyed talking to you, even though I've forgotten your name.'

'No you haven't. People often tend to ignore what I say.'

'Why?'

'Perhaps it's my manner,' she said candidly. As candidly as a twelve year old might.

'I'm a babe in the woods when it comes to this kind of stuff,' he said. He was too awake now to go back to sleep.

'Corruption is endless.'

'I'd like to meet. Maybe we could have lunch…'

'It's predictable that you should ask, but I've already told you, I'm married.' Her voice became very girlish. 'And one last thing.'

'Yes.'

'You should take care who you lunch with.'

'Why?'

'*Buenos noches, senor.* And sweet dreams.'

The line went dead.

Clyde lay on his bed and mimicked sleep.

The cold drizzle on the unopened bottle of beer. A favourite shot for commercial camera angles. Rich tears that roll down the neck of a fresh-from-the-cooler bottle. They soaked into the softened, ragged edges of the label. There's another camera angle. It's too early to be drinking.

The lines he had written lay in front of him and he searched them for some sign, some clue. Some arcane message. After all, the whole of the material universe was just a form of coded information. It was a matter of being code literate. You had to stare into the stinking guts of prophesy and draw your own conclusions. Cities burn in the guts of the sacrifice. Within those smouldering entrails, the thin bright thread of the poem. Few see their own faces and live.

With a quick flick of the wrist, he twisted the screw top off the beer and poured himself a few gurgles. It was too early to really *drink* and until the true subject of this poem was disclosed, the true source of it, that thin bright thread could only move this way and that through the smouldering entrails, blindfolded, tunnelling across the blank page in search of spaces. It was not a means of writing poetry he felt at all comfortable with. He preferred something palpable, visible. Preferably an object, within the compass of which might be disclosed its own vision of itself. He was suspicious of too much of this internal shit, these bright ethereal threads that too often led nowhere. As ephemeral as they were ethereal.

The beer settled with a cold, familiar comfort in his gut. He wandered out onto his deck to have a look at the late morning and think about what the hell he should be writing. The Greenpeace article was there, trying to turn an honest profit. There were depths in there too, *cliffs of fall*. A poem was there, but only half begun.

He thought of consulting the cabbage tree, realizing rather sadly that such matters were beyond the tree's jurisdiction or interest. The article, he realized sadly, wasn't really worth jackshit. No one really wanted to know about that kind of horror story, how they were being shafted by chemical companies – what he really needed was to be laying down the foundations for some kind of novel, something he could *sell*. His publisher was big with ideas on that score. That reminded him to ring his publisher before he pulled the plug on the phone and got serious about the morning's writing.

A neighbour across the valley was burning something off. Streaks of haze veiled the bush and trees, making them look a long way off, as if he were floating away from them. He remembered his dream conversation with the precocious voice. He found written on his pad the words 'spray drift' with an arrow to 'molecules of glyphosate.'

Two lines came into his head and he returned to his desk to get them down. The telephone rang. It was his publisher, George Stockman.

'The English publication of *Madagascar* has fallen through,' Stockman said without preamble.

'What a shit. It was a long shot.' With brief regret Aichen thought of his first novel. It had caused a brief sensation, been suitably praised and reviled, and quietly forgotten.

'They're all fucking long shots,' Stockman said without rancour. 'What are you writing now?'

'Ah… some poetry.'

'Oh yeah.' Stockman's voice cooled a few degrees. Poetry took a quick trip to Siberia. Then the enthusiasm returned, 'Have you heard my idea for an urban terrorist novel, set right here in Auckland?'

'A little bit,' Clyde said cautiously, making sure he got the lines down before they went out of his head, two more followed rapidly and he sensed a quickening pool of words.

'It's never been done properly here. You could take an average bloke. Mr Ordinary. Weird things begin to happen to him and he goes berko, off the deep end. Serious psychological stuff. You're good at all that head-tripping stuff, Clyde. That's your forte. Prose-wise, I mean.'

'Ah-huh.' Clyde doodled stars and spaces. He checked out his old smoking doodle with its malicious grin. Doodle knew something he didn't. Bride of Doodle was hiding something she shouldn't. The whole thing was looking dodgy.

Stockman's voice crackled down the phone. 'Something with plenty of violence. Your hero gets tied up in something bigger than he can understand, right? And he goes paranoid. He gets obsessed with some particular thing. He starts to believe that mysterious forces are moving against him. Maybe in his past he's lost someone dear to him and it's unhinged his mind. Maybe he gets jilted. I'll leave that to you. That's your forte, too. Anyway he gets into revenge on a grand scale.'

'Uh-huh.' Clyde patrolled through his lines on the screen, searching for clues.

'Now he's not stupid, in fact he's very controlled, and very sharp. And very organized. He deliberately places his rational mind in the service of his obsession. Spooky stuff. To him it's an act of bravery; only the reader can see it's an act of madness.'

'Very cunning, Stockman.'

'You've got no idea. So you've got a sociopathic killer with a mission to right some evil in the world. That would really upset our wimpy liberal readers. Have him say something really trendy then cut some trollop's heart out just for practice. A wonderful disjunction, you have to admit.'

Clyde admitted nothing, but Stockman barrelled on, 'He organizes a few loonies, social misfits with nothing to lose. Maybe he makes contact with some dissident Black Power members. You could tap into the Big Fear that these gangs will become politicized. Shit, I could set you up to meet some of those fuckers to give you a bit of local colour. These guys will cut your balls off if you smile on the wrong side of your mouth. Imagine them running around with explosives and AK47s! You could have a love interest, say between a yuppy career woman journalist and a Maori lesbian activist, or maybe the loony hero herself who kills her and eats her. You could have fun with that one. Great sex, great cuisine. Plenty of soul searching.' He was generous. 'As much soul searching as you like. And a cop. You'd have to have a cop who's on to them, who's one step behind them all the way. Or maybe a step ahead. Or a corrupt cop, which we're not supposed to have in this country, who gets off on what they're doing and helps them. You could make him a bad bastard, a leftover from the Red Squad 1981 Springbok days. You're good at bad bastards. They could rob the Bank of New Zealand building say. Christ, the BNZ's been robbing everyone else for years. They could shoot up someone just for fun before they left, like in that movie The Wild Bunch. Red blood all over the garish green carpet they have in that place. Have you seen that carpet? A great social statement. You can't go wrong.'

'Sounds great,' Clyde said in a deadpan voice. 'I'm sure there are writers who are very good at this kind of thing. Live by the pen, die by the pen.'

'Don't be so precious! You could do it better than anyone. And it's bound to be big, I mean everyone's fed up with the way this country is going. We've got plenty of disaffected loonies, make no mistake. I should know, I'm one of them. Our loonie could become their avenging angel. Some kind of popular hero vigilante type. Yeah! And maybe sex is the only thing that calms him, like a soporific. A good excuse for plenty of sex, since our hero needs lots of calming down. And lots of violence too, shoot-outs and executions. All logical and well organized.

'I get the picture.'

'I wonder if you do. Look,' Stockman became almost philosophical, 'people like to see things blow up in front of their eyes, especially things like mirror-glass buildings. You could have them plant a whole lot of bombs all around the city. When she blows, every major mirror-glass building goes up. The Rob Jones tower – boom! The BNZ tower – boom! Elder's Resources – boom! The Regent Hotel – boom! Tacky modern Capitalism – boom! And then the guy just vanishes back into the community. Puts on a smile with his tie in the morning. His motive is general and his method random. Christ, what a movie!'

Clyde couldn't see it but knew what it would look like, his publishers face, lean and dark with a lock of black hair falling over his right eye. At this moment he'd be grinning like a maniac.

'The other terrorists of course are a right bunch of screwballs. Have you read Conrad's Secret Agent? Academics don't appreciate how funny that book is. The whole thing's a big send up. You could do the same, take the piss out of all sorts of people in no uncertain way. You'd enjoy that. That's another of your fortes. You got lotsa fortes.'

'Ah-huh.' Two more lines appeared. There was heat and mystery in them, but none of the language he was used to worked, none of his old tricks cut any ice. He sipped his beer. The article could wait.

100

Stockman's voice lowered a register. 'There's another aspect to this, something I've given a lot of thought to. Did you know there are books whose publication or distribution in this country is banned, and they're not porn. They are urban terrorist manuals. Full of all sorts of fascinating info. Like how to make napalm out of Cold Water Surf. How to assemble a plastic explosive. Info on timing devices, weapons assembly, the works. A few skilled and dedicated people could fuck a whole city up, did you realize that? I've got the contacts, I can get these books. I can't publish them, but if the essential info was smuggled into the fabric of a novel, a thriller, what the hell could they do?' His enthusiasm reached a pitch.

'Christ, with a bit of luck they would be forced to ban it! Imagine the U.S. sales! A novel that is a revolutionary manual in disguise! Shit! I've thought of a couple of scenes. You see the book could begin with a description of some weapons assembly while two of the terrorists are talking. They could be talking about peace or brotherhood or their girlfriends. While they talk, what they do tells the reader how to put together some lethal motherfucker of a bomb out of everyday materials. And you could have a bizarre sex scene in which these two people put together an automatic weapon while fucking. I don't know any other writer in the country that could pull off a scene like that.'

'Great idea, Stockman.' Clyde sipped his beer and looked at his lines. Until he saw it, until it stared him in the face or kicked him in the backside it would go on like this, a cat and mouse game played between words and stubborn silence.

'Sure as shit it is. Done the right way, a book like that'd clean up. Some kind of literary equivalent of *The Terminator*, you know, that Arnold Schwarzenegger movie.'

'I'll think about it.'

'It's a damn good idea. It would be a great vehicle for all kinds of social comment. You could put a strong antiviolence message in it if you wanted.'

'Sure.'

'That would really bewilder the critics. Imagine *The Listener* review.'

'You have a point.'

'Hell. It's only an idea. I wouldn't tell you what to write. I wouldn't dream of it.'

Clyde Aichen slipped into a quiet bar in his favourite pub, the Queen's Head, like a schooner slipping into a bay after a long, stormy journey. Heinz Major was already berthed, nursing a beer, prodding sceptically at a hot pie on the counter before him and muttering imprecations at the advertising industry.

'You would not believe,' he said as Clyde placed his full glass carefully down on the table, 'the activities of so many intelligent people directed to such trivial ends for so many boring hours of a day. The celebration of a biscuit, the deification of a chocolate bomb, the glorification of a piece of soap. If you're lucky you score a contract with a car company and do 'creative' ads, every one like a mini Arnold Schwarzenegger movie.'

'*Monstrum horrendum, informe, ingens, cui lumen ademptum,*' Clyde said with satisfaction, sipping his beer, pondering the cultural impact and influence of Arnold Schwarzenegger.

'Sounds impressive. What does it mean in the language of ordinary mortals, *kiss my arse and I'll kiss yours?*'

His prodding had produced a blood like trickle of gravy from the side of the pie. It spread in a viscous pool on its oil soaked paper-bag.

'A monster fearful and hideous, vast and eyeless.'

'That's my wife you're talking about.' With a nihilistic gesture, Heinz left off torturing the pie and threw back his beer. 'It's all very well for you poets to point the finger, spout Virgil or whoever the fuck you're spouting.' His lips formed a contemptuous arch. 'Occupying the moral high ground, eh Aichen? Even though the waters of materialism do lap around your feet, still you remain pure of heart. And on the Benefit, or whatever passes for the Benefit these days.'

Clyde snorted. 'Only in death is there complete purity, even an old hack like you should know that. The same waters that lap at your feet, do lap at mine, brother my brother. The *Monstrum Horrendum* will swallow us all with no more thought than you give to swallowing that pie.'

It was Heinz's turn to snort. 'Bullshit. There's nothing pure about death. Your *Monstrum Horrendum* is all wormy and rotting corruption, brother my brother, my arse. Not for you. Every day's Cruisy Tuesday part-time at the College, with adoring young females over you like a rash.'

This was the usual banter, but Clyde could hear the whiplash of envy. He shifted uncomfortably in his seat. 'Courtesy of the Benefit, of course,' Heinz went on, 'thoughtfully provided by the taxes of honest labourers of the world, like myself.' He pulled away a pastry corner of the pie, revealing a dark, glutinous interior, held in place by a wrinkled skin of cooler gel.

'Greenpeace pays,' Clyde said defensively.

'Is that a fact? Fifty dollars a thousand words, I suppose. Two bucks an hour. Let's be honest, Shakes, where honesty is clearly lacking and truth walks with a begging bowl. It takes an old liar like me to spot an honest man, you know, and I can always spot a man who's living off someone else's taxes.'

'Talking of honesty, did you know you're getting bald on top?' It was true. It looked as if a chicken had been scratching around on the crown of the ad-man's head.

'Thanks for the update, Shakes. And don't try to change the subject. If you're on the hook, the least you can do is wriggle.' Heinz lumbered to his feet, sweeping the two empty glasses into a hairy fist. 'What did Jesus say? Before looking at the bags under your friend's eyes, you should look at the suitcases under your own.' But the heat had gone out of his voice, the banter had returned to ritual. The pie looked cool enough to almost eat.

The second beer appeared before him, full of amber fury. Heinz sat down, picked up the pie in both hands and stuffed it into his mouth, one half of it anyway, chewed briefly and swallowed noisily.

'I suppose you're a vegetarian?' he said.

Clyde watched the ad-man eat the pie and rub the pastry off his hands with the gestures Pontius Pilate might have used to purify himself of human affairs.

It was an image that lasted him well into his third or fourth beer.

Clyde Aichen had stopped counting the beers. He was sitting very still, thinking about Madeleine Farquar; he was not able to stop thinking about her, but he did cling to one simple understanding: his hallucination of her was not her. The smiles he saw, the laughter he heard, were not hers. They belonged to creatures inside his head that dressed up to look like her. Like a good story, he was making her up to suit himself.

A few more beers and the problem would not even exist.

'I think you've been avoiding me, buddy boy,' Heinz said, watching Clyde sourly from over the rim of his glass. Clyde's long silences had apparently unnerved him.

'Not successfully enough, obviously,' Clyde said without friendliness. He didn't want to talk bullshit with Heinz right now. He just wanted to sit there and drink beer and think about Madeleine Farquar. To indulge himself in a wash of thinking about her, so he could see. Just so he could see. See how far he could push it. How far he was prepared to go. Just how far thought could take him.

He'd be best off buying a bottle and getting out of there.

'I'm not spoiling your drink, I trust,' Heinz said. The man had a hide as thick as a rhino's. Clyde grinned as he thought of Betty, the Victorian maid, and the ethereal Cleo. He hadn't thought about Cleo at all. She had gone the way of luminous wings and fairy dust, into the rubbish file (it was a question of good taste), but now, after a few beers and the sight of Heinz's sozzled face, she was brought out and dusted off for inspection once more.

'How's the Toxic Avenger? New Zealand's answer to Hunter S Thompson? Whose goose are you cooking this week? Look out Monsanto, here comes Clyde Aichen?' He ducked beneath the table, laughing, his laugh turning quickly into a chesty cough.

'Stalled by the truth. I haven't even started writing yet.'

'How's the poetry business? Or should I say the con business?'

'Suspended, right now. I'm in suspended animation. I can neither read nor write nor think.'

'Lying's something you can always do, but Christ, you should be an ad-man. We've got more suspended animates in our office than any other. Booze is all that keeps most of them on their feet.'

'No different from a P.E.N. meeting.'

'Point conceded! Even an ad-man knows the truth when he hears it.' He held out both palms in surrender.

Thinking about Cleo offered an escape from thinking about Madeleine Farquar. Now that he knew Madeleine, it was ludicrous to think she worked nights in squalid downtown parlours. That was the trouble with imagination – it never knew where to draw the line. He was left, however, with that peculiar impression of similarity to account for. There was a simple way of putting it to the test and getting rid of that whole silly business for good.

He drank and thought about it.

'I used to be like you,' Heinz said, pointing a drunken finger in the direction of Clyde's heart. 'I used to be in love with words. When I read Mallarmé, I would caress them as if they were my first virgin surface. Ha ha. I was fucking wrong. Words! Watch them! Words have no integrity of their own. They're whores, even the pretty ones, and they'll lie down for any cock with the cutes or cunt with a clue. They are inherently debased, and can be further debased at any given point. This is the ad-man's creed. No job is too craven for them.' He nodded with satisfaction. He was, once again, not Heinz Major the ad-man, but Heinz the barroom raconteur. The word basher at work.

Clyde stood up. He had to get rid of Heinz if he was going to do what he thought he was going to do – and he was drunk enough to do it.

'I'd love to stay, Heinz, but I've gotta move.'

'What's gotta about it? You sat on a fuckin tack or something? You don't look normal.' He peered up at Clyde, puzzled.

'I'm already late.'

'Gotta date, have we?'

But the ad-man had lost it. Whatever he was looking for in Clyde's face had eluded him. 'You know, the heavy-duty Christians, the fundies, believe that the Father of Lies is writing a great long book using human hands to do the writing. There go all your novels,' he made a farting sound with his lips, 'there go all your plays,' he made another farting sound with his lips, 'your poetry! That's all just Old Nick laughing up his sleeve.'

'Are you thinking of converting?'

The ad-man's face grew serious. 'Christ! It's too late for me, I'm already damned.' He stared gloomily down at his beer.

Clyde patted him on the shoulder and left the bar and steered down Queen Street, possessed of a single, fixed idea. It was that hour, after dark, when the streets emptied and the bars and movie theatres filled up. He walked fast, the shop windows going past like so many blank faces, ignoring the creepy lure of the mannequins. As he saw it he was caught within the terms of an inherited male myth-woman whose legs were in the whorehouse and over whose shoulders hung a divine luminance. It was the Old Testament dispensation; and it was the most profound bullshit to grip the human heart. Yahweh had decreed that man should have the knowledge of the gods and the nature of the beasts. Men and women were doomed to be stretched between these contraries. Separate the animal and the divine and string them across a piece of bone, set the bone upright and walking, fill it with blood and heat and slippery fat. There's your human being. What a work is man!

If he saw Cleo again, his beery brain told him, he would debunk for good any lingering impression that she was Madeleine Farquar and explode the myth of this whore-angel duality right at its source. Confront his projections with the reality and shake loose from the mythic power of the thing. All he needed was to talk to her, just for a few moments; he'd know soon enough. This mission, as he conceived it, transformed him at one stroke from a Drunkard into a Warrior of the Heart. Who could confront his archetypes and plumb the nature of their power over him. A man, in this case, who could tell Yahweh to get fucked, and seek a new dispensation. Who would refuse to idealize on one hand and degrade on the other. A Warrior of the Heart who would enter even the Satin Chambers of the Damned to put their Graven Images to the Sword.

'...twenty dollars for a warm-up,' the fat blonde woman was saying patiently, her earrings hanging still. She gave no sign that she recognised him.

'I'd just like to see Cleo for a few minutes,' he said.

'Cleo?' She jerked her thumb towards the door to the inner reception. 'She's busy. You can wait. Twenty dollars warm-up fee, fifty to finish.'

'Look, I just want to talk to her for a moment. It's a personal matter.'

'Talk to her?' The blonde's level gaze took him in. 'You can have a rap session if you wish. For a twenty minute rap you pay...'

'I don't want a rap session. I just want to talk to her for a moment.'

The blonde's eyes wandered down to the desk in front of her.

'I'm not a customer. I'm a friend of hers.'

'Give us your name. Leave a message – we'll pass it on.'

'I have to talk to her, personally.'

The blonde made a decision.

'She's working. Either leave a message or pay up. Or get out.'

'Can't I go in and have a drink.'

'It's your funeral. Drink up!'

'I just drank last time. Talked to the girls.'

The woman grimaced with distaste. 'You came in here with Captain Knickers, didn't you? We had to throw the bastard out.'

The large Samoan appeared from behind the curtain and glanced disinterestedly at Clyde. For himself, Clyde couldn't understand what all the fuss was about. All he wanted to do was to see Cleo for a moment, speak a word with her. A mask could hide a face, but a clear voice like Madeleine's could not be hidden or faked.

'An overboard case,' the woman said to the Samoan. 'Wants to "talk" to Cleo.' The Samoan grimaced tiredly, glanced over at Clyde and, with an unmistakable gesture, jerked his thumb towards the street door.

Clyde held his irritation under control. It was a simple matter. He decided to speak to the Samoan, who didn't look like an unreasonable person. He had huge, sloping shoulders but a wide, agreeable face. He was wearing a brightly coloured shirt patterned with palm trees.

'I have to see her for a moment,' he said apologetically. 'I'm happy to buy a drink.'

The Samoan made a negative gesture with his mouth and jerked his thumb to the door, inviting Clyde to leave with a formal incline of the head.

Clyde's patience was running out. It was time to stop being so fucking reasonable and put on a bit of heat. 'I've a perfect right to see her. A simple, ordinary fucking request, Christ!'

The Samoan gave the blonde a resigned look and a moment later Clyde was on the street on his arse, wondering what had happened. Above him, like an apparition, loomed Heinz, swaying and smirking virtuously.

'What did you do, Aichen? Go for their bung-hole or something?'

Aichen got up and shook himself loose of Heinz, who was now consigned to oblivion.

He found twenty dollars and walked back inside.

Cleo took him by the elbow and led him into the same small cubical they had been in before, with the peephole.

'What would you like me to do, Clyde?' she said, with the appropriate degree of provocative shyness. Beneath her Nu mask her face shifted, the way the texture of the surface of the sea does when the wind moves across it.

'You could take off your blouse.'

'That would feel good.' She took off her blouse and shivered her shoulders forward a little. When he saw her high, smooth breasts he realized how young she was. He drew her forward and took her warm body in his hands. Up until this point everything had been a play of shadows; a dance, the steps of which they played without their true bodies. Using their dream bodies. With the feel of her in his hands, all of that changed.

'That feels nice,' Clyde, she said, softly. 'Gentle and strong.'

'It's the pretence that frightens me,' he said, standing away from her. He was thinking of the quality of any event to become instantly memory. He couldn't pretend with his hands. He turned for the door.

'We could have the light off. Then I could be anybody you want. Or somebody you want and can't have.'

'No.'

'Wait a minute, Clyde.' She reached over and cupped him between his legs. Long enough for him to feel a tingle of response. 'There's something you want, that's for sure, Clyde.' Her lips parted. She could have been his fair angel after all. Her voice had that clarity of diction, her body the same clarity of line.

'You're right,' he admitted. 'I wonder what it is.'

He turned away from her and went out the door.

Clyde Aichen, retired Warrior of the Heart, swore off the booze.

He woke early enough to hear the morning's tui repeat the same clear passionate note, over and over. While it was there, ringing through his head, cutting through the materialism of his hangover, he swore off the booze forever and a day. Well, a day at least. Unhappily, events of the previous evening had not been lost in the blood haze. Words like debacle, fiasco, disaster, crowded into his mind. If he'd been sober, none of it would have happened. His Warrior of the Heart was none other than Don Quixote of the Bottle. When he had held Cleo between his hands, one on each hip, sensing the whole compass of her between, he had discovered nothing but the capacity to act like every other man who had held her like that, in that place. If he'd been sober he would have known that. He was grateful now that he had not gone through with it. Fucking Madeleine Farquar by proxy would have been ruinous.

He got out of bed feeling peculiarly lucid and clear. It happened like that some mornings. He'd have drunk enough to fell an ox and come morning greet the day smelling like a rose. He'd probably flake out in the afternoon, half a day's writing down the tubes. What was left of the tubes.

It was time to put the booze away.

A piece of sunlight had fallen across a blank page on his desk; he took this as a good omen as he put the jug on and prepared himself a strong pot of English Breakfast tea. While the jug boiled he turned the radio on.

'…the most we can hope for, as far as the environment is concerned,' a voice from the radio said, 'is a damage control operation. Seventy percent of the earth's ecological damage has been done in the last thirty years. We have ten years to turn that around. So far the governments, and their partners the corporations, are doing little more than *talking* green.'

'Is it already too late? Has the process gone too far? I mean for the planet.'

'For the planet, no. The planet will go on, but we're a different story. We mammals live within a pretty strictly defined range of biological conditions. And we're interfering with those conditions on a massive scale.' The voice laughed. 'Call me a creative pessimist, if you like. I think we should all be out there, doing it, whatever we can to reverse the process. Ten years. That's all we've got. It's a last chance decade. And watch for the backlash.'

Clyde poured his tea and snapped the radio off. He went over to his desk where a shaft of sunlight still illuminated the blank page. He picked up the South American novel that lay beside it and shut its wars and revolutions firmly between the covers. The booze had played a ubiquitous role in this sorry story right from the beginning. He sipped his tea and thought. The hovering angel he'd seen in class was probably some fluctuation in his brain cells caused by a hangover, the hallucinations of dehydration. He raised his pen and held it over the page. It made a long, thin shadow across the lines.

Again the cry of the tui came, this time closer to the house. Not wanting to frighten the bird by a sudden movement, he pulled aside one edge of the heavy, lacy curtain (left there by the previous owner), and peeked out at a clear, bright morning. His view was across his deck to his flax and cabbage tree in the foreground, and across to the bush of the opposite valley where clematis was threaded through the manuka blossom. The clematis hung in wreathes of white across the spring green. Everything was clean and freshly rinsed, shiny side up. He was looking through a lacy peephole into a brilliantly lit world whose light was spread voluptuously across the softened curve of the hill.

Acting on intuition, he let the curtain fall and crossed to his mirror. His own face was there, in place, looking back at him with good humoured irony. And something more. A mischievous twinkle. How come he felt so good? How come he wasn't lying out on the deck with a jug of cold water nursing a headache and cursing the folly of the night before? His face was handsome, in a lived-in sort of way. Expressive. His mouth had a sense of humour. Right now the face in the mirror was having a joke at his expense. The face in the mirror knew something that he didn't. The Mona Lisa beginnings of a fatuous smile. You'll be the last to know, the face told him.

He went back to his lacy peephole upon the world. The same strong light infused everything. The tui cried out the name of its ancestor and dropped out of the sky with the flash of a white wing-bar into the flax.

The slim black stem swayed with its weight.

Something infinite and gentle held the world in place.

When the tui cried again its repeated note rang out as a blessing upon the morning. When the bird turned on the stem, its coat gleamed a dark mother-of-pearl. Raising its head between dips into the dewy black seedpods to look around alertly, the bird drank with a ferocious and dedicated attention.

We have just ten years, he told it. Ten years to change our lives, to turn this thing around. The canaries are already falling over, the tuis will be next. The syllables of its ancestors will die as the bush dies. Ten measly years.

The tui vanished, flung from its perch. The flax stem quivered.

The first lines came out fluid and strong, supple, and prickly. He pulled the plug on the telephone and wrote several more lines. The quality of inner search intensified as fragmented pieces, compelled by the gravitational tug of some unknown force, fell towards a comprehension of themselves.

He got up from the screen and walked around the room, enjoying the windless magic of the morning, the buoyancy of the air, the intimacy of the light on the oiled pine of the deck. In the wrists, where his hands joined his arms, there, the ache of words. At the same time his puzzlement deepened into unease. He had entered into a world of enchantment and paradox, a world in which he was oddly powerless. A territory reigned over by strange tutelary deities like the evil, foul-mouthed, drunken Heinz (did he really see the ad-man while on his arse outside the parlour?), Cleo, the fallen angel of the parlours, and Madeleine his scarred angel of beauty. A world of unexpected parallels and peculiar reversions. Impossible things. Hangovers that turn beneficent. Tuis that turn into prayers when they take to the wing. Poets that turn virtuous. Lesbians with lizard tongues. Enlightened anorexics. Angel eyes and fairy dust.

And a poem that would not disclose itself in its chosen language.

What could account for this diverse phenomena? Even booze, guilty on all counts, could not carry the can for all this. He began to smile and write down lines, and the lines came hard and clean straight after, announcing love, and the occasion of love, in quiet straightforward language, the momentous nature of the declaration balanced by restraint of tone, precision and particularity, the old Aichen trademarks.

It's a confession, he thought with amazement, getting up and rushing to the mirror. The whole thing's a fucking confession. His treacherous face told him the rest. He blushed, as they used to say, to the roots of his hair. Then the blood left his face completely and he stared at an ashen image of himself, his own rigid Nu mask. Being in love is no joke. A disaster in fact.

He walked slowly back to his desk and looked down, stunned at what he'd written, sat down and wrote more of the same. With its subject declared, it came out in sinuous pieces, linguistically resilient but fragile as an eggshell. A forward, warm, open movement, full of crosscurrents, voluble and strong; and a counter movement towards contraction and focus, particularity and essence. At once stringent and vulnerable, these lines made no concessions, gave no quarter and asked none.

Love poems! for the love of God. And for the insufferable Madeleine Farquar, the tawny lioness.

At the top of one page he wrote Charles Olsen's dictum, *only emotions endure.*

Olsen should have known better.

This changed everything. The innocence of their little tête-à-têtes for one thing. It should been obvious. His search for her in Cleo. Even Cleo understood. *We could have the light off. Then I could be anybody you want. Or somebody you want and can't have.*

He went back to bed and slept and dreamed of Jeannette. Her body was covered in fine down, such as babies are sometimes born with. He was walking along a beach, trying to catch her up, but could not lessen the distance between them. The faster he moved the greater the distance became. He understood that this is the law of inverse proportion that always applies in dreams. He watched her until she was no bigger than a gull's wing against white sand.

A group of tattooed warriors came down out of the sand hills and took him away. This was tapu ground, they said, sacred, ancestral ground; he would not be permitted to destroy it with his poisons. He tried to talk to them, to explain to them that he didn't want to destroy it, he merely wanted to fish there for oysters. But the warriors were not listening to him. They were listening to a secret sound inside their ears. They showed him a place in the sand where there were graves. He opened one of the graves and found the skeletons of bone-winged angels, a mass grave of birds, with each skeleton preserved to perfection; the delicate, lacy wing-bones; the light, tightly curved ribcages.

He got straight up out of the dream, flipped the top of a beer, and went to the desk and wrote. He let the beer fizz in his mouth to wake him up as he wrote. The words moved through his body onto the cold, clear, dreamless space of the page. When courage came, he went back through previous lines, weeding and thinning.

Then he returned to bed and dreamed that his tui flew into the room and dropped a flax seed in his mouth. It tasted of almond, or sperm. His body glowed like a glow-worm in a cave of nights. His flesh was damp and moist, as if it had been tenderized with kisses.

He got out of bed and went to the mirror. The face had lost its knowing grin. His eyes were like two dark lamps in his head. He should stay away from the mirror, or get rid of it.

He peered through his peephole out to what he took to be that peculiar predawn dark which is intensified by the faintest luminosity. The flax bush was a rustle of shadows.

He went to bed and did nothing, staring at the home made tongue-in-groove ceiling, reddish, macrocarpa the previous owner builder had scored in a cheap job lot. Scored from one of those demolition outfits that had sprung up in the wake of the tearing down of the old Auckland warehouses. It was full of knots and sinuous shapes. His body wriggled between the sheets like a hot worm. He could smell his own heavy, musky odour. He got up and wrote again. As he wrote he let the predawn chill bite into his naked body.

He wrote until he went back to sleep again.

Sylvia walked into his life through the front door, in the normal way. She was carrying so many bags it looked as if there was more than one of her. Or she was planning on moving in for the next two years.

'Thank God you're here,' she said. 'There's something wrong with your phone.' She looked around the room. 'Good Lord, have you been on a bender or something?' She was looking at a pile of empty beer cans by the desk. He had no idea how they had got there.

'Writing,' he said. He tried to say more but couldn't.

'Don't tell me you can write in this state. You look like the morning after the morning after.' A fresh wind came through the door with her.

He smiled sleepily. He couldn't take offense, writing had wrung all offense from him.

'Well, now that I've properly insulted you, I have to ask if I can stay a couple of days. I need a break, honest to God, Clyde. I came here like a homing pigeon. I didn't think about what I was doing. Silly me! I only remembered you and Jeannette had split when I was halfway here.'

She was blabbing. It was from embarrassment at having landed on him like this, festooned with suitcases. And catching him in *flagrante delicto* with the poem. Her connection was really with Jeannette. He sensed she didn't realize how embarrassing it could have been until she was standing outside the door, when it was too late to do anything else. That was just like Sylvia, Sylv, Jeannette had called her, much to Clyde's distaste. Silly Sylv.

Jeannette was always in despair at Sylv, because Sylv's life was always a mess.

He smiled again. His body felt pleasantly rank, seedy and loose. His tatty shirt was out at the waist and he was wearing a pair of baggy old jeans held up by a piece of string. In contrast she looked brisk and smart in a knee length skirt and fresh white blouse buttoned to the neck. She looked as if she were about to step into an office for another day's executive money grubbing. He remembered vaguely that she made pots of money moving other people's credit from one place to another.

'You won't get much sense out of me, Sylvia.' He was determined not to use Jeannette's Sylv. He gestured to his desk, 'I'm writing.'

'Go on ahead writing or drinking or whatever it is you're doing. I just want to vanish from the world for a couple of days.' She walked over to the French doors and looked out onto the deck, tapping her fingers on the aluminium frame. One foot was raised onto its toes, as if she were wearing high heels and needed to show the curved, muscled line of her leg. The sun hit her face and all the tense, bright smile lines left her face, the city posture drained out of her body. She was exhausted.

Clyde decided it wouldn't work. He was writing. It was hard to write with others around. Even Jeannette. Especially Jeannette, whose subtle presence had pervaded his most private moments. 'You can try the spare room.'

Jeannette had told him once he should learn how to say no. He did, and said it to her. Fuck Sylv for arriving here and bringing Jeannette in the door with her.

He showed her the spare room beside his room. It was the room he and Moira had turned briefly into a love nest after Jeannette left. Both he and Moira were too superstitious to make love on the bed where he and Jeannette had lain.

'I can take it from here, Shakes.' She was standing at the door to the spare room smiling amusedly at him. Her hair was light brown and casually but carefully styled around her face.

'There's only one other person I know who calls me that.'

'Who's that?'

'A guy called Heinz. Writes advertising copy.'

'I remember him. You brought him back here one night. Jeannette was pissed off.' Her smile became wider.

'I don't remember that.'

'You were both very drunk. You made asses of yourselves. Heinz spewed on the rosemary bush. You pissed on the cabbage tree.' She was laughing now. He had to join her. It's hard to laugh with your mouth clamped shut.

'It's a good thing I don't remember it,' he said, turning for his desk. He was amazed to find he had an untidy stack fifty pages. He had no memory of writing so much, and no clear direction for writing more. With Sylvia, the world had entered the house, its indifference and carelessness, the implicit cruelty of its swift judgements. A world that apparently had ten years to turn itself around or face some heavy music. His poem would never bear the weight of that world, for it was fashioned from nothing more substantial than the scratches and gaps of the heart. His publisher would be about as interested in a book of love poems as in a truckload of rocks. In fact, he'd probably be more interested in the rocks. Stockman wanted a book that would blow up a building. With ten years to pull up our socks, it was as good an aim as any, wasn't it?

He kept working, pushing against the resistance of the lines or suddenly riding with them. The awareness of Sylvia moving quietly into the spare room faded from his mind. The initial flood of words was over, and he was working with a steadier hand. He knew that this phase was the beginning of the drying up process that would eventually see the end of even the richest run. On the other hand it was a period of the process during which he had the most control, and during which some of the best work was being shaped.

At the same time it was no less vulnerable to avid eyes. Never had he been so self exposed, so stripped of philosophic, linguistic weight, so exacting in the particularity, or austerely fitted to the great white silence of the page. As creator, his position was becoming invidious. Here was the emperor with no clothes. It was being written, he realized, for one set of eyes only. It might not be fit for any other set of eyes. It might be fit for no one's eyes but his own. Bottom drawer material. Face down, bottom drawer. He had a few of those.

At first he was concerned that Sylvia would peek at it, but when he realized she was not interested he relaxed. That was one advantage of having a completely self-absorbed visitor. That didn't stop him from turning the top page down when he walked away. She didn't appear in the room or speak. Once he looked out the window and saw her sitting on the deck in the sun. She'd changed into a short, casual frock. Her face was dreamy as she looked across to the opposite valley.

She's like me, he realized. She'd rather be alone.

He wrote until he couldn't write anymore and got up to have a beer. We must abandon the poem before it abandons us, he quipped to the fridge, which replied by disgorging a cold lager into his hand.

It occurred to him that Sylvia would be a good distraction from the poem. He could talk to her for a while. Say some normal things. He seemed to remember that she liked movies. They could talk about Alfred Hitchcock and Dario Argento, and whether or not Arnold

Schwarzenegger could act.

With this intention he headed back across the room, finding himself, however, back at his desk, looking down at what he'd written. Many of the lines had already abandoned him. He sat down and revised with a cool manipulative skill, picking up this and putting down that. He could do anything but tamper with the core of the poem.

It was dark when he lay down on his bed. The house was quiet, as if he were alone. His body was emptied of dreams. He floated in the cool, lucid medium revision had brought with it. The poem could not afford to be a soft, pulpy thing, like ripe fruit on the tree, and it was not that. Its strength, he perceived, lay in its surrender, its surrender to the fact; and in that surrender there was devotion. This devotion had nothing to do with the worship of an image, more like an acknowledgement, an admission.

He'd only loved once or twice in his life and he'd never been prepared for it.

He wasn't prepared for it now.

Sylvia slipped into the bed and lay beside him, not touching him. They lay that way for some time without talking, breathing quietly. Clyde was surprised. Sylvia had never indicated any interested in him in that way, and suspected that mostly she still wasn't. There was a matter of factness about her that belied any sexual tension. Her attitude seemed to be that, since they were both unattached and alone in the house they might as well sleep together.

He didn't argue.

He didn't feel like doing anything much, so he turned, sought and found her nipple and began to suck like a baby. When his body was filled with the warmth and comfort of sucking she started on him, lapping and nibbling at his body.

Neither of them were that interested, but they just kept doing it. It was better than doing nothing at all. Render to body what belongs to body, and to love what is love's, he thought lazily. You can eat me but I cannot be consumed. Lap me and there's still a lap to go. Lovers speak in tongues. He would hold the faith, he would not let go.

When they'd finished, she rolled off and lay beside him, her body a little separated from his, breathing heavily. She lay facing him, her breasts just touching him when her ribcage rose.

'Jesus. I hope that's ok.'

'It's fine,' he said dreamily, feeling the cool air drying her sweat on his stomach. Now he was enveloped in the greater, larger medium of the air and the night. It was pleasant.

'But you didn't come.'

'There's more to life than coming,' he said. It was something else, infinite and tender.

'Well, I came all over the place. Did I need that! Jesus! I hope it's all right just hopping into bed with you like this. I needed it, I can tell you that. People tell me I can be quite masculine in the expression of my sexuality.'

'Really?' He touched a scar on her upper arm. 'What's this?'

'I had a tattoo removed.'

'What was it?'

'It's kind of personal. I'm a changed woman.'

'Alright.'

'You're on heat, did you know that? I can smell a man on heat. I smelled you as soon as I came in. I looked around for the woman. There was the sense of a woman everywhere, and this smell. The air was thick with pheromones. I thought there must have been an orgy going on. Then I realized it was just you. A male on heat smell. I knew it would be ok between us when I smelled that smell.' She rubbed her scar with a forefinger.

'I probably haven't had a bath for a few days,' he said, stroking the stubble on his chin. One thing he was grateful to the eighties for was the fashionable designer stubble look, the unshaven, just out of bed look. Such men seemed to have on their arm blondes with mussed up, just-out-of-bed hair.

'I'm glad of that.' That was about the most they said to one another. It didn't matter to Clyde, neither talking nor not talking affected his state. Later that night they did it again, and again he did not come. She had a practical attitude to sex, what in an earlier decade would have been called 'healthy' or 'therapeutic'. She needed lovemaking, she said, for her physical balance, which was sadly lacking. It went along with good diet, exercise and walking or jogging as part of a vigorous woman's healthy balance.

Afterwards he got up and wrote. Sylvia made herself scarce. She didn't try to cook or take up any domestic role, and he was glad of that. They made no effort to work in social times together. She came to him only when he lay on his bed, and she never commented on the fact that he didn't come. Sometimes he had a semi ejaculation, but it was not an orgasm as he knew them, there was none of the satisfying emptiness he associated with sexual release. Once or twice she tried to bring him, to pull it from him, but she wisely did not let it become a quest. She didn't try to vary her on top position which she enjoyed. He sensed she was happy enough with the arrangement, since he was there for as long as she needed him for her pleasure. The rest she left to him.

Once or twice they talked. He told her how the voice on the radio had given humanity ten years to turn around the ecological slide. He told her about Don Bealter and the pesticides industry. She got tight-lipped and angry.

'These doom spreaders will say anything,' she said. 'Scare tactics.'

'Sometimes it pays to be scared,' he said.

'These end-of-the-world types piss me off.'

They left it there.

He kept writing, ploughing the words out of his body back onto the page. He now had a hundred and forty pages. He had no idea how long he'd been writing. He worked more slowly, revising as he went, constantly rereading to pick up threads he'd dropped in the haste of the first burst.

There was a hankering, here and there, for the old certainties and solidities of the Aichen style, but these were clearly backward glances. There were moments, too, of grand funk when doubt doubled him over, wrecked his posture, slumped him across his notebook in a fury of negative analysis.

Why did he expose himself in this way, and for what effect? He hated this sort of self-revelatory stuff in other poets; he was always warning his class about it. There was something gratuitous in it. No social value attached to it. It addressed no social issues. It did nothing to arrest the ecological slide. Broached no new ground. All its lines pointed back in, towards its source. It had no commitment but to the felicity of the moment. Some parts of it were ok, some of the best he'd written, perhaps, it might even be published, but for what? For people to laugh at him behind his back, nod and wink at one another, and over a few beers decide that Clyde Aichen had gone soft. Male menopause, they would say as they raised their glasses. Fuck them all. He was better than any of them. And so on. And so on.

None of this made any difference to the writing, which continued regardless, sometimes through storms of such abuse. Or he'd crack a can and sit on the deck waiting for the tui to land in the flax beside him in a madrigal of wings and offer him the secret of its poetry. He'd heard it one morning, half in dream, repeating the same theme over and over. He dreamed of drowning, the cry of the tui borne to him by ocean currents. Schools of small, shiny fish poked through his guts. It wouldn't be much longer now, he was back into the old breeding ground from which the first lines had sprung. Death came and took up residence in the lines. He reminded himself of the deeper meaning of death as standing for rebirth or change. He had a presage of a grief yet to come but could not turn his lines towards it; they belonged to another time, another poem.

He floated in a fluid medium which bore him up. His tiredness didn't matter; his despair was irrelevant. He wrote and slept and dreamed of making love to Moira on a beach of white shells. He dreamed that Madeleine Farquar turned into a heron. He dreamed he was a little boy with his father at a river mouth. They had caught a huge salmon which leapt and bucked on the wet stones. Neither he nor his father could control it. Finally his father took a flat stone and slammed it behind the head, threw it into a sack and tied the top. The hook lay on the stones with a piece of the salmon's lip speared on it. He dreamed he was Orpheus, searching the huge dank caverns of the underworld for Euridice, but there was no Euridice. The caverns were empty, the feast overturned. The Lord of Death was out hunting. The heron flew effortlessly across a blue sky.

The lines came slowly now, in reluctant surges, crawling into his fingers on caterpillar legs. Sometimes, when he lay down, Sylvia would come and lie on top of him. Once she said, 'You really are working, aren't you? I just thought you were sitting there hitting the piss.'

'I've given up the piss,' he replied, half asleep. He had a hundred and sixty pages, but their bulk was a false comfort. A lot of stuff would have to go. Already the stack was beginning to diminish rather than grow.

Sylvia's attitude toward him was changing. His ongoing passivity, the offering up of his flesh in that way without consummation, which at first excited her and filled her with delighted greed, came to bother her and frustrate her in a way that was not entirely therapeutic or healthy.

One night she came and lay beside him without making a move towards him. He lay quietly, allowing the lines he'd just written to slip away. He enjoyed these moments when everything left him, when he could fill up with nothing but emptiness. Then he felt the body beside him go rigid.

'Are you ok?' he asked, cursing himself for asking. A little question like that might open a Pandora's Box.

'You just lie there. You never come,' she said in a small voice. 'I just use you like you're a living dildo or something.'

'Be my guest.'

Clyde thought it was a fair description. It didn't matter to him, and she sensed that; she grasped the true root of his passivity and didn't like it. It frightened her. It wasn't natural. Then it angered her. She couldn't get a grip on him at all. He offered his flesh, but it was no more than a subterfuge, a decoy.

She felt cheated, but knew she had no recourse. Despite all her happy orgasming, she felt frustrated. The situation had become demeaning. She'd brought it on herself of course, as she usually did. After all, what did she expect? She went back to the spare room and slept there, wondering why she always involved herself in these bizarre affairs, wondering if perhaps she was one of those Women Who Love Too Much.

Clyde slept alone and dreamed of salmon. His father had shown him how to slit the guts, and cut the pink meat along the backbone. The great fish slithered in and out of his dreams as through a transparent veil. He dreamed he was standing by the College Bookshop when Death came up and took him by the hand. She was shy and wore her face veiled. Death reproved him for making so little progress in his lifetime, saying, *Only fools dream of eternity when I come around.*

When the dream finished Clyde got up and went to the fridge for beer. Sylvia was standing by his desk, the sheaf of poems in her hand. She's crossed the line. As soon as she looked at him they both knew it was over.

'Who's Madeleine?' She sounded just like Jeannette.

This violation made Clyde numb, but he had to face this, and more than this, if any of this were published.

'I thought I was using *you*. I felt as guilty as shit. Now I find you were using *me*.'

He shrugged. If ever there was fruitless territory, this was it. He took the poems from her and put them on the desk. Already his eye was running over the lines, probing their weakness, their evasions, seeing them through someone else's eyes. He stood quietly by the desk, thinking about the poems. He heard Sylvia move away. An hour later he had the house to himself again. It didn't matter.

He had written the last lines.

Clyde went downtown, checked his postbox, shuffling through the letters until he came to the one he thought he was looking for, shoved the rest into his bag and made for the nearest watering hole. Not quite the nearest, for he walked past De Bretts' *el-plastico* bars to reach the Queen's Ferry, where they still poured stout out of a tap.

He lined up a beer and considered the envelope, which was plain and brown with no sender's address on the back. He tried to remember the name behind the strange, girlish voice on the phone. Two documents fell out. Attached to one was a piece of paper with a name and address written on it. After studying the piece of paper for a moment he turned to the documents. The first was in the nature of a scientific report entitled, *Ecological and Public Health Implications Associated with the Use of Glyphosate Herbicides.* It was dated 1988 and emanated from a Dr David Monroe, a Consultant in Environmental Toxicology and Public Health.

Clyde took a swig at his black-and-tan and started to read. Someone had underlined a piece in the first paragraph, and Clyde's eyes gravitated towards it:

The formulation also contains 15% various surfactants shown to be the primary toxic component to fish and humans (Formar et al., 1979; Swada et al., 1988). The surfactant in the Roundup formulation has been identified as polyoxyethylene amine (POEA). The formulation also includes roughly 3% isopropylamine and 0.1 ppm nitrosoglyphosate as contaminants. The remaining inert ingredient is water.

So much for your industrial secrets, Clyde thought. And so much for your inert surfactant. Why had the company hidden this for so long behind the 'sensitive commercial secrets' argument? His eyes fell on an underlined piece in another document: *This surfactant, lethal to salmon fry at concentrations in water of 2.6 parts per million, is four hundred times more toxic than the Rodeo formulation which contains glyphosate and no surfactant... POEA... has been reported to cause adverse gastrointestinal and central nervous system effects and damage red blood cells.*

He took further swigs on his bitter beer. The surfactant, he went on to read, along with the formaldehyde resulting from glyphosate breakdown, has a greater potential for contaminating water, and poses a significantly greater hazard to wildlife and human health than glyphosate itself. Although: *observed acute and subchronic toxic effects of glyphosate at high doses include mortality, central lobular hepatic necrosis, chronic interstitial nephritis, proximal tubule epithelial hypertrophy, diarrhoea, nasal discharges, stomach haemorrhage, decreased food intake, decreased body weight and convulsive seizure.*

Paint me a pretty picture. Could low doses induce these sorts of effects in chemically sensitive people, he wondered, swilling his beer around in the glass, unwilling for a moment to drink. And yet he could still not make a direct link between all this and Don Bealter, lying in bed with his huge hands slumped uselessly on the sheets by his side. He could see what Sue Hyde had meant; there was no *provable* link between

Roundup and Bealter's illness. In fact he only had Bealter's word for it. So he sprayed Roundup on the day he got sick, so what? He probably drank coffee and cleaned his teeth too. And elsewhere there were people spraying Roundup and not getting sick. There was a logical gap here, a wedge in words through which some vast filthy machine had been driven, spraying poison to the right and left. The *Monstrum Horrendum*.

Swada et al (1988) reported 56 cases of Roundup poisoning in Japan between 1984 and 1986. Reported symptoms included gastrointestinal erosion, vomiting, pulmonary oedema, severe pneumonia, hypotension, haemolysis, and clouding of consciousness. The clinical description of Roundup poisoning was hypovolemic shock.

With morbid fascination he read on, his eyes skipping down the paragraphs... *'accidental exposure to glyphosate herbicides have resulted in bronchial constriction, nausea, headache, pleuritic chest pain, conjunctivitis, corneal ulcer, contact dermatitis, swelling of the extremities, and nervous system disorders.'*

As he tossed the article to one side in favour of his beer, he noticed that there was no data available on the mutagenicity, immunotoxicity, neurotoxicity or the developmental and reproductive toxicology of Roundup. And he noticed how blurry the printing was, as if this paper had been photocopied so many times that the print had grown uncertain of itself.

He rounded up another beer, glanced at the spoof clock behind the bar which moved backwards through the hours, returned to his stool and sat staring, without thinking, at the three fruit machines side by side at the back of the bar. They were new, these things, appearing in bars and clubs and sports clubs like some alien invader with their constant blipping and beeping. No matter where they were put, they were never unobtrusive. Another little delight of the decade, he could tell by the amount of money people were pouring into them that they were not going away anytime soon.

Sitting in front of them on bar stools were three operators mechanically pushing coins through the slots, wholly concentrated on their tasks and oblivious to each other. One was an older man in a crumpled white shirt hanging around his wrists. He had a roll-your-own in the corner of his mouth and watched the icons as they bounced into place through the heraldic wreath of smoke with a stoical calm, picking coins out of a plastic bag. A woman beside him did the same, pulling the coins from her purse and taking quick, sideways puffs on a tailor-made, never taking her eyes from the ever-rolling display.

As Clyde watched, the older man hit a jackpot and coins spewed out into the tray below. On and on they went, falling with a heavy, dull sound. The man's face didn't change. The woman beside him paused, said something briefly to him, and turned back to her machine.

Screwing one eye up against the ascending smoke, the man swept the freshly spewed coins into his plastic bag, placed it back in the tray and, with the same profound indifference, began feeding the coins back into the machine.

The second document was of a very different nature. Headed February 19th, 1990 and distributed by The International Independent Agent Orange Network based in Washington, it related to an appeal Monsanto had made against a 1989 conviction for a Dioxin spill at Sturgeon, Illinois, in which they'd been fined sixteen million dollars. The document was taken from the brief entered into evidence in support of the earlier court decision being challenged by Monsanto.

Clyde flicked through, reading the underlined bits.

Monsanto's chemical engineer, Donald Edwards, testified that for at least seven years in the 1970s Monsanto was dumping 30 to 40 pounds of dioxin daily into the Mississippi River... this dumping was continuing as late as 1977 although Monsanto officials recognised the potential health hazard from Dioxin getting into the Saint Louis food chain through the river...

Monsanto's Stantophen is the active ingredient in Lysol disinfectant and cleaning products. Monsanto's analytical chemist, Fred Hileman, testified that Monsanto knew that Lysol is recommended for cleaning babies' toys, and for various other cleaning activities involving direct contact with the human body... Hileman testified that he knew people who used Lysol were contacting three parts per billion of Dioxin 2,3,7,8, and that 2,3,7,8, is extremely toxic... Hileman testified that he knew people were spraying their lawns with products containing Monsanto's 2,3,7,8, and these people didn't know it.

...Monsanto knew Dioxin was in its 2,4,5-T as early as 1957 ...Monsanto's 2,4,5-T is present throughout the world...

His beer growing warm, he flicked through a couple of pages

concerned with how Monsanto deceived its workers on the health risks involved in working at their plants, and came upon this passage,

Monsanto's cover up of the Dioxin in its products included, of course, the deception of the purchasers of the products. The testimony was that there was no evidence that Monsanto ever notified any of its customers that any of Monsanto's products contained Dioxin...

He put the document down on the table and watched as a little spilt beer soaked into its outer pages. Vague as yet, the article for Greenpeace started to form in his mind. The human cost of our commercial, agricultural practices, would be its theme, firmly focused on Bealter. He would juxtapose slices of Bealter's medical record with juicy pieces from Monsanto's history of deception and cover up. In the conclusion he could press hard for the kind of Governmental review Sue Hyde was after.

He was surprised to find his half pint glass empty, but decided not to get another. He had a class to teach later. And he would see Madeleine. He was grateful to his class and to Madeleine for taking his mind off the nightmare the Bealter story was becoming. Glancing down at the document without focusing on the words, he felt the whole story was becoming one huge bottomless cesspool into which he might sink and never emerge. The deeper he sank into it, the dirtier and murkier it became until visibility was nil. He grinned cynically at his empty glass when he thought of the commercial clamour for a 'level playing field.' It was a hot new phrase. When historians looked back at the eighties they will say, this is the decade that levelled the playing field, and fell to the invasion of the pokies.

He knew what that 'playing field' would look like in decades to come: a denuded, treeless landscape with sour, wreaked soils and lifeless, poisonous rivers.

As he put the document back into his bag, some underlined sentences caught his eye,

Probably the most appalling feature of this story is Monsanto's effort to convince the World that Dioxin is harmless. Dr Suskink testified that he advised Monsanto they should publish experimental findings so as to better defend their position on Dioxin. Plaintiffs' exhibit 1552 is a March 3, 1978 memo from McPhillips to Monsanto's Callis saying, 'The monkey is on Monsanto's back to show Dioxin is acceptable, as Dow's Penta has less Dioxin than Monsanto's.'

At the fruit machine, the man who had hit the jackpot continued to feed coins into the machine, one stoical eye screwed up against the smoke from his roll-your-own.

A few amber drops ran around the bottom of Clyde's glass.

Behind the bar, the hands of the clock ran backwards.

'The trendy slogan is, *the personal is the political,*' Clyde Aichen said, pacing before the class, fully hitting his stride, 'which seems to do the trick, but I wonder if we don't interpret this slogan in a political way. We politicise the personal instead of personalizing, I mean humanizing, the political. Anyway, our writing is caught in the squeeze between. The truly personal, and therefore most profoundly political, is in danger of being disenfranchised in terms of language. May have already become so.'

Where was Madeleine Farquar? The class had perceptibly thinned, as these classes invariably did. The brash young man had ceased coming, but his presence still lingered on in his seat, an abrasive vacancy. The three golden oldies had collapsed to two. The woman with the braids was starting to fall away. The blonde with the red scarf was a surprising survivor, since she seldom spoke or shared her work and was associated in Clyde's mind with the brash young man. He felt those who were left were starting to get intense about their writing. And where was Madeleine Farquar? What was she getting intense about?

Her absence was like a blow to the heart.

'Are you talking about the exhaustion of lyrical language?' someone asked.

'Maybe.' He felt uncomfortable with the notion that lyrical language could become exhausted. He had a picture of an aging bunch of tired metaphors and overextended similes slumped around on chairs like dehydrating flowers.

'We can be deceived by figurative language, which always moves sideways and away from its object. That's the nature of comparison. Metaphorical language can be placed in the service of deception.

Politically and personally. The Romantic engagement with metaphor took them, I mean the Romantics, to no final truth, despite Keats' dictum about truth and beauty. The Father of Lies can still quote scripture, write it even.'

As he said this he became discomforted at the thought of the poems he'd just completed. Surely this figurative bent lay at the heart of his own work, and if so, might not he be deceived by it even if no one else was? He wanted to run out of the lecture room, jump in his rust-bucket, drive home and read his poems again, as if the lines themselves would reassure him.

He knew they would not, could not, by their very nature, offer him this assurance.

'I believe we need to keep our essentially humanistic aims in mind; a joining of perception and language to reclaim love for an ecology of the emotions. No literary devices or style can guarantee us that.'

The alarm bells were ringing again at the back of his mind, but he shut them out. If he listened hard enough, there'd be alarm bells ringing all the time.

Madeleine Farquar met him outside the lecture room. She was sleek and flushed. They hugged quickly and she stepped back.

'These are some poems I wrote,' she said, as they sat down on their now familiar park seat. 'I hope you've time to look at them.'

'I have time.' Even if he didn't, he did.

There was a restlessness in her today. A sense of unfinished physical movement.

Now that he knew he loved her, he had some context for dealing with the flood of emotions her presence released in him, the burn of new, hitherto unsuspected chemicals in his blood. He stepped into a crystalline realm where every detail was etched sharply against its background and stained on his memory. Greens soaked up blues, blues saturated browns; time changed gear. Her voice came up at him out of the spirit world as if another being spoke out of her chest. Her face filled all the gaps in the world.

Clyde had to learn how to function in this new medium, put one foot in front of the other, one thought in front of the other. He could do it. It was all words. He could learn to breathe underwater. He could talk and laugh and do all the things people normally did. He could sit with Madeleine Farquar on a park bench as if the human world didn't have just ten years but an eternity in which to work itself through, as if a poem were something other than a thin skein of words, and held living flesh rather than the shadow of its memory. Love is not blind but sees with true sight, he quoted to himself without a single detectable trace of irony.

She gave him a small sheaf of poems and smiled. Her smile made the world possible again. 'I'm feeling my age today. I looked in the mirror and saw lines I've never seen before,' she said mischievously, 'but I suppose you'd know all about that.' She drew one long, elegant leg up onto the bench.

'From my lofty heights?' He waved an experienced hand. 'I feel better than I ever did, to hell with the mirror. I've always thought mirrors were spurious things.'

Her grin turned to a knowing laugh. 'I, of course, am obsessed by them, I look into every one I see. I study my beautiful face every morning, just to make sure it's still beautiful.'

'It is,' he assured her.

'Anorexics have a strange faith in mirrors.' The other leg, equally long and elegant, came up to join the first and she hugged them both.

'Are you that self-involved?' he asked, knowing the answer.

'Totally.' She directed her self-involved gaze out to the sweep of the park and placed both feet back on the ground. Clyde picked up the poems. I mustn't pretend that I haven't got some stake in this, he thought, that I'm just some kind of impartial observer.

The light bounced white and bright off the page. He could feel her watching him as he spread the poems out. While he read he worked as intelligently as he could at tracing the nature of his reactions. The sensation of being enveloped by her, stemmed, he perceived, from the power of her concentration. It was more than just an intellectual force, her ability to focus wholly upon something and take it in, candidly absorb it into herself. It was an ability to be wholly there in any one moment, just as she could be wholly absent in another.

Love and sanity don't mix, he thought.

The poems were clear and boldly stated, if unspectacular. Only two or three of them, however, brought the movement they initiated to a satisfactory conclusion. Two were love poems, and he had a foolish moment imagining something before she spoke straight to his thought. 'These are written for my previous… boyfriend.'

'Is this the addictive relationship?'

'That's right.'

The poems had moments of acute observation of what it felt like to be inside her skin, a growing engagement, through the senses, with herself. Of course, herself.

'What was addictive about it?'

'He was trying to follow a sort of wacky spiritual path. He had some strange beliefs. I was Desire Personified. Diana in all her mythic forms. I had to crawl to him. That was my role. It was his role to resist me.' She placed one long, elegant leg over the other. 'I had to bait myself on the hook of my own body to get him to fuck me.'

Her lips shaped her distaste. There was a quality of revulsion in the way she withdrew into herself, away from the memory. He understood the loathing that lay there. The scenes folded out and away in her mind like a deck of cards being flicked. He considered their relative positions on the park seat and the discrete, emphatic distance between them.

'We are trained to lead lives of denial,' he murmured, suddenly thinking of his mother. The massive denial of her silence.

'Aren't we ever!'

They shared an affirming moment. Clyde threw away a few bits of his sandwich and they were surrounded by sparrows. One flicked into a branch right above their heads, pausing to give them the quick once-over. Madeleine put her head back and looked up.

'God, I just love birds.' She laughed, and in that moment of unalloyed delight, beauty broke over her in a wave. He should have looked away but he couldn't; her head was framed in a glaze of turquoise. He'd seen the colour before but couldn't place it. Clyde lost all sense of irony and distance. He was inside her as surely as if they were welded in flesh. While her lean body form might be feline, with the energies that implied, her spirit really was like the wounded bird she'd written of in her story, quick and light and with a love of air.

'Do you like the poems?'

'Most seem unfinished.'

130

'Are you avoiding the answer?'

'No.'

There was an awkward moment.

'I have trouble with endings,' she said.

'Don't we all.'

'Tell me.'

Clyde sat back and talked about himself. Some of it. The unfinished bits.

Two Maori men dressed in rough clothes came up and sat nearby. Her attention shifted to them. When he looked over, they were in the act of pulling out a joint and lighting up, talking to one another in quick deep phrases between tokes. After the first couple of rounds, laughter broke between them with the same quick phrasing. It was a knowing, complicit laughter.

They had already checked out the two pakehas sitting opposite them.

What they saw was a classy, long legged woman with gold tinted hair and skin who didn't want to look at them. And an older dude. She was a looker, dressed in red, loose silky pants with a pale, stylishly shoulder padded jacket who moved around a lot and waved her hands when she spoke. The dude was nothing special, an ordinary guy with a bent nose, dressed in a white shirt and olive green, unhemmed baggies. He was hanging on to what the looker was saying, watching her hands as if he were at a tennis match. The looker and the dude were too hung up on each other to care about a number passing around, although the dude noticed. The looker pretended not to notice. After the second couple of rounds they forgot about the pakies. The sun fell benevolently on their faces. Alice would be along soon.

Clyde felt the movement of Madeleine's mind to judgement. It was not exactly prejudice but the visceral reaction which precedes it, which underlies it. She struggled briefly with this reaction, pushing her hair back up with an impatient gesture. He could see where, in the mornings, the lines of disappointment would sour her face. In the tension of her upper lip, which was slightly contracted as a consequence, he could see the potential for bitterness. It reminded him so much of Jeannette's self-loathing he blinked the image away.

'Jeannette was my second wife. My first wife was Elaine, that was a teenage marriage.'

'Do you still see Elaine?'

'From time to time.'

'What sort of person is she?'

'A lovely person.' And that was true. If he hadn't gone out on a bender and never returned he might still be with her, a family of three or four. He would never have taken the long road with Jeannette, and he wouldn't be sitting here with Madeleine Farquar, his heart labouring in his chest.

With a quick indrawn breath Madeleine gestured to the bench where the Maoris sat, 'Look at that woman,' she said under her breath so fast Clyde might not have heard it, or imagined he'd heard it. He looked. A young Maori woman was approaching the two men, a smile on her face. She was fat, and wore a tight mini-dress that accentuated the girth of her thighs. As she walked the nylon of her stockings rubbed together producing a synthetic, scratching sound. She had long hair and plump rosebud lips. The men cried out a hearty greeting, calling her Alice, forgetting about the two pakeha covertly watching them. They made a space for her and Alice sat right down between them, her knees touching their knees. The joint was immediately passed to her. Somebody put a match to laughter.

Clyde grinned. He felt the first stirring of rebellion against the stringencies of his position. He wanted to blow it wide open. To leave Madeleine and wander over to the other seat. 'Hey bro,' he would say, 'that smells good,' and they would hand him a joint and he would fry up in the sun with them there and then, blow some holes in his day.

Madeleine's lips shaped in the same distaste he'd observed earlier. Her eyes were shaded almost dark, hidden by half descended lids, but he saw it anyway; the ugliness, the brutality of judgement, the shiver of revulsion, and the self-hatred that attended these things like a shadow.

The three on the bench hardly noticed the two pakehas get up and go. Hemi caught the eye of the looker, whose posture was upright and strong. He went to light up the roach but the final, smokable piece had fallen into the grass where it was giving up the last of its ghost into the shadowy air beneath the park seat.

When he looked up, the looker and the dude had gone.

Quick and light, a flock of sparrows flooded the empty park seat.

'I've sent these poems to your publisher.'

'Stockman?' Clyde tried to imagine what Stockman would do with them, and failed. He tried to imagine what Stockman would do with Madeleine Farquar, and succeeded. Stockman wouldn't think twice.

She nodded. 'Will he publish them?'

'It's not likely. He's developing an aversion to poetry. Or to poets, maybe. He's become all bitter and twisted.'

She laced her fingers together and placed her chin on the flexible bridge provided, her elbows resting firmly on the table. Clyde blew a little distance across his coffee cup, and watched the play of animation on her face.

'I'm sorry to hear that.'

'I think he likes it that way.'

'Hello Madeleine.' The interloper was a fresh faced man with light, curly hair. There was something wrong with his face and it took Clyde a moment to see what it was. Youth.

'Hello.'

'Are you at University this year?' Freshface asked.

She inclined her head. 'What are you studying?'

'Majoring in Sanskrit.'

Clyde and Madeleine were both turned towards the fresh faced young man majoring in Sanskrit. They wanted him to go, and it didn't take him long to see it. There was an exclusiveness in their relationship he recognised instantly; neither of them suffered fools lightly, nor interruptions with much patience. This time was for each other. He felt absurdly pleased.

'And I've met a friend of yours,' she said, as the young man walked away.

'Who's that?' For a grotesque moment, Clyde thought of Heinz the ad-man.

'Moira Andrews.'

Clyde nodded. 'I've known Moira for a long time.'

'She makes beautiful sculptures.' Her fingers unlaced and inscribed fruitful shapes upon the air. The sludge in the bottom of Clyde's coffee cup fell into the shape of a star. A strand of amber hair fell across Madeleine's forehead. People passed to and fro carrying food, balancing drinks. Taking her knife, Madeleine cut a piece off her slice of cake and placed it fastidiously in her mouth.

'I envy you,' she said, putting her knife down, wiping back the strand of hair and picking up bits of crumb with her fingers. From the strange look she gave him he knew that it was true.

'I don't like being envied,' he said. Above them hung large black-and-white pictures of the 1980's Bob Dylan looking shattered and stubbled. *You gotta serve somebody.*

Envy was not what he had expected from her; whatever she envied, he wasn't that.

'You have all the time in the world to write.'

'What gave you that idea?'

'Effectively you have. Your writing's well received.'

Talk like this made Clyde Aichen uneasy. Ambition made her mouth tense. Her body resumed its dissatisfied, restless movement against the tight lines of her clothing. She picked up the knife and cut off another slice of cake with slow, preoccupied movements. She was aware of his scrutiny, the intensity of it. He looked away, down to the dry star on the bottom of his cup and made a decision, or rather, reversed a decision he'd earlier made not to show the poems to her.

'The classes are finishing. Shall we keep meeting?' His tone was light and free of implication.

'I would like that,' she said.

He would show them to her, of course he would. Why else had he written them?

134

The party at Moira's was already in at least half swing by the time Clyde got there. He was not in a mood for crowd scenes.

'I thought this was going to be a quiet get together, a prelude to our little outing in the car,' he said to Moira. Out of the corner of his eye he saw Snake and a broad hipped Maori woman confer briefly, their arms around each other's shoulders. Snake gave him a slow-lidded wink.

'That trip in the car is becoming a standing joke,' Moira said. 'That date you were always going to take me on, Clyde Aichen, but never quite made. It's a ghost date. It'll happen in some other universe.' She was on her way to getting drunk. Aichen had some catching up to do, but her thick-tongued volubility made him think of dope.

'By the way, how's Madeleine Farquar?' Moira said, pulling him over to the sideboard.

There's nothing sacred, Clyde thought, looking at the arena of bottles. He was standing beside a big built man who had long, straggly hair.

'You're Clyde Aichen, aren't you?' the man said, flicking the cap off a bottle of beer with a practised gesture. 'I very much enjoyed your novel, I'm glad to say.'

'Which one?' Clyde decided to stick to beer.

'The one about the solo dad and his daughter, how they slowly lose their relationship. Bloody sad. Was it autobiographical?'

'I don't remember.' Moira gave Clyde a silly smile and a shrug of the shoulders. Not my fault, she seemed to be saying.

'Bloody sad,' the man repeated. He raised the bottle and gurgled some down. It was a new craze, this drinking straight from bottles, flashing them in the air. Heinz had told him that the breweries encouraged it because of brand identification. Like having everybody waving little flags in the air.

'It was called *Blood on the Table*,' Clyde said, hating himself for his lecturing tones. 'And the main character lost his daughter through his own foolishness.'

'There's lots of solo dads,' the man said emotionally. 'They have special problems no one cares about. These days anyway. It all goes to the women.' The man drank again. He was knocking it back.

'So I've heard,' Clyde chose a lager. Turning his back to the man with the emotions, he said to Moira, 'Have you been prying into my affairs,

Moira Andrews?' He opted for mock reprove.

'Affairs? My! My! We have progressed, haven't we? The old Aichen charm.'

A stupid grin was creeping onto Clyde's face. Moira knew what it meant.

'Cheers!' Their glasses met with the sound of scissors snapping empty air.

'I'm glad you chose to write about that,' the man said, making Clyde turn to him. 'It's very relevant to people's lives. Some of these wankers don't know what they're writing. I picked up a book the other day by some fancy writer and it was all about a college professor's affair with one of his students! Can you beat that? They've got nothing left to say so they write about their grubby little love affairs with their grubby little students. What a con! One hand on their typewriter and the other between their legs. It's not fair that people like that should get fuckin literary grants, *grants* mind you! Taxpayer's money. Everybody's on the tit.'

'It's disgusting.'

'You can say that again!'

'It's disgusting. I pay my taxes, like a good citizen.'

Moira snorted into her drink.

'But you're different. You wrote about a dad separated from his daughter.' He took hold of Clyde's arm, his voice trembling, 'The courts don't seem to realize that the mother is not always the best person to have the children. Men's rights get tromped on.'

'All you can do is pay up and shut up,' someone on the other side of the man said.

'That's right,' Aichen's admirer said, turning to this new source of support. 'My ex is perfectly capable of going out and doing a day's work. Instead she sits at home on a benefit, whining.'

'That's heresy,' the other person said.

'That's bloody right. And if you kick back they'll turn around and accuse you of sexual molestation. We've got fathers afraid to comb their daughter's hair or kiss them off to school in the morning. We got unemployed who can't put food in their kids' mouths while our writers write about diddling their students! Christ!' He turned belligerently to

Clyde, 'Literature has some sort of social responsibility.'

Aichen agreed, and guided Moira away from the righteous dads. He owed no explanations to Moira. She was not his wife. Once a path had opened up in that direction and he had not travelled down it. Sometimes it seemed to him that he and Moira lived out a ghostly marriage, real in that other dimension she had just talked of, the path not travelled, the rose garden whose gate is never opened. There were moments of awkwardness and confusion as that unstated, unlived relationship intruded upon them the gravitational tug of its hidden mass.

'Have you been spying on me, Moira?' He took a swallow of his beer, deciding he'd take it easy on the booze. He was virtually on the wagon anyway.

'Wherever you go, Clyde Aichen, someone is watching you.' He put down the solemnity of her tone to the dope, which he could smell in the air. At the same time it gave him a shiver.

'That's exactly what I was afraid of,' he said.

Moira laughed. There was a glazed, wild look on her face. 'I'm in love, Clyde, you should congratulate me.'

Clyde stared at her stupidly. 'But...' As always, understanding arrived ridiculously late. It was her pleasure to watch it register on his face.

Clyde remembered the last time they were together, Moira and Snake dancing with wild exaggeration, Moira's face full of reckless heat. He thought of how it must have been afterwards, after he blacked out, both of them lying brandy sodden on the bed, Snakes huge tongue, slithering like a fish in and out of Moira.

'You know nothing about this, Clyde Aichen, so I don't want to hear any smart-arse comments.'

'I can make some assumptions.'

'They might be wrong.'

Clyde remembered the last time he and Moira had made love, how swollen her vulva had become as he'd stroked it, how wide her mouth opened when he first intruded the tip of his cock between those swollen lips. Behind that there was an image of Sylvia doing her gymnastic twists up on his hips. Clyde shook his head to free himself of these clinging images. Too much thinking about sex. Couldn't be good.

A pair of fingers appeared before him, holding a burning joint. The fingers were attached to a hand which was attached to an arm which was attached to an army shirt and topped with Snake's smiling face.

'This is the man who can quote poetry while falling over drunk,' she said to the broad hipped Maori woman beside her. Clyde took a quick hit at the joint and handed it over to Moira. If he wasn't going to get drunk, he wasn't going to fry either. It was moderation all around for Clyde Aichen.

'Kia ora,' the broad hipped woman said.

'Kia ora,' Clyde said. 'And it wasn't much poetry, just a few lines.'

'Bullshit. You went on and on. Half an hour at least. This is Grace, by the way.' Grace gave Clyde a sleepy, friendly smile.

Moira was sucking heavily at the joint. 'That's his party piece,' she said. 'He can do "Ozymandias" and Yates's "The Second Coming".'

'Like old Billy on the guitar,' Grace said. 'She only knows one song, but she plays it like she knows dozens.' She had a rich, musical voice.

Snake and Grace laughed. Everybody was laughing a lot, jokes or no jokes.

Moira handed the joint to Grace and leaned heavily on her arm. Two more women joined them at the sideboard.

'I zink it is berry important to be committed to zis action,' one of them said.

'This Is Heidi,' Moira said. 'And this is Clyde.'

'Hi-dee Heidi,' Clyde said.

'Kia ora,' Heidi said in an earnest German accent. She was broad and thick set.

'Heidi has organized environmental actions in Germany,' Moira said. 'She's only been here six weeks.'

'And she doesn't know a fuck from a feed when it comes to the Maori scene here in Aotearoa,' Grace said.

'I do!' Heidi said, grabbing Grace's free arm. 'I understand about zis Treaty of Waitangi. It is berry strange, this treaty.'

'A berry strange treaty indeed,' Grace said.

'You have it easy here,' Heidi said to Clyde. 'In Germany, you have a demonstration, for fifty demonstrators you have hundred fifty police.'

Grace spat an imaginary gob of spittle to the floor. Heidi put her arm around the woman's shoulders. 'I do understand. Fuck, I do,' she said in a low, intense voice. Grace stared moodily at the floor.

The woman who had arrived with Grace said to Clyde, 'I'm Aria. No one's going to introduce us.' Aria was an angular Maori woman with a small, gaunt face. 'Yous a friend of Moira's?'

Clyde nodded and sipped at his beer. Aria passed him the joint and he took another token toke. Bit more this time. Just being sociable.

'For a minute I thought you were the other guy,' Aria said.

'What other guy?' Apparently Aria did not hear.

'I know this group of people over at Coro,' Snake said to Heidi. 'They're all Germans. A big group of them all living together. It's weird. Feels like you're in Europe and you're just over in Coro.'

Heidi nodded. 'I know zeez people. Zey are Germans. Zey hide here. Zey hide from mad zings.'

Clyde found himself nodding and grinning like the others. It was always a good idea to stay clear of mad zings.

'Refugees,' Snake said. 'From western culture.'

Moira suddenly picked up a dishcloth and began energetically scrubbing the sideboard where someone had spilled some beer.

'And I know about za French tests too. Za fucking French, zey activate the whole Pacific Rim. All the big volcano, in Philippines, Japan. Zey all begin to rumble.'

Clyde slipped away, hoping Moira would follow. She didn't. The party looked more like a series of small meetings than the usual chaotic shift Clyde was used to. People were gathered in small groups around speakers who were holding forth on different subjects. Clyde found himself in a group of people listening to a gentle faced man with a long greying beard and shoulder length hair. He had a joint bogarted in one hand while he used the other to assist his argument. Occasionally the joint, held firmly between the fore and middle fingers of a fist, was brought in to do service in the form of a forward, punch like movement which, when repeated several times, created from the smoke a wavy and dissolute calligraphy.

'We're all going to grow old together,' Greybeard said with a broad grin, extending his arms to everyone as if welcoming them into his home. The Baby Boomers from World War II. This big bulge of us. When we're gone the country will be half empty. We can sit around in our wheelchairs, smoke a quiet joint or two and hear stories of how our friends are going out the back door with heart attacks or brain haemorrhages or whatever the fashion might be. There'll be no pensions of course, no savings,' his grin grew broader. 'By that time the country will have been stripped to the bone. Well stripped and looted by the big money boys.'

The smoky fist punched the air.

'I thought this guy was Father Christmas,' somebody next to Clyde said. Clyde recognised the voice. It was the brash young man who stopped coming to class.

'He's left his bag of toys at home,' the brash young man's companion said.

Greybeard held up a hand. He ticked off the items. 'The assets will be gone. Dams, railways, golf courses, TV channels, communications, the electricity grid, all painfully built up over the years from the taxes of your parents and you. That's one. Any large sums of money, like pensions, savings schemes, will be moved by legal impoundment into the Consolidated Fund, which is, properly speaking, neither consolidated nor a fund, but never mind that, the money will be history. That's two. Any productive base will be fucked because it's always cheaper to import from some country where the workers work sixteen hours a day for the smell of a rice bag and no one worries too much about environmental laws. That's three.' His grin broadened even further. 'Need I go on?'

'Then why the fuck are you grinning so much?' The brash young man's companion heckled.

'It's this goddamn weed, this wacky baccy,' Greybeard said hoarsely, shaking his head and waving the fist with the joint. 'This Coro killer gets me grinning like I'm spinning.'

There was a burst of spontaneous applause from his audience, momentarily drawing the attention of other groups. The brash young man turned to Clyde. He was wearing a t-shirt which said, *die yuppie die.*

'Isn't that a bit out of date,' Clyde said, gesturing to the t-shirt. 'The yuppies went down in the crash of 87, from what I've heard.'

'That's why I'm wearing it,' the brash young man said. 'It's a cultural artifact. It's history. I wouldn't have been seen dead in this in the 80s.'

Clyde took another sip at his beer.

'That makes sense,' he said.

'I enjoyed your classes,' the brash young man said. 'I enjoy writing but I can't stay with that. There's other media.'

'The commitment to words is a primal one,' Clyde conceded, thinking of his first writing, the first frenzied, self-conscious lines, how the Angel of Terror rolled out the words for him.

'I'd like to make movies,' the brash young man said.

'So would I,' Clyde said.

The brash young man smiled and Clyde realized he was not brash at all, just young; and quite shy.

A party, like an organism, has a life and development all of its own, the principles of which are governed by the law of alcoholic entropy – or at least the parties Clyde knew did. Stable conversational systems fall apart, people drift into other rooms, someone turns the stereo up good and loud for AC/DC and five minutes later someone turns it down again, people arrive who have never been seen before and the likelihood of a punch-up increases exponentially with the number of caps flying off bottles.

It's about this stage that the hostess gets pissed off.

From its first hesitant, awkward steps around embarrassment and shyness to its final, maximally dispersed, brain-dead state, there is a predictability, an inevitability in stages of a party. Moira's party was just at the point at which it would take a sudden, quantum leap into chaos. Moira could not be found, the front room was full of people Clyde didn't know, and an interesting woman he had been working towards disappeared. The party had phase-shifted. Clyde headed back towards the bar (as he thought of the sideboard), which was at least some sort of stable reference. Now, of course was the right time to slide out from under with the smart ones and go home. He'd find Moira, say goodbye, and do just that. He changed direction and headed for the hall. It was empty but for a couple kissing fervently up against the wall and a group clustered around the front door.

Clyde moved the other way, deeper into the house towards Moira's studio. As he passed the spare room he heard the unmistakable gasping of a woman in pleasure. Immediately he thought of Moira. He remembered the peephole and the picture that covered it. Heinz and the Victorian maid. Taking a deep breath he slipped lightly into the room and stood inside beside the door. The stark light of a street lamp fell across the bed though the tall, arched windows, lending a bloodless luminosity to the sheets and the figure in the bed. It was Snake lying on her back, her arms thrown out. The bedclothes had been pulled down below her breasts by a shape moving under them, the outline of a head lifting up and down. The effect was of some shadowed, shapeless breast feeding.

Moira! Clyde was gripped by a sudden jealousy; Moira was growing away from him, evolving through some territory of experience where he could not follow, and there was no place for him. Snake was beautiful, there was no denying that, and the portrait of her pleasure upon Moira's bed was of unabashed voluptuousness. Her cries of pleasure pierced his flesh. Had Moira not done something like that to him, once?

The sheet slipped back and the head beneath appeared. A dark haired face lifted, as a bird's does when it drinks, and Clyde caught the profile. The sharp-nosed, long jawed face was not Moira's, it was Stockman's. The maniacal grin could not have belonged to any other face. There was a trickle of dark saliva from the side of his mouth, and, just before he went back beneath the sheets, Clyde glimpsed a peculiar dark mark on his shoulder.

None of this was possible. Stockman had not been at the party, at least Clyde hadn't seen him, and Moira and Snake were supposed to be an item. The L word had been bandied about.

Clyde stepped back out of the room and went looking for Moira.

Moira's studio was cool and empty, and Clyde was content to sit on her stool, where she worked, and cradle a lager, plundered from a half finished bottle on her workbench. Moira's potting room still held the same mortuary chill in the stillness of its corners and in the competed work that stood in rows on racks, some fired, some ready for firing. Perhaps it was from all this clay the cold exuded. The unfired pots looked dull and blank, shapes without animation; the fired pots glowed with their own strength, disclosing their form. He'd been told of Moira's superb kiln work, he could see it with his own eyes.

He closed his eyes, leaned back on the stool and tried to imagine how it must feel, this earth art. The rush of clay. A feel for the inherent movement of a curve. A vision of colour. A wrestle with mud. And when you finished you had something. Something that might have been dug up out of the ground with garlic and sapphires. Something cultural. An artefact.

You don't get that with words, except in theory. The old, pre Madeleine, Aichen poems, the ones he was known by, strived for the status of artefacts. He'd put the glaze on them, the sheen – but that was so much deception. With words themselves, no matter how densely packed, the product had to be that much more diffuse, their constructs an insubstantial thing of the mind, something you could fall right through, and as time-bound as the actor's voice which rings out into the air in the moment of its expression and is immediately dissolved into memory.

Up till now his own work had not conceded this, his poems had acted as if this were not so, as if they were in the world the same way as a piece of fired clay was. They pretended, through the metaphors of form and appearance, to a status they could not truly own. Only his new work by its very helplessness refused solid form, maintaining a determined diffuseness, a surrender to immateriality.

He opened his eyes upon a colour that brought him to his feet. He'd seen it before, that blue. The deep water blue of turquoise, almost. The pots on that rack looked like they were part of a finished, paid consignment. His feet took him to a particular pot and his hands brought the pot to his eyes. It was small enough to fit neatly in the hand, nicely rounded and curved into a thin-necked top. A small vase for a single flower. But it was the colour, that edgy blue for which there was no adequate word. How crazy, that there should be no word for it! Or at least not a word that everybody would know, and put in mind this colour. Ultramarine was nice, but not quite it.

Then he remembered. Madeleine's face, framed by the same hue. It was not the sky, not a natural colour for sky. Driftwood sometimes burned with that colour. It was her colour. The colour she wore like a mantel. It accounted for the fairy-dust effect he'd been feeling so embarrassed about. That sparkle in the air wherever she went. It was her colour. Madeleine's aura, her magnetic body or whatever you wanted to call it – Clyde didn't give a shit. He'd seen it; that was enough for him. He'd seen it, a bright cowl over her shoulders.

His hands stroked the pot. It was cool and firm. The colour shone up from beneath the glaze. Then his fingers conveyed it into his pocket with the most professional of shoplifting gestures.

Clyde steered back towards the kitchen sideboard, the pot bulking awkwardly in his pocket. Heidi walked past, her face grim, Aria scampering along behind, a rag in her hand.

'Grace zinks zat just because I'm German I know nozzing. I know about za struggle here. Za struggle for za land. It is everywhere, zis struggle.'

Aria nodded and grinned apologetically at Clyde as she went past. Clyde didn't know what any of this meant. The *colour* was everywhere, burning like an after image upon the air. A little more than turquoise, and little less than aquamarine.

Moira took him by the arm.

'Moira, where have you been?'

'*To a nunnery.*'

'Let's not start up on that. I'm going soon. I mean now.'

'What's wrong? The party's just starting. I'm going to put some music on and snap some of these zombies into action.' She rubbed her hands, 'we're going to have some fun.'

'I don't think so. The party's pooping.'

'Watch me.'

'Are you too stoned to have a conversation?'

'Of course I'm not. Fuck you, Aichen.'

'Let's have a chat on the porch.' And don't go anywhere near the bedroom.

'I'm never too stoned to talk to you, Clydie-Clyde.'

Clyde lead her through the hall to the front porch. They passed a tall, handsome Polynesian talking vigorously, 'The Indians owned everything,' he was saying, 'the shops, the businesses, the land...'

'I want...' Clyde had almost forgotten what it was he wanted. Maybe he should tell her about Snake and Stockman.

'You want to talk about Madeleine Farquar.' Moira tried to smile maliciously. Heidi barged past them, a large paint brush in her hand. Aria trailed behind carrying a paint tin. They were heading down the front path.

'No. You were making big hints before, as if you know something I don't. Two can play at that game.'

The grin fell off Moira's face. She gripped his arm hard and pulled him off the porch and back down the hall to the workroom.

'He's talking racism,' somebody said loudly as they went past.

The chill silence welcomed him once more. The pots on their racks stood guard.

'We don't owe each other anything, Clyde I know that. You've gotta live your life.'

'You too,' Clyde said, one ear set for the movie clichés. *You've gotta live your life*. In his pocket, his fingers closed around the stolen pot.

'But you've reached that stage, Clyde, that stage,' she nodded solemnly to herself, 'when you could make a fool of yourself.' Her pupils swam up out of their drowned irises to fix on Clyde.

'By stage you mean age, don't you, Moira?' With a quick motion he downed the lager he'd left there earlier and wished he had another waiting. He could see what Moira could see, the whole scenario. Madeleine rejects his love. His already bad poetry turns maudlin. He goes a little mad. Drinks heavily. Makes absurd phone calls to Madeleine, who stops answering. Goes down to the parlour seeking echoes in Cleo. He's already been once (twice); he's broken the ice. He would become a regular and the fat blonde woman would be nice to him. He would get to know the girls, have a drink and talk to them while waiting for Cleo. They could all have a giggle about Heinz. He would hold Cleo's ghostly flesh between his hands. Seventy dollars a week. He could have a beer with Captain Knickers himself beforehand. He and Heinz, arm-in-arm. He would slip towards fifty with evasive eyes and pale, treacherous hands. His writing would become rote and lustreless – like one of Moira's pots before firing – or too withdrawn and internal. Publishers would start to complain. He would lose his readership. Christ! What a pretty picture.

'You don't give me much credit, Moira.'

'Credit! When did you ever ask me for credit, Clyde Aichen? I'm not a bloody bank.' Her head hung from her spine, her eyeballs hung themselves on his face. She looked so smashed he wondered if she was really following the conversation. If indeed there was a conversation.

'Listen, Clydie Clyde, you're setting yourself up. I've heard about this Madeleine Farquar. She can cut men dead, with her eyes. Get close to her, or try to, and she'll ice you out. You'll say 'hello Madeleine, my queen,' and she'll look right through you. Like shit on her shoe, she'll scrape you off.'

Clyde shivered. He could imagine it. That quiet amber fury. No longer disdaining to destroy him but destroying him in one glassy stare. Oh the bitch! he would say, oh the bitch!

'What have you got in your pocket? Is that a little bottle of some special poison you have hidden away?'

'No, Christ, I wish it was.' He clamped his hand tighter around the vase. 'Why are you telling me these things?' He exhaled noisily, wishing he had a beer, wishing he was at home rounding up the poem. Oh the bitch, he would say in his annihilation. He would have to put that in the poem.

'No, Clyde,' her voice had taken on the quality of a chant, she rocked backward and forward. 'I'm not jealous. Of *her*. What did they say? Been there, done that. Remember? Everybody had been everywhere and done everything. Nothing new could happen to anybody.'

'I remember.'

'I gave up on you long ago. What the hell are you clutching in your pocket if it's not booze or that other thingy you have down there?'

'It's nothing.'

'Like fuck. What's that stupid grin on your face? I swear…' She did her best to lunge forward and grab his pocket; he did his best to fend her off with his other hand. The result was a clumsy fiasco of a struggle in which the vase came free. Moira turned the colour of white clay. She stared at Clyde, her mouth open, then swung the same gap-jawed stare up into the rack where the vase ought to be.

'You'd steal from me, Clyde Aichen?' She had just the cracked trace of a voice. The words crumbled away in her mouth. They made no sense to her. They were words played back through her ear in a dead language. She saw the zonked man in front of her avoid her eyes in shame.

'Shit, Moira, I just put it in my pocket for a while. I was stoned, I couldn't resist the colour, see, that glaze,' he pointed, 'I could see it was part of a consignment but I just had to have it. A moment's madness. I would have told you about it. I would have paid you. Fuck, you've got to believe that.'

Moira had ceased to listen. Her eyes turned to some inner quarter no man had seen. Whatever she saw there, she closed her eyes against. When she opened them they were focused on the vase. The colour. The preternatural blue.

'You were going to give it to her,' she said.

Clyde couldn't remember deciding any such thing but now that Moira had said it, he could see she was most likely right. That's why he'd put it in his pocket. Love and sanity don't mix.

'What an incredible arsehole,' Moira said aloud, not seeing him, trying to figure it out. 'An arsehole of truly cosmic proportions. I've been living in a fool's paradise where friends are friends.'

'It's a tribute to your work,' he said, attempting gallantry. 'I probably wouldn't have left of the house with it. I'd have sobered up…'

'No you wouldn't.' In her hatred she was implacable. Her logic followed the fall of axe on his neck. 'You'd have got drunker. And more wasted. You'd have left with it. In the morning you would have found it and thought about returning it to me, which you couldn't do without lots of embarrassing explanations. You've taken more than you realize. You might as well give it to her. Wrap it up in some shiny paper with a little ribbon tied in a bow. That'll bring the colour to her cheeks.'

Clyde looked at the vase. Its colour seemed impossibly remote. A glaze from another world. And yet it was, after all, just a thing. Something shaped by human hand. Out of earth and pigment.

'Goodbye, Clyde Aichen.' She held the vase out to him. He pondered the symbolism of it dropping on the floor. The idea offended his aesthetic principles. The vase was not a symbol. It was evidence.

His hands closed around the vase and he walked over to the rack, placing it with reverential care in the exact spot he'd taken it from.

'Goodbye, Moira.' Without looking at her he turned and went back out into the party. A late hour revival was taking place. A doomed rally before final collapse. Somebody had put on some music and wrapped the volume up. Some more booze had appeared. The whole room, was full of the sweating mixed human odours of dancers, many connecting thighs in the current fashion. Dirty dancing, another gift from the egregious eighties.

He went to the sideboard, had a quick drink, and glancing around to see if he were observed, slipped a half bottle of vodka into his side pocket where the vase had been.

In the hall a remnant of talkers remained. A short, thickset, balding man with round glasses was talking hoarsely. '...of the cabbage trees,' he said, as Clyde slipped past.

'What are you saying?' Clyde said, stopping reluctantly, thinking of his own cabbage tree. Any mention of cabbage trees seemed to impinge on his personal territory.

'I'm just saying that the cabbage trees are dying,' the man said. 'All over New Zealand the old cabbage is karking, and nobody knows why.'

'Is that true?'

'You can read about it in the newspapers. The scientists haven't got a clue. There's no bug or virus or mould or anything. But the ecologists have a theory.'

'What is it?'

'It goes something like this. The cabbage trees are fucked up. They don't know what season it is. This may be due to the Greenhouse Effect, or some particular response of the cabbage tree to the increased ultra violet light due to the hole in the ozone layer...' The speaker paused to scratch the back of his head with a bemused look, '...but whatever it is it has the cabbage tree fucked up badly because it's flowering all the time instead of in season. It can't stop flowering so its whole cycle is fucked. It's received instructions that the only way to survive is to go through its sexual cycles constantly, like an addict. It's sexing itself to death.'

'Jesus,' somebody standing next to Clyde said.

148

Heidi and Moira pushed past. Clyde stepped back. Heidi, still carrying a tin of paint, had an exultant look on her face and Aria was covering her mouth. From the porch Grace watched them, expressionless.

Clyde turned for the door. 'Nice night,' he said to Grace as he went past.

From up the street a little, he looked back at the house. Grace was still on the porch, someone else was with her. Clyde could not see if it was Moira. He saw the glow of a cigarette. On the fence facing him in dark, clear lettering, still fresh and dripping, was painted:

HONOUR THE TREATY.

Clyde headed for Jervois Road.

The door opened.

'Mr Aichen?'

Clyde stepped forward, smiling towards the shape of the man shadowed by the light behind.

'Thank you for seeing me, Dr Thurgood.'

When the man turned his face into the light, Clyde could see it was glistening with sweat. Strange lines which came and went on his face shifted and changed as if the skin could not find a comfortable spot to rest upon the bones beneath.

'Please make it brief. I don't see many people.'

Dr Thurgood walked with difficulty, guiding Clyde into a small lounge and taking a seat opposite him.

'I was involved in a serious motor accident, Mr Aichen. I have ceased taking painkillers and am trying to control the pain with special meditative practices.' The muscles around his eyes twitched.

'I'll be brief. As I told you on the phone, I got your name from a contact I made investigating a case of chemical poisoning.'

Thurgood nodded. 'I know your contact. She told me she had given you my phone number.' He didn't sound too pleased about it.

'You're a Doctor of Pharmacology. You worked with chemical poisoning cases in the States.'

'Ten years with the FDA. I was mostly involved with one-off massive exposure victims; people who had drunk half a bottle of 245T, that sort of thing.'

'What do you think of the danger of low dosage exposure?'

Dr Thurgood was sweating hard. His eyes shifted in their sockets and every so often his face would crumple like a piece of wet paper.

'It's hard to collect data on that sort of thing. It's the same problem you get when you try to gather data of low dosage radiation effects.' The skin around his eyes twitched as if pecked at by invisible birds. 'I saw a woman on TV drink a glass of Roundup and walk off still smiling. I've seen a guy in the Forest Service here in this country eat 1080 laced possum bait to prove a point.' He patted his hair, trying to plaster it back into place.

'Mr Aichen I don't know what you want to hear, but I'll tell you a story before you go. Why I came to New Zealand. I was part of team working in California in this valley where the cancer rate was sky high. Everybody had cancer. Even the kids were getting it. We tested the river where the kids used to play and where they got their water, and found it chock full of carcinogens, poison waste, dioxin. We had no idea where it was coming from. There were no factories, no big farms where there might have been pesticide run-off, nothing. Then I found out.' He smoothed his face over several times with his fingers and closed his eyes.

'Dumping, illegal dumping. Have you heard about it?'

'I can guess.'

Dr Thurgood face twisted into a rictus of pain. His skin crawled down over his cheekbones. His limbs jerked. 'From a pesticides plant fifty kilometres away. The trucks would dump their chemical sludge twenty miles or so upriver from the town. Some local authority was being paid off. That's when I decided to get out of the States.'

'Which company was it?'

'I could tell you but it won't do you any good. You can't use this stuff, I won't put my name to it.'

'You mean I can't quote you, even in general terms.'

Dr Thurgood shook his head and stood up. Clyde stood too.

'I don't want any more to do with it. I've left it behind. I'm sorry I wasn't more help to you.' He tried to smile. 'You've run into a wall. And that wall's bigger than you.'

On their way out Clyde noticed a photograph on the windowsill of a pretty young woman in a knee length flared skirt. She was giving the camera a very private look.

'My wife,' Thurgood said, opening the door.

'Is she with you?'

'She was killed, in a crash, right here in Auckland a year ago. A truck. A truck came out of nowhere. I should have been the dead one.'

His eyes stared through Clyde like empty boreholes.

Clyde opened a new file and began entering data from the Bealter documents: quotes from doctors, selected bits on Roundup and Monsanto, personal testimonies. He penned a quick backgrounder on Agent Orange and Vietnam, and thought of the things he could do: contact the Army with some pointed questions, the Vietnam Veterans Association, the Medical Association, the Health Department, Monsanto... There was no end to it, the story would suck him in and never let him go. He remembered now his visions of a quick, clean, throw together story for a spot of cash.

Working rapidly, from the medical records, he built up a sketchy narrative of Bealter. Bealter as the reader would see him. A stocky, competent, practical man, a conscientious, intelligent farmer who just couldn't bear to see the gorse grow. A once energetic, robust man whose immune system was so undermined by his 245T exposure that he spent much of his time helplessly sick, dragging himself from one incompetent medical authority to the next. He wrote up Lorna Bealter too, her dwindling hopes and energies, how the black hole of her husband's illness had swallowed her life.

He went on to describe the farm, the area, and the farms around, deftly incorporating the barking dogs, the modern well-kept look of the place. He took the reader into Bealter's bedroom and introduced them to the shadow of the man lying on the bed.

Finally, he began to write up some more detailed notes on dioxin.

He could see where these notes were leading. Monsanto had covered up the dioxin in its products, tried to lie and cheat its way out of the truth. And why shouldn't Roundup itself be contaminated with dioxin? After all, according to the information in his mystery package, Roundup was contaminated with POEA, a substance known to be lethal to young fish. Looking back now at that information, he confirmed that the presence of POEA made Roundup four hundred times more toxic than one containing glyphosate with no POEA.

If dioxin was also present, it would provide a direct link between Bealter's Vietnam exposure and his subsequent illnesses. Once poisoned by Monsanto's contaminated 245T, only to be poisoned by the same crowd twenty five years later with another contaminated product right in his own backyard. There was a kind of grim persistence in it, a taste of fate and doom. And no proof.

Surely, if this were so, someone would have tested for it. There had to be a quick way of confirming that. Cursing at the time all this was taking he opened a new file and wrote a quick letter to the Ministry of Agriculture and Fisheries in Wellington, asking them if Roundup contained dioxin, and if the Board had tested for dioxin. At the same time he asked for confirmation of the existence of the mysterious POEA in Roundup, throwing in the names of a couple of other common brands of pesticides for good luck. Fuck them, he'd check them all out. It took him three or four lines which he didn't bother to spellcheck, content to print it out, sign it, and shove it in an envelope.

Weary of the work, he opened the file menus, eager to revisit his poems to Madeleine, eager to banish this chemical nightmare from his mind. What had the strange childlike voice on the telephone said? – *and when the canary stops singing…* Going back to the poems would be like seeing Madeleine again, reading the lines would bring her presence into the room, which felt very empty and huge. Perhaps the poem was no more than that, an incantation to summon her image.

To his bewilderment her folder was empty. There was no poem. The folders were there but no files were in them. Not a single file anywhere. He was trying to absorb the implications of this when another box appeared on the screen. There was a bomb, an old fashioned one with a spluttering fuse. Beside it was written, *Sorry! Systems error, please restart.*

Clyde didn't argue, pressing the restart button. Immediately it began to boot up again, unfolding the installation icons like cards being laid down by an invisible hand. The desktop pasted itself onto the page and there were his folders, with their files. He opened the poetry folder and clicked into the Madeleine poems. They didn't make it. Before they could appear, the same bomb with the same instruction jumped up. The screen began to flicker horribly. He broke the circuit again and the machine patiently rebooted. He tried to open a file and again got the bomb. He did that five times until he accepted the fact that his files were out of reach. Not just the poetry, all of them. Including the Bealter notes he'd just made. Gone.

A systems error had occurred.

The Westmere Rest Home looked exactly as it did when he'd left it a few days earlier. The same skinhead lawn. The same old people waiting at the same bench for the same cargo. The buildings and their grounds had all the appearance of a timeless zone, a redbrick and lawn no-man's-land hovering between the fifties and the eighties. Like a crematorium. Nothing ever happens here, the Rest Home proclaimed. The grass never grows, the windows never get cobwebs, the sheets never get soiled; it is a kingdom of varnish and glass across which the shadows of mourners cross without a trace.

Clyde had brought a daffodil to symbolize spring and a packet of chocolate wheaten biscuits. His mother would eat the biscuits and ignore the flower. Clyde would check out the level of her gin. The weekly ritual would be enacted.

She sat in her usual spot at the table looking out toward the street. As always, he tried to penetrate her silence and, as always, he failed. Her short, grey hair hung limp and unmoving at her temples. Her skin did not hang loose on her face in the manner of old people, but was stretched tight across the bone and possessed of a peculiar sheen.

'I thought you were dead, Mother,' he said cheerfully, putting on a jug for a cup of tea. 'You were sitting so still.' He returned and sat by her.

He passed his hands across her eyes and there was no response.

'Are you dead, Mother? Can you tell me what it's like?' He opened the packet of biscuits and placed it in front of her. Her hand moved from the arm rest, scooped up a biscuit and placed it in her mouth with the gesture of one posting a letter. Clyde grinned. 'There's powerful magic in those biscuits, huh, Mother?'

His mother's jaw moved mechanically sideways.

He picked up a biscuit and ate along with her. He wanted to tell her about Madeleine Farquar, but an ancient restraint forbade him. He trembled on the point of tearing those restraints to pieces, shocking her with personal revelations and obscenities. Instead he went into the kitchen and located the gin, meditating on the massive abdication of her silence.

Since he was, technically, off the booze, he was not due for a gin right now, so he contented himself with a quick, undignified sip at the bottle from the kneeling position, immediately returning it to its hiding place among the liquid soaps and cleaners.

The kettle boiled and he took two cups of tea back to the table. He imagined her silence was different today, deeper and more thorough, as though the process of withdrawal from the world had progressed that much further. Numbness had taken her throat. Her spirit had already departed from her body, or rather was tied there by the thinnest of threads, consisting of chocolate wheaten biscuits and the level of the gin bottle.

She's drowning, he thought, standing up again, not knowing where to go. Drowning in her silence. He got up and walked into the bathroom, not knowing why he was going there. The bath was half full and occupied by a pubescent boy who looked up at him, startled. He had the soft, girlish appearance of a twelve or thirteen year old, before the male body hardens into its muscular, adult shape. There were a few silky hairs around the boy's genitals. All around him, in the water, there were toy cars, half or wholly submerged. One clung with declining chances onto the upper side of a sponge. The boy's surprise turned to fright and his fright to fear, and from fear to shame.

Clyde closed the door and re-joined his mother.

'Who's that in the bath, Mother?' he asked. He sensed her on the point of replying, but her lips never moved. There was more than silence in this, surely. His mother was playing some game, just as she had always done; taking her revenge, just as she'd always done. Up to her old tricks. Not even silence could keep her quiet.

'Who's that in the bath, Mother?' he said again, sharpening his voice, as if the implied threat could possibly have any meaning.

Of course she didn't answer.

He walked back into the bathroom and the boy was still there. As Clyde watched, the car on the sponge slipped off into the water. The boy didn't move. A flannel covered his genitals. He looked up at Clyde defiantly. As Clyde watched, he brought a car up to the surface of the water and moved it forward as if it were a boat, making a childish humming sound.

Clyde wanted to take a step forward, into the bathroom, but his power to move was trapped within his body as surely as his mother's voice was trapped inside hers. The boy had stopped moving the car and was watching Clyde's face, his defiance collapsing into fear. What does my face look like then, Clyde wondered, trying to turn to the bathroom mirror, still finding himself powerless to move.

'I'm having a bath,' the boy said in high, emphatic tones.

Clyde had no voice to answer.

Recovering the power to action, he shuffled backwards and closed the bathroom door. He went back to the table, noting that at least four chocolate wheaten biscuits had been eaten.

'Who's in the bath?' Clyde said sharply in a no-nonsense voice. His shirt was sticking to his back. He was sweating as if he'd been in a sauna.

'Who's in the bath!' he shouted. 'Who's in the fucking bath?' When his mother didn't answer, he leaned forward and slapped her briskly, once on each cheek. Some sound issued from her throat so he slapped her again. This time her head snapped against the back of the chair and Clyde stepped away from the table. He was displaced from his own body as if it did not belong to him. His mother's cheeks began to mottle.

Clyde went into the kitchen and recovered the bottle of gin. He was off the booze, sure, but there was no sense in being fanatical about it. He splashed some into a glass and topped it with water. His hand was shaking like an old drunk's. What if she can't speak, he wondered. Got lost in the middle of a sentence and never found her way out. A pause between thoughts that went on forever.

Carrying the gin, he went and sat back down beside his mother. He knew who the boy in the bath had to be.

'Why am I always one step behind, Mother?'

He had come here looking for a sign, to hear once more the oracle of the dead speak through her mouth. Instead he had found a memory. He understood her silence now. It was a massive mirror reflecting him utterly. A screen upon which his own feelings were writ large. In herself she was nothing. An absence. A monumental cypher. What he read there was only what he'd written.

Understanding this brought a little peace. Finally, the gin warmed his gut. A strengthening sunlight came through the lace curtains and fell on the table. He noticed that the old people had gone from the front lawn. The sight of the empty seat made him feel curiously sad. Their cargo had finally arrived. The sunlight fell on the small table beside his mother's bed. The photograph had changed. This one was of his mother as a young woman. She wore a bridal veil and a smile to match.

'And where are you, Father?' Clyde said aloud.

Sweating, Clyde cautiously hoisted the pack carrying his Mac P onto his back. He had misjudged the weather and had overdressed, easy enough to do in Auckland in spring, and was now wishing he could remove everything from his back and take off his winter singlet. He trudged the distance to the Opal Towers like a pilgrim with a burden on his shoulders and a confession to make. His eyes he kept carefully on the pavement before him, trying not to dwell on the consequences of slipping and falling.

Opal Towers, rinsed by overnight rain, gleamed with shining commercial promise. Behind these glass walls people sat hunched over their keyboards and screens moving money. Clyde walked into the foyer and headed straight for the lifts and waited patiently by the closed doors. Everything gleamed, the floor, the walls, the steel lift doors.

The lift arrived, took him to the fifth floor and obligingly opened for him, but Clyde didn't bother getting out. Fantastic Computers were gone. The whole floor was empty except for the shelves and the blue-grey carpet. There was an abiding emptiness here, cushioned and echoless, as if the rooms had never been occupied. Just like the decade itself, he thought. Throw up a few appearances, create the illusion of substance, make some money, or try to, then disappear overnight. Evaporate in the incorporeal air.

The lift waited patiently for him to make a move. He did the same. Eventually it gave up and closed its doors. The vision of the empty room vanished and, as the lift began its first few moments of ponderous movement, Clyde thought of Madeleine and the poem. The poem! That uneasy collection of thin lines had always had, it seemed, a tenuous hold on the world, and now their hold was more tenuous than ever. They were lost, somewhere in limbo, a pattern enfolded upon a piece of silicon. In what sense could the lines be said to exist? They were memory now, just memory, with no more substance than memory has. A dream of time.

The bottom dropped out of his stomach.

His head caught up with his body and the lift door opened. He was back in the gleaming foyer, his burden still on his back. On the street he looked, up and down, uncertain of directions. He had to wait for his direction to arrive.

Instead a big, sloped shouldered man walked up to him and clapped him on the back, as far as was possible considering his burden, and said, 'Shakes, old son. You look as pale as old Hamlet's ghost. What have you just seen? The affrighted globe?'

'An empty room.'

The big man looked at him acutely and nodded as if he understood. He gestured to the tall, office blocks around them, 'There's plenty of empty rooms around here, matey. More businesses folding than you can shake a stick at.'

There was something different about the ad-man and, as usual, Clyde had to wait for the penny to drop. The ad-man wasn't drunk! Clyde had never seen Heinz sober before, maybe Heinz felt the same way about him. They wandered along the street and Clyde told the story of his technical problems, deftly not mentioning the poem to Madeleine. The big man listened gravely and nodded sympathetically.

'Get ready for the nineties, Shakes, old son. The eighties are fading fast.' He licked his lips. 'Someone has been staring too long at the bottom line. The freeze-dried, quick-fried decade leaves lots of empty rooms.' He made a sad gesture towards Queen's Arcade, 'This week's cosy little coffee house becomes next week's beauty salon. A stationary shop turns into a cheap-priced wool store selling jersey seconds from trestle tables. Next week the same place is selling remainder books, four for ten dollars or three bucks apiece, from the same trestles. Look over there,' he pointed towards Custom Street, 'a video parlour becomes a blue-movie house with peep-show provided. Actually it's just another derelict empty space.'

'You've nailed it.'

'It's a sign of the times, boyo. Everybody wants to bet on the win-win, but somewhere there's a loser.'

'That's me.' Clyde gestured to his burden. 'I've just lost all my data.'

They had stopped walking. Heinz was smiling a gentle smile. 'You do look melancholy, Shakes, even beyond the requirements of fashion. You got the bomb did you?'

'With the spluttering fuse.'

'A bad sign, but take heart, Shakes, old son, I know a man who knows the right cyber spells to make those nasty little bombs go away, my own pet Neuromancer. You are aware of William Gibson's novel, I presume.'

Clyde was aware.

'Best book of the decade. When they look back on the eighties they'll say, *Neuromancer* rules. Follow me, I am the way and the light. He lives not far from here.'

Heinz's neuromancer turned out to be little man in a wheelchair crippled by arthritis. He wielded his hand as someone might wield a prosthetic. There was a quarter bottle of whisky beside him, and several empties on the floor. He wanted $200 up front. While he worked on Clyde's computer he drank and swore. Heinz didn't drink but circled around the bottle like a hyena around a carcass.

After several hours, the magic moment came and the neuromancer proved his wizardry by booting up the machine and restoring Clyde's folders to the desktop. They had been conjured away, and now they had been conjured back again. Poet meets poem, poet loses poem, poet finds poem again – and everybody lives happily ever after.

'Do print-outs,' he advised Clyde, 'and transfer everything onto a floppy disk as back up.'

Clyde promised faithfully, like a child at the dentist promising to clean his teeth. He meant every word of it.

'This place stinks of booze,' Heinz said. 'Let's go have a drink.'

The poem existed. He had firm, material evidence of that now he had done a printout and had in his hand what they called *hard copy*. Fresh and blinking in the hard light of the page, his poems tried to make sense of the world while Clyde tried to make sense of the poems. It was a remarkable one hundred and eighty pages, but his eye was immediately drawn by a messiness and unevenness of quality, as if during their lost days in cyberspace the lines had subtly degraded, making quantum alterations of their own in an attempt to subvert him. He saw minor pieces, verbal doodles, lapsed lines, lines that were no more than direction finders for other lines, lines that wandered away into la-la land, and some that stayed so close he hardly recognised them. Some of the lines suffered an even stranger and more horrible fate, for, although they retained the same outward form that he had given them, all the spirit and passion had drained from them; the black flame that animated them had died. These were no more than the ashes of love, and it would be his pleasure to backspace them right out of existence. Cut and cut and cut again!

It would all cut back to about eighty or ninety pages that held tightly to their purpose, precarious as that might be. He worked rapidly, cutting, shaping, paring, occasionally reconstructing. He knew the way the lines should feel now, even though he still did not entirely approve of them. They needed to be taut, thin and defenceless – yet strong as wire.

He began in the morning. There was a bright strip of light on his decking but he refused to be distracted by it, or even by the thought that he should go out and look at his cabbage tree. The one that was flowering itself to death. He resisted a moment's temptation to open the Bealter file. Soon the sky clouded over and rain crimped the polished wood. At midday he did a second printout and went to work once more, pressing even harder, testing the resistance of the lines. Midway through, he stopped and spun around in his chair. If Madeleine were there now, he'd sketch her, just as a painter would, but from words. The image alerted him to something he should see but couldn't. I'm one step behind again, he realized. When it catches up with me, it will be too late, too late at least for this moment.

The phone rang.

'Hello, arsehole.'

'Moira.'

'I've heard that line before.'

'What can I say?'

'Try *sorry.*'

'Sorry won't cut it.'

'You're right, but I've decided to forgive you anyway.'

'I'm in your debt.'

'I know. That part of it feels great. As for the rest, I've decided you are not in a rational state. You are like a child. And with a child, you tell them off when they steal, but you can't hold it against them. Children pick up shiny things because they get lost in their dream and forget what the universe is really like.'

'Thanks for the affirmation of faith.'

'It's my big heart. I'd make you one just like it, for the fun of humiliating you, but I would never be able to get that special *colour* again.'

Clyde's eyes raced back over his words. How would they sound, for example, in Moira's ears? He doubted she would have much patience with them.

And how would they sound in Madeleine's ears? Like sweet music.

'How did the party end?'

'I never found out. I went to bed.'

'You told me you were in love with Snake.'

'I told you I was in love.'

'I'm finding this hard to believe, Moira.'

'I knew you would. You thought I was in the wings, hanging in there, waiting for you.'

'There's enough truth in that to sting.'

'Thanks for saying so.'

Clyde hit the *delete recall* code and several lines he'd just cut leapt back onto the screen. He looked at them hard, trying to figure out why he'd cut them, why he'd written them in the first place. It was a problem of promise and delivery. These lines were like chocolates which promise a hard centre and which prove to contain only marshmallow. He deleted them again.

'I'm discovering the real source of my sexuality, Clyde. It's such a relief, like coming home again.'

'I'm happy for you.' He jabbed at the *delete recall* code and looked at the same lines again, trying to delete the memory of Stockman's maniacal face beside Snake in bed. He doubted that was a real memory. More like a bad trip. Flashback to the old acid days of the sixties.

'Don't be flip, Clyde. All those years I stayed emotionally unconnected and I never knew why.'

Clyde remembered her body again, quick and dark against him, her teeth on his collar bone. He stared blankly at the screen. The lines were marked by a faint quantum jiggle, courtesy of cyberspace. Their off-again on-again existence had made them nervous.

'I know we had Jeannette's ghost in the house,' Clyde said, 'but you and I had some pretty good times, Moira.' He was surprised at the tremble in his voice.

'Yeah, Clyde. We had good times, but that's all we had. There was no deeper fulfilment.'

'But sexually...'

'I know you feel threatened by this, Clyde, that's very understandable. I know what you were going to say.' A note of asperity entered her voice. 'You might be able to separate your emotional and sexual life, but I can't. Maybe that's easier for men.'

'Don't go that way.'

'Why not? Generally, there's something wrong the way men relate to women, or haven't you noticed? Women are getting bashed and raped all the time, and that's just the upper edge. It's symptomatic. We're projections of men's desire, and because we can't conform to that, we won't conform to that, we are battered, either emotionally or physically, until we are numb, then raped. That's the world I live in, what kind of world are you living in, Clyde?'

Losing his temper, Clyde, slammed *delete* once more. The weakness of the lines had run into the bones of his arm. He wanted to see Madeleine right now, to ring her up and hear her voice.

'You're being grossly one-sided and one-eyed about this.'

'Am I?'

'You're very fucking quick to dump on Madeleine. To issue mysterious warnings and act like a jealous wife or something, while at the same time,' he hit *delete recall* again, 'you produce this Snake creature and announce...'

'Forgive me, Clyde, but you don't understand the situation at all and I'm damned if I'm going to enlighten you.'

'Sure, sure.' He stared balefully at the Jack in the Box lines. Until he knew why they rankled him, he was reluctant to consign them to permanent oblivion in cyberspace. There was an emptiness in them, but not the right kind of emptiness, a so what factor totally at variance to his intention.

'The difference is this. I am a thirty-five-year-old woman who has finally discovered her true nature, after much pain and misplaced faith, which is more often than not the lot of a woman. No don't interrupt. Hear me out. I believed I should be feeling things I wasn't. I pretended things I didn't feel. I ended up alien to myself. Now I've found someone who values me. Seeing and understanding all this is like coming up for air. For the first time I have a context for understanding my life. My bisexuality. I can breathe again. I can do my art again. Whereas you, Clyde Aichen, are a forty-two year old misogynist hung-up on a beautiful young image with deep dreamy eyes who doesn't, and won't ever, love you.'

'You've got incredible cheek, Moira.'

'You bet. She's leading you by the nose. No. Let's be kind to her and say that you are leading yourself by the nose into a cloud cuckoo land, an imaginary world where you love her and she loves you and you will walk through the wilderness of this world holding hands like a pair of chickens, I mean children. You are like the child who wants to eat a daffodil so he can be as beautiful as its bloom. It's not going to be like that. She is a mirage. You are simply exhibiting the typical middle-aged

162

male syndrome. Christ, can't you see that?'

'Have you been drinking, Moira?'

There was a long silence. The receiver crackled and spat as the phone cleared its wire throat. He stared right through the lines on the screen. They were stare through lines alright. Behind the screen there was a miniature gun mounted, spraying him with radiation as it projected his words into cyberspace. He'd seen the screen glow in the dark after he'd turned it off at night, a ripple of electrical memory through folding frames. Outside a tui leapt into the flax and gave its clear, insistent yodel. Ten years, he thought; ten measly years.

The sky in the east lit up with a stab of lightning, thunder hovered on the horizon. Tiny manuka leaves went scudding across the deck.

'Is that all you can say?' Her voice sounded small and far away, as if she was holding the receiver away from her face.

'Does Snake drink in the morning too?' Rain was coming in across the hills in the lee of a grey cloud.

'Clyde. I didn't ring up to fight or argue. Actually I rang up to give you a chance to apologize for trying to rip me off by taking me for this wonderful drive in your battered old Toyota out of the city somewhere. You know how you get ring fenced sometimes, especially when life gets intense. I need some air.'

He went through the doubtful lines again and a new idea occurred to him. He'd been through these same lines many times, over many rereads, and he'd found them fit to form. He'd rung them upon his ear and had found them true coin. Now he found fault with them. How many other passages were there like this, ready to emerge from the seam of the text into the shadow of dubious connections? The whole poem might thus be borne away like the sons of time in the old hymn.

'I don't really care where we go. Just a quiet place.'

'You know I've said I'll do that.'

'I mean now, numb brain, right this very minute.'

'Moira, I'd love to, truly I would. But I am in the middle of a showdown right now. High noon.'

'Are you writing?' Storm rain swept across the decking. The light outside went yellow.

'No. Yes. I'm facing undecided lines.'

'It's always high noon for you when you're working, Clyde. Every line is high noon. I wouldn't ask this often.'

'And I wouldn't be so totally tied up often either.'

'What are you writing?'

'Poems. A collection of like-minded poems, you could say. A gaggle of consenting lines.'

'And you can't leave them?'

'I do, often, but not right now. I'm on the verge of seeing something.'

'I hope you see it.'

'So do I.'

The phone went dead. He pulled the plug on it and sat back on his chair.

The problem of the dubious lines was simple. They were not up to scratch, that was all. They did not fulfil their own terms properly, and in failing to do so, ceased to be the real event. Rather, they were imitations. Unsteady simulacrums. Which would taint the whole work. The solution was simple. Cut them out. Return them to silence, and any others upon which the taint of suspicion might lie, until only the irreducible remained. The bedrock. Core of the movement itself. To tamper with that was a violence he would not undertake.

He got up, went to the fridge and extracted a can of beer, giving thanks to the God of the Fridge for the bestowing of Eternal Cans. It was always like this finalising a manuscript; the obsessional last minute changes, the calling of the whole enterprise into question. Words alone do the trick or fail to do so; intentions count for nothing. Experience goes begging. Some manuscripts had failed to make it through this last minute gauntlet and were consigned to the uneasy oblivion of the bottom drawer where intentions fester against the yellowing of time. This manuscript was not to be one of those, there was too much at stake in it – something new. He had his title, and he would not let an attack of vague anxieties deflect him now. There was no escaping history in any case. All lines must bear down before time's occluded eye. What is the half-life of a poem?

The rain had gone as quickly as it had come. He worked till evening, stopped, had another beer, and prepared an envelope. There was no stopping now. No fatal hesitation. If he didn't prepare them for posting now, he might never do it. They might end up in the bottom drawer through sheer default, default brought on by cowardice.

He did a final printout and took one last look, marvelling at its transparency, disturbed by its fretful cohabitation with silence, shamed by its evasions.

He placed the manuscript with a covering letter inside a sealed envelope and threw it into his briefcase. To hell with Stockman, Stockman probably wouldn't even read them. He'd just put them in a pile with all the other poetry manuscripts he hadn't looked at and never would. Let the College Press have them. They'd been after him for another book, or so he liked to imagine on the basis of a friendly conversation with the editor.

It would have been nice to have heard the tui. That bird, he felt, approved of the poem, had watched over him as he wrote it. In any case, its absence was merely the absence of an omen, not an omen in itself.

Randomly, on a sheet of paper he wrote: *this little piggy went to market.*

Clyde had just begun writing the Bealter article, at long last, when, sighing, he pushed the keyboard aside and pulled the telephone over. Like human corruption, every story is endless, a bottomless pit; but for practical, time bound, journalistic reasons, there has to be a cut-off point. And yet… and yet this story deserved just one more turn of the wheel, or the screw or whatever it was. A final touch. *A coup-de-grace.*

As the phone rang he set himself up with his doodles. They were still there, Doodle and Bride of Doodle. Doodle looking rather cynical with a cigarette hanging out of his mouth, Bride of Doodle looking off into a distant future happiness.

'Mr Gladwin,' Clyde said smoothly when he got through to the person he wanted, 'I'm a researcher, Clyde Aichen, doing a background article on our local fruit and vegetable farming.' His voice was light and easy. The word *journalist* was far away. 'I discovered that your product, Roundup, is the most popular herbicide on the market.' He put a lift into his voice at the end of the sentence, as if he were congratulating Mr Gladwin.

'That's right, Clive, we…'

'Clyde.'

'Sorry, Clyde, bad line. Yes, we have an edge in the market because our product does the job. No weed is safe! People buy it once, they'll buy it again.'

'Worldwide you have a multi-billion dollar business with that one product.'

'In excess of a billion for sure, Clyde – who did you say you worked for?'

'The Auckland Herald. We're doing a weekend horticultural feature.' He tried to give Doodle a liar's face but Doodle' face was full up. There was no alternative but to increase the family. He drew another head with a wide, liar's grin. Brother of Doodle.

'Well,' Mr Gladwin grew expansive, 'Roundup is probably the most successful herbicide in the world right now.' His voice was as crisp as a cucumber, bright as a blade.

'Who are your major buyers?'

'All sorts of people, Clyde. Schools, local authorities, park boards, conservation groups, farmers, and just your ordinary Joe Blow backyard gardener. No garden shed is complete without it!'

'Did you say conservation groups?'

'I sure did. Royal Forest and Bird, for example. They buy it to keep the ginger plant and other nasties out of our native forests.'

'Is that right?'

'I'm glad you brought this up, Clyde. Few people realize that without products like Roundup our native bush would be completely overrun by stronger exotics. There would be no native bush. Roundup is on the side of the environment one hundred percent, and some environmentalists are becoming aware of that. The smart ones. The ones who see we have no choice.'

'That's an interesting angle.' Beside his liar's grin, Brother of Doodle took on shifty, liar's eyes.

'There are a number of invasive species that simply cannot be controlled any other way. Our native bush is facing extinction from these invasive species and few people realize it. I mean the urgency of it.' Mr Gladwin's voice was large and expansive. And urgent. He made Clyde wonder what Clyde was doing about his ginger plant, in a corner of his property quietly strangling some native ferns.

'Some of the farmers I spoke to were thinking of going organic, do you see that as a threat?'

Mr Gladwin's voice was very tolerant, 'We've no quarrel with organics, Clyde, no quarrel at all. Our product is biodegradable too. The active ingredient, glyphosate, is not much more toxic than common salt. Salt will kill things too, remember? In future organic farms will probably stock Roundup.'

'For use on crops?' Clyde allowed a trickle of incredulity into his voice. All liars hold a secret tension in their faces, and Clyde would like to have been a good enough doodler to capture that in his new doodle face. He contented himself with vague, suspicious looking lines along the cheekbones.

'On driveways, around fences and gates and buildings, steps, paths, roadsides – that scrubby area behind the garage you want to get cleaned up. That reserve you want protected. That runaway gorse and tobacco weed springing up everywhere.'

Clyde decided he was getting nowhere fast.

'Mr Gladwin, why hasn't your Company submitted all the tests and toxicology data on all of Roundup's ingredients to peer scientific scrutiny?' Brother of Doodle acquired a hat, tipped at a rather gangster-like angle.

There was a pause while the open line hummed its own music. Mr Gladwin's voice, when it came, was slightly less expansive. 'All the data necessary for registering Roundup with the EPA has been provided, Clyde. If you've done that much research you'll know that.'

'Yes, I know that. You've done what is legally required. What I'm asking you now is, why haven't you gone a step further and done what is *morally* required and opened up free access to all your data?'

Mr Gladwin gave a little laugh, apparently tickled at Clyde's naivety.

'There are commercial sensitivities involved. There are plenty who'd love to pirate the Roundup formula for their own purposes.' There was a coolness in Mr Gladwin's voice now, a new steeliness.

'But Monsanto actually sued the EPA to prevent it from releasing the data.' He was at an impasse with Brother of Doodle who refused to accept either a beard or glasses.

'Of course. The EPA had already registered Roundup. They accepted the data. From the public's point of view, that is the key thing. The EPA says Roundup is safe. The move to release the information was motivated by our competitors. We feel no *moral* requirement at all to release that data, Clyde.'

'Given already existing doubts, however…'

Mr Gladwin jumped in, quick as a flash, 'What doubts, Clyde? We have never had one verifiable complaint about our product.'

'The fake tests of the seventies. All that initial fake data submitted to the EPA.'

Mr Gladwin gave a tired sigh. 'That's ancient history now. All those tests have been duplicated. Look, let me try and explain something to you Clyde, and save you from perpetuating some silly myths. Our product is safe when used as directed.' He coughed. 'Some people claim to have been poisoned by Roundup, but not one of them can prove it. It's more likely they're suffering from chemophobia.'

'Chemophobia?'

'Fear of chemicals. All part of the lunacy of our modern age. People want to hang their problems on one simple thing. A scapegoat. Roundup gets blamed for everything from pins-and-needles to heart-attacks. You should read Dr Amos, Clyde. He has an interesting perspective. He points out that humanity has always been surrounded by poisons. There are poisons in the common cabbage. There're poisons throughout nature. Evolution has provided us with a body that can deal with these poisons.'

'You don't think dioxin is dangerous?' Abruptly, evoking creator's privilege, he swept away Brother of Doodle's hat and replaced them with horns. Now he had it, the old Father of Lies himself, with a somewhat swollen head where the hat once was.

'Sure it's dangerous, but so are a thousand other things in your life. It's not the end of the world. Did you say you worked for The Herald?'

'Yes. Just one more thing. A question of impurities. Is there any dioxin in Roundup, Mr Gladwin?'

The heartiness had gone right out of Mr Gladwin's voice. 'Certainly not.' His voice bent through the wire like a piece of steel tubing. 'And I see no reason to even raise the issue.'

'Thank you for your cooperation, Mr Gladwin, just one more thing. Do you use Roundup yourself?'

The voice became expansive again, 'I sure do. Especially on kikuyu. Roundup works like a wizz on kikuyu. You can tell your readers that!'

'And do you use full protective gear, goggles and body clothing as recommended by Monsanto in its material safety data notes?' Clyde's voice was as smooth and as slippery as soap.

There was a fractional pause. 'I do, yes.' The voice came stronger. 'Of course I do.' But the enthusiasm had gone out of his voice.

Clyde put down the phone and got to work and did the writing.

He stood on the Downtown square, facing Queen Street, looking from the Post Office to the Downtown Shopping Complex and back to the Post Office again. Beside him, the stone Maori Warrior looked the other way, out to the harbour.

He had paused to watch a little old man dressed in Bavarian costume and wearing a long-nosed mask play a fiddle, tapping his foot as he did so, activating through the medium of some wire attached to his foot a puppet dressed as he was, playing a fiddle and wearing the same mask, dancing in tune. A little old man playing and a dancing with his simulacrum. People clustered, fascinated at this dual image, one knee-high to the other, and some threw coins into the fiddle case. Clyde juggled his coins against the prospect of a later beer.

Madeleine Farquar came out of the Post Office and wandered across the square at an angle to his vision. Although not especially tall, she gave the appearance of staring out over the heads of the moving crowd towards some distant goal as she strolled forward, oblivious to everything around her. She lives in another world, Clyde thought, thinking of Rilke.

There was a dreaminess in her movements he did not wish to intrude upon, or disrupt her world of thought forms with its colours bright and interior. Clyde slipped into the anonymity of the cluster of people around the Bavarian fiddler. The little puppet danced and played. Clyde knelt down and examined it carefully, noting the clever resemblance of the papier-mâché head to the mask the man wore, and how precisely sewn its little jacket and knickerbockers were, as if cut and put together by elvish tailors. The fiddle too, was a beautifully formed miniature, strung with golden hair-like threads.

Moira may be way off beam, he thought, his fingers closing around some coins in his pocket, in suggesting that Madeleine cuts men dead with her see-through stare, her withering eye. That see-through stare may be no more than simple truancy, or forgetfulness. Perhaps she did not even recognise them at all, so massive her absence.

He took the coins out and juggled their false brightness in his palm. Such a moment of forgetfulness might be forgiven anyone, he thought, his mind turning towards his mother. Perhaps his mother simply walked into such a moment and never emerged.

Clyde Aichen's Waitakeres retreat was bathed in the new season's light. A spring sun with a summer intensity to its heat. Aichen himself, prize winning poet, lay naked and spread-eagled on the warming planks of his deck, buoyed by the firm timber and the cool fizz of a beer in his belly. He was here, there was nothing more he could ask of himself, nothing more he could do.

He didn't have to go anywhere, do anything or make any sort of effort to please anybody. He was not even under any obligation to write anything. His collection for Madeleine was with the publishers, the Greenpeace article was all but written. As for poetry, the universe would go on without another Aichen poem. The world would turn, the great jellyfish consciousness's whose bodies were galaxy clusters would continue to swim their sidereal hours through. One poem, more or less, was not the straw that would break the heart of love.

The mind is a wondrous, whoresome thing, Clyde thought, feeling his outstretched body turn. It has no boundaries, and, since there is no way of apprehending it other than through its own mechanisms, there is no way to get an overview of it. He'd heard of medical freaks, people born without brains, nothing there but a smear of cells in an empty brain cavity, and these people were able to lead a normal life – work, love, laugh, do maths, have dreams, maybe even write poems.

He resisted the urge to get up and do something. This vacuous doing was a form of madness. Busy work. Even the urge to the fridge for a second beer was an errant one. He could see all the future beers he would ever drink stacked away inside the next like Matryoshka dolls. If he didn't have the next, that is where they would stay.

His body was melting into the planking. He was floating above the earth, connected to it by a long silver thread. He didn't ask to be the hero of any hectic, first person narrative, bound by duty to push the plot forward with every scene. Turn on the spit of love with every heartbeat. He could take time out. Like God he could rest. Look back at his creation. He could give himself permission to do that much.

It was ok to be spared.

Clyde and Madeleine walked beneath the great elms and birches of Albert Park, down towards Victoria Street, the shadows passing over their faces like ghostly palomino horses.

'There's some sort of crisis coming up in my life,' Clyde said. 'I can't see what it is, but I can feel the shadow of it.'

Clyde was not telling the whole truth, but it was as close as he could get at that moment.

'My life is changing too,' she said. 'In fact something has happened to me.'

'What's that?'

Through the porous membrane connecting them he sensed the differences in her. Her fear was to the fore, but behind that there was an emotional excitement, a flush, a spring in her stride. Her hair swung out from her head full of kinetic energy. He'd read how the Islamic leaders of Iran believe that a woman's hair contains 'special rays' which drive men mad, which is why a Muslim woman should cover her hair in a public place. Of course it was funny, in a horrible way, but for a moment they had Clyde's sympathy. It is the fairy-dust factor, he thought, grinning to himself. Those rabid old ayatollahs had caught a little of the enteric sparkle.

'I'm in love.'

Below them, Victoria Street West fell away to the big Queen Street intersection. Pedestrians were rushing at random angles across the barndance. Arnold Schwarzenegger looked up at them from the Civic Theatre billboard.

She said, 'It's scary. I mean it's wonderful too, but it is very scary. I mean, I was recently in a scary relationship.'

'Some feelings you have to trust,' Clyde said. They paused at the steps leading down to the street.

She sighed, almost unhappily, 'I know that's true.'

'It sounds like a burden.'

'Not altogether. We, that's Philip and I, went for a walk on the beach. There was a lot of joy. But I'm aware of the pitfalls too.'

'There are many.'

'That's why I'm scared. Truly, I'd almost rather not. I didn't anticipate this. I was thinking of being celibate. I find the idea of celibacy very alluring.'

'Celibacy derives from the Order of Angels,' Clyde murmured. 'I think angels are celibate.'

'It's a practical alternative, for a woman,' she said. 'But I want children.' She looked meaningfully at Clyde. 'Nowadays, when I'm with a man, I don't so much think of what kind of good time he's giving me, but what sort of father he would make.'

'That shows uncommonly good sense.'

'I had to fight against all this feminist conditioning just to admit to myself that I did want children. Talk about blocks!' She tried to laugh.

They went down the steps onto the street. Clyde stood in a glaze of car lights, as in a Fassbinder movie. Lights sliding all around.

'We're not... sleeping together yet. I don't know if I want to, just yet.'

'Save it up,' Clyde said, pushing the pedestrian button. Once, twice, three times.

'Yeah. Wait till the desire gets too much.'

'That should do it.'

Like the parting of the Red Sea, a channel opened up in the traffic and a distant beacon told them to *walk now*. They obeyed, and the beacon began flashing a red warning sign at them. Walk faster!

'You know, Clyde, I can't talk with any other man the way I can talk with you.'

Clyde smiled. His first for the day.

They crossed Victoria Street West and into High Street. Clyde saw his reflection slide in and out of the doorways of shops. A new Video Games parlour had opened. The Video Parlours, like the pokies, were signs that in the eighties we suffered an invasion from Mars, just never noticed it. They Live! Mr Carpenter.

Clyde paused and stared in at the youths standing at the machines lost in the flash and twitter of cyberspace battles.

'Are you doing any writing?'

'Hardly any. Some stuff in my notebook.' Carelessly, 'A few poems for Philip but they're not up to much.'

'Most love poems are not up to much. More often than not the emotion outruns the poem, so it ends sentimental or maudlin.' He should know. Rejection poems might be a lot easier.

They turned into Simple Cottage looking for an empty table.

When the phone rang in the middle of the night, Clyde knew who it was. It was the Westmere Rest Home. His mother was dead. Heart failure. Peacefully. Found half an hour ago. The voice was like the Rest Home itself, professionally reassuring. Of course Clyde would come at once. Clyde put the phone down and went to get up. His limbs would not cooperate. He lay pinned to the bed. Dreams came in and went in fixed orbits like planets. His mother, dead at the bottom of the ocean. A grave full of the skeletons of birds. Under a pewter sky, the wide sea. More silver than any reflection. Warriors wave a warning to him. He must come no further or be drawn himself into the sea of the dead. Their tattoos twist about on their faces like wreathes of smoke. *Moko*: a fine sounding word. The song of the fishermen is the sutra of farewell; Clyde may hear it from a distance but may not sing the notes. For ten years he would consecrate his silence to the wellbeing of trees. He searched the beach for his sorrow and found the guts of fish. The dawn was the colour of salmon flesh.

Clyde tried to break the spell and get up. The spell he knew was nothing more than the chaos of his mind. He also knew that once his limbs began to move, the irrevocable would be set in motion. He existed now in a suspension of time in which his mother was not dead, the phone had not yet rung, the dream had not yet ended. His mother was sitting at her table and eating chocolate wheaten biscuits, and checking the level of the gin. She drank gin and watched the wind blow the street along outside her window. She went to bed and dreamed of drownings.

She was drowned. Her last words, if Clyde had not imagined that. What did they mean? It was herself she was talking about, Clyde decided. She had drowned herself in silence, which had crept into her veins, made its dark way up to her heart. Her heart had stopped beating because it made too loud a noise in her ribcage.

He got up and went to the fridge and grabbed a can of beer. The world in which his mother was still alive went tumbling away from him. He drank the can, threw it in his aluminium recycling bag which was full to overflowing, and headed for the door, for his trusty old Toyota. I couldn't have heard the tui, he thought, it's not dawn yet.

He'd never seen the Westmere Rest Home at this hour. Well lit from the street, the rest home kept up appearances. It is stuck in the same dream of time that I was, he thought as he went up the familiar well manicured, well sprayed path past the rose bed, the inhabitants of which looked blood-dark in the hard streetlight. It has fallen into the same gap between sleeping and waking. He stopped and, with thumb and forefinger snipped off a small bud, thinking of his mother's vase with its now kneeling daffodil. Looking up, he saw he was being observed by a man in a black suit standing on the path.

'That's alright,' the man said. 'I think that bush can spare one flower for your mother.' He introduced himself as Roy Peace, manager of the Westmere Rest Home. He spoke quietly, his tone grief soluble in a professional, sympathetic way. He led Clyde to the darkened entrance

174

of his mother's unit, speaking quietly of how well liked his mother was at the home. He assured Clyde the Rest Home could facilitate funeral arrangements. His quiet authority suggested that Clyde could put his mind at ease for here was an experienced death broker.

The deregulated Crematorium probably pays the Rest Home by the head, Clyde thought as he went inside. Roy Peace gets his cut of the action, the gardener gets paid to put in the roses. The Crematorium ups its operating costs. Clyde pays.

His mother was lying on the bed, a white sheet pulled up to her shoulders.

'This is a bit final, Mum,' he said, sitting down. His mother did not answer. That was par for the course, and Clyde was obscurely disappointed. He'd expected something different, some change, but nothing had changed; she was possessed of the same, stubborn silence. He got up, as he usually did, went to the kitchen and got out the gin. True to form, the level was at the exact halfway mark. Clyde got a glass and filled it to the brim. This much at least would change. The bottle would never be the same again.

He took the glass over and sat it, without spilling a drop, on her bedside table.

'I'd like to grieve for you, Mother,' he said, but there is a problem.' He brought the glass up to his mouth and swallowed some down. Death is probably like an endless bender, he thought, a great rudderless journey. He swallowed more. 'The problem is, I think I grieved for you a long time ago, I can't remember when. Perhaps when you stopped talking, perhaps before that even. When I was a little child.'

He noticed the rose he'd picked lying on the table. He got up and sought the vase which he found on the table beside a photograph of his mother and himself he'd never seen before. She was standing on a low mudflat, her shadow reflected in the shiny mud. Clyde, about four or five years old, squatted by her digging in the mud with a stick. His mother had gumboots on and a bucket in her hand. She was laughing, mud smeared over her face. Clyde wanted to peer into the bucket. He knew it would be half full of mussels. That was not the photo she usually had there, the one of her in her wedding dress.

'What are you trying to tell me,' Clyde said, picking up the photograph.

Even in death she was playing her old games. Filling up the gin. Switching photographs. He looked around for a plate before remembering he didn't have any chocolate wheaten biscuits, realizing that his sensation that nothing had changed was a dangerous illusion. Everything had changed. Death had come through. He was talking to a corpse.

Her body had lost the last of its tenancy.

He returned to the glass and drank half of it. I'll go around and see Moira, he thought. We'll get plastered, go to bed and have a wake.

His mother's eyes were closed. Her face had the same, set, tight look he remembered. Even death had not erased the Puritan line of her mouth, the rigidity of her jaw. That line would remain, even as the flesh fell away. He would know the skull when he saw it, the clamped smile. It was an ancestral cast of bone he'd be lucky to escape himself. All those words still shut away behind the same lips, only rotting now from the inside, dropping syllables, crumbling the arches of the alphabet. Rubbing language to a fine babbly powder, a muddle of morphemes.

As he watched, an ant crawled out of her nostril.

He downed the rest of the gin and walked into the kitchen to get another. The bottle was less than half full. He waited at the sink, the bottle suspended superstitiously over the glass, for his mother to speak. She would wait till he had his back turned, as she did last time. It would be just like her to end her life in silence and speak from beyond the grave.

'I'm supposed to make my peace with you, Mother,' he said, returning to her side, 'but if I didn't make peace with you while you were alive, how can I do it now? It takes two to make peace.'

He felt his mother's secret approval of this conclusion. The dead do not want to hear our confession, he thought, turning towards the window, deciding to give his glass a break, or break the glass. Nor do they pity the living.

And I doubt if the dead are interested in our tears, he thought. And he wept. It was the little boy who wept, but that was alright. The little boy had something to weep about.

It didn't take long for the dreams to come, and for his mother to come through the dreams. There were a lot of people. Most of them Clyde didn't know. There was a party in full swing. They buried his mother in a pit oven, cooked her over hot stones, dug her up and ate her. Everybody got drunk. He ate her flesh happily, and buried the bones in the graveyard of birds. Then he vomited into the empty pit and watched his bile fizzle over the stones. But the pit was not empty. There were two figures making love, heaving and groaning on the burning ground. It was Madeleine and the poet Rilke. The images of them came up before him like two entwined genies out of a bottle.

The dream shifted to a beach. He was lying on the sand, half dead, nothing in his mouth but the wash of the sea and the crush of waves on small stones. The world smelled of rotting seaweed. A tui arrived and sat on a piece of driftwood shaped like a deer horn. It sang about its childhood in the sky. A figure approaching along the water line turned into his mother. He waited for her approach but she walked right past without turning her head even once.

Sweating and awake, the gin burning a spiky hole in his gut, Clyde got up and wandered from room to room. The house was full of creatures. Some of them had sharp faces, some woeful. Around them the air tingled with a flickery static. Their bodies were pale lizard shadows and their faces were of foam. Some jumped in front of him and others simply smiled at him with sickly smiles. He was on the borderland of something; a submerged realm vast and silent, boiling with the half appearance of wispy things. It's the booze, he thought. The fucking gin.

He went straight to the sink and drank as many glasses of water as he could stand. He thought of the beach and the tangy sharp taste of wet stones, the taste of the dream. He put his head under the cold tap and kept it there until he thought he would go to sleep, stood up and went out onto his deck. It was the only safe place left. His blood was sick with prophesy. There might have been an hour of dark left before dawn. The flax made short, scissor movements.

It was the hour of the morepork. The eyes of the *ruru* were turned his way.

He waited, superstitiously, for dawn before he went back to bed.

Madeleine Farquar put his poems down and blushed hard. Being so fair-skinned, she blushed beautifully. Her Vogue magazine face lit up.

'What am I supposed to say?' she said.

Clyde had no answer. The poem was not a question.

'Am I to simply comment on this as a poem or what?'

Clyde sat on the floor of her living room, his arms limply at his sides. Around them were scattered the pages of his new manuscript. She had her journal clutched tightly to her chest. He had made no plans for this moment, he had no strategies. He had decided to show her the poems, that was enough.

'I mean, what are you showing them to me for?'

Clyde shrugged. What else was he to do with them? Of course he would show them to her. They were written to her. He would show them and damn the consequences to hell.

She looked at him for a long time, studied his face as if it were new to her. 'I think this is genuine,' she said finally.

'It's genuine enough all right,' Clyde said, feeling like a fool. 'I have some understanding of myself.'

'But what have I done to deserve all this, to merit this?'

'What gave you the idea love must be deserved, or merited?' Like a good poem, love comes of itself or not at all, he thought.

She considered this quietly, with that meditative calm he admired in her. He pulled together the pages of his poem as if he were cleaning his toys up off the floor. He remembered when they'd stood outside the College Bookshop and Radio BFM had played Steppenwolf. Out of nowhere a hard light had fallen upon him. He'd been grateful, then, that she could not see inside him – now he had no such protection.

'What I mean is that I'd like to take some kind of responsibility for this, admit some part in it.' Her voice had a faint, remote quality, as if her throat had become detached from her chest.

Clyde said nothing. It was not his job to convince her of this or that or talk her into anything. His respect for her was a touchstone.

'You've cast me in this *femme fatale* role, haven't you?' She turned her great, calm eyes upon him.

'I haven't,' Clyde said, but she had her proof in front of her. She gestured to the poem.

'This is based on a projection, this is not me. You're projecting it all. That's the bases for an addictive relationship.'

Clyde nodded. He was disappointed with this utterance. He felt it did not do justice to either of them, but then, the matter was out of his hands. He would not attempt to intervene; disaster lay that way. Disaster lay all about, in fact, if he moved a single muscle.

'If you think I've formed some sort of unreal, glamorous image of you, you're wrong. I think I see you very clearly.'

'I find that hard to believe.'

Clyde got up. He wanted to walk. It was an old remedy for agitation. They left her place and walked out into the night. She had a room in a house in Herne Bay, and it was a brief walk down to the water. The quick, snappy wind jumped about them. Clyde was relieved to breathe the open air, feel the larger universe above. It was a Conrad sky, he thought, sodden with cloud, pregnant with a brooding, electrical darkness.

'I'm sorry,' Clyde said. 'I really am sorry.'

'I'm sorry too,' she said.

'Don't apologise. Don't apologise for feeling something. I'm not sorry for feeling things. I'm sorry for jeopardizing that which is valuable to both of us.'

'You haven't,' she said.

But he had.

The bay was deserted and windswept. A single yacht lurched on the fragmenting water. The harbour bridge loomed behind like something out of Disneyland, arching away into nowhere.

She said, 'I'm trying to work out if I have caused this in any way. You don't know how shaky I am.'

'Not the cause but the context,' he said. 'The intensity and closeness of our communication.' And those long, fashionable legs on park benches.

She turned her head away when he said that. She was there and not there. And she would not acknowledge what he said. But it was ambivalence he saw in her face, not love. She was in love with somebody else, remember? He'd left his run too late.

At the end of the beach they found a dinghy, half sunk, moving listlessly to the pull of the current. The piece of driftwood from his dream was there, shaped like a deer horn. Madeleine trailed her fingers along the dinghy's rotting sides. Clyde looked at the sunken boat, marvelling at how the sea turned everything it touched into myth.

Madeleine came and sat by him. Clyde could think of nothing to say. He reached out to touch her hair and she knocked his arm away with a simple movement. It all happened so rapidly it might not have happened at all. She didn't move away immediately. The tide shivered around their feet.

'You remember that part of your poem where the lines say something about love coming when you saw me close the back door of my car.'

'Yes.' Their quietly stated action was full of intensity and desire.

'My car doesn't have any back door.'

He laughed, and tried to recall her car. 'That doesn't matter. I wanted that everyday action.'

'But what were you seeing?'

He shrugged. It didn't seem like an important question. He'd found the image he'd needed for those lines, that was all; the shape of the car was irrelevant.

'Such an ordinary moment, I mean – to fall in love with somebody for… just opening a car door.' She couldn't quite believe it.

She got up and they walked back towards her place.

'That's what I wanted, the ordinary moment.'

They stood outside her place. She didn't invite him in.

'Shall we meet again?' he asked.

'Yes.'

Clyde opened the door of his car and looked at her significantly. She laughed.

'Maybe one day you'll do something heroic like opening a car door and I'll fall in love with you.'

One day.

Clyde slept without dream and awoke in a state of mortification. This he hid behind a funeral mask. The funeral was a drab affair. A few of his mother's old friends turned up, those who had stuck with her through the silence, and a few who remembered her before that. Some relatives turned up and put flowers on the coffin. Most of the mourners were fellow residents of the Westmere Rest Home who sat about on the narrow pews in the same attitudes they assumed on their park benches. Roy Peace was the soul of tact. All Clyde had to do was sign cheques. Since his mother's silence had been, in the eyes of some ministers and priests who had visited her, vaguely blasphemous, there was no friendly officiator to make a personal speech. Clyde himself got up and read some pieces from the Dharmapada:

'Better than a thousand words is one single word that gives peace. Better than a thousand verses is one single verse that gives peace. Better than a hundred useless poems is one single poem that gives peace... How can there be laughter, how can there be pleasure, when the whole world is burning. When you are in deep darkness, will you not ask for a lamp? Look at these grey-white bones, like dried empty gourds thrown away at the end of summer. Who will enjoy looking at them... When a man considers this world as a bubble of froth, and the illusion of an appearance, then the king of death has no power over him. Come and look at this world. It is like a royal painted chariot in which fools sink.'

His voice in the small chapel had a curiously detached sound.

Afterwards he was given the ashes in a small jar. They were grey, gritty and unexpectedly heavy. Roy Peace, death's faithful broker, had arranged a small plot marked by a rose. Clyde scattered the ashes and planted the rose. Here it was, in a tiny, tight row of like roses with their shiny plaques. This was a different notion of death to the sprawling tombstone mansions of the earlier part of the century. This was where it ended – the chocolate wheaten biscuits, the gin, the photographs, her precious silence.

An apartment in the City of Death.

The farm looked the same. The same cow looked up from the same munching. From the cow's point of view, he might have passed by only a few minutes ago, or never.

The dogs leapt out, barking and choking themselves. Lorna Bealter came to the back door and watched while Clyde got out of the car, making no effort to silence the dogs. Clyde plucked his briefcase off the front seat.

As he approached the door, Lorna Bealter put some effort into her smile. She looked tired and there were dark rings around her eyes, but her voice was bright.

'I'm glad you came.'

Clyde took his dark glasses off and a new, hard, pre-summer light rained down on the farm. He squinted towards Lorna Bealter. 'Does everyone get such a welcome?' he called over the tumult of the dogs.

She led him into the kitchen. Don Bealter was sitting at the kitchen table spooning porridge into his mouth. He paused to smile broadly as Clyde entered.

'This is a surprise,' said Clyde. Don nodded, his mouth full, and motioned Clyde to a chair.

'Don's better now,' Lorna said. Her voice had a tone to it, like somebody patting a pillow back into shape.

Clyde took out his briefcase and took out Bealter's diary and medical record. Don Bealter didn't look at them as Clyde put them on the table. 'I'm glad you're better,' Clyde said lamely, realizing that this was not entirely true. There was, in fact, something almost improper about the farmer's robust looking good health, as if he did not belong at the table, spooning porridge into his mouth, but in bed, staring out into the large airy gloom of the bedroom. That was the role Clyde had assigned him, and had written him up that way. Bealter was ruining a good story.

'I feel like a new man,' Don said.

Clyde said, 'Of course it's consistent with the medical record. Sudden illnesses and strange recoveries.'

Don continued to eat, moving his jaw rapidly back and forth through his porridge, 'Maybe, but I'm under a new kind of treatment. Homeopathic remedies. Have you heard of Dr Twizzle? He has a machine he uses to test for poisoning. God! He identified Roundup straightaway, without me having to say anything.'

'Two days after he started taking them, he got better,' Lorna said from behind Clyde. 'He was up and walking around.'

The farmer gave a hearty laugh. 'A lot better. And I could eat, too.' He waved his spoon in the air.

'I'm really glad,' Clyde said, wondering why he felt so uneasy. Lorna put a cup of tea in front of him and Clyde sipped at it gratefully. Nothing was said and the hard bright light from outside poured through the window and filled up the drab room. The Formica tabletop gleamed dully.

Lorna brought her tea and sat at the table opposite Clyde.

'I can get a few things done around here,' Bealter said with satisfaction. 'What kind of machine is it?'

'It's called an EVA. It makes a kind of whistle. Looks like an overgrown battery with a few knobs and dials to me,' he shrugged. 'It seems to work.'

'What's in the tablets?'

'An extremely diluted form of Roundup, would you believe.' He gave the same hearty laugh. 'It's pretty nutty when you think about it. If it didn't work, I wouldn't have believed it myself.'

Clyde pulled a wad of paper from under the farmer's medical record and opened it up. 'I did the article. I'd like you to see it before it goes to print. I mean I want you to be happy about it. You could keep this copy and read it and maybe give me a ring.'

He gave the pages to the farmer who held them with one hand, continuing to eat porridge with the other. He glanced at the opening paragraph, stopped eating, put the spoon down and concentrated, frowning as he read.

'I brought a camera,' Clyde said, patting his briefcase. Maybe I could take a couple of pictures of the farm. And you, of course.'

Don didn't answer. He was moving his jaw slowly, as if he were still eating porridge. Lorna concentrated on her tea, blowing the steam across the face of the cup. Her husband flicked through the pages of the article, pausing here and there. Finally, he pushed it to one side and turned back to his empty plate as if there were still some porridge left.

'Mr Aichen, we appreciate what you've done, putting us in your article and everything, but...'

He looked at his wife for moral support. Lorna was looking through the article with the same frown of concentration her husband had used.

'We don't want you to use our real names,' she said to Clyde. She paused awkwardly.

'Or photographs,' her husband said quickly, following up with a short, embarrassed laugh. 'This farm's in a hell of a mess.'

Clyde took a deep breath. 'I know you feel better,' he said, hearing his voice rise. 'But you might get sick again. It's happened before.'

'I think this medicine's fixed me,' Bealter replied with a strained smile. 'You write for Greenpeace, don't you?'

'Sometimes.'

'Greenpeace isn't all that popular around here,' Don said with difficulty.' He didn't look at Clyde but fiddled with his spoon.

'We've got to live in this district,' Lorna said.

'What do you tell people when you're sick?'

'Just that it's some old war thing.' Don showed Clyde how he waved the thing away. He didn't meet Clyde's eye.

'He's better now,' Lorna said, her voice as bright as enamel.

'There's the human side to this story,' Clyde said firmly. 'It'll take the heart right out of the argument if we can't show who we're talking about. The fact that you are not anonymous, the fact that you are who you are is very important to the story. Hell, you've got nothing to hide.'

'Maybe you could use other names. Fictional names.' Lorna Bealter smiled at Clyde. 'You know, where there's a little statement at the beginning saying the people don't want to be named, and in the article they're called Tom and Joan.'

'Tom and Joan,' Clyde repeated as if there were something wrong with his brain, which there well might be.

'I've seen that done often. Even in the Woman's Weekly.'

Clyde was supposed to nod glumly, as if this last piece of evidence was some final truth, the Woman's Weekly some ultimate standard. Instead he said sharply, 'Mrs Bealter, didn't you say people should know? Remember?' Clyde seemed to remember a moment they had shared, right in the kitchen doorway as he was leaving. The intensity with which she'd spoken as the sick man lay in his bed like a vaporous shadow of himself. A moment of truth. A moment in which some unspoken compact had been made between the woman and himself. He seemed to remember a sudden hope in her face. Now she considered her tea cup, staring into it as if it were a crystal ball.

'Well people should know,' she said finally. 'But they don't have to know that it's us. I mean, would it matter we were someone else? I mean, the point is it is happening to somebody. Does it matter who that *somebody* is?'

'It does to me,' Clyde said emotionally. And didn't know what else to say.

'There's a lot of fine work in this article,' Don said to his wife, tapping the pages. 'Mr Aichen's done a good job.'

'He has,' she said hastily. 'It's only different by changing names.'

'And the location,' her husband took up. 'I'd like you to be a bit vague about the location.'

'You see there's bits in here about the neighbours, about how their spraying made Don sick. We don't want our neighbours hating us for things we're saying about them.'

Don nodded in agreement. 'I mean we borrow stuff off them and they borrow stuff off us. It's a community.'

'Sure as hell sounds like one,' Clyde said viciously, standing up. 'Look I'm sorry, I need to use your lavatory. I understand of course.'

'I knew he'd be good about it,' Don said, nodding to his wife who nodded in return. Their heads nodded up and down to each other.

The farmer spoke. 'We've had a rough time, Mr Aichen. It's been a big strain on us, especially Lorna. She's had to carry everything. Now I'm on these new pills I feel a lot better. Almost completely better.'

'Almost?'

'Ninety-nine point nine percent. We're going to make a fresh start.' He put his hand over his wife's arm. For a moment the tiredness fell away from her face. 'Dr Twizzle says…'

'Wait a minute, weren't you the one who told me that the doctors don't know shit from shingle? Isn't that what you said?'

'But Dr Twizzle is different. He's a homeopathic doctor. He's helped lots of people like me, he's got hundreds of patients.'

'I'm sure he has. Do none of his patients ever get sick again? Have you read your own medical record lately?'

'The new pills…'

'Are magic remedies, but I need to go…' he gestured to the hall. Mrs Bealter slid her eyes sideways to her husband who nodded briefly. Clyde smiled politely as she showed him the door to the hall.

The door swung shut behind him and he saw immediately that the darkened hall was full of the same kind of horrid quasi-life he'd seen in his house the night after his mother had died. A surge of chattering, snickering creatures rippling up and down the hall. He stepped right through these undulating shadows on his way to the lavatory, and passing the open door he'd previously noticed, he saw that the flickering light was not entirely imaginary. A television set still played a darkened room, and he thought he could tell, from the colours that fell against the wall, that it was playing Star Wars.

Curiosity held him at the open door. Why should a television set be continually playing Star Wars to an empty room? With a surreptitious glance down the hall, he stepped quickly into the room. It was a bedroom with the blinds pulled down. The television set was in the corner and Luke Skywalker was doing a breathtaking swing through the clean, sanitised vacuum of space. Sitting in front of the television was a child, a boy, nine or ten, staring at the screen. Slowly he turned towards Clyde, his profile caught in the brilliant blue flicker. He wore thick spectacles which enlarged his eyes to two globular orbs, and his head bobbed up and down on his shoulders as if on a spring, like Noddy's head. He focused on Clyde but showed no reaction. Then, slowly, his mouth unhinged itself from his jaw as it swung open. A line of dribble came out of his mouth and down his chin. Chittering shadow creatures surged all around him in a tide, apparently energised by the motions on the screen, jumping in and out of his mouth in slithering leaps.

Clyde slipped back into the hall, his own shadow moving in front of him like a dark tongue. A white glare filled the hall and Clyde made for it. Lorna Bealter was standing at the door looking at him curiously. Don Bealter was sitting at the table, Clyde's article in front of him. Clyde went to the sink and helped himself to a drink of water. Two drinks of water.

'Well…' he said, 'the article will be alright. You're right. It doesn't really matter what your names are, it's what has happened to you that counts.'

And the boy in the room you never talk about.

The Bealters gave each other relieved smiles.

'I'll send you a copy when it comes out.'

They both nodded. Don got up and went and stood by his wife.

'We appreciate very much what you have done for us, Mr Aichen,' the man said solemnly. 'Nobody really cares, until it happens to them.'

'Understand that. Thanks for the tea.' Clyde headed for the door. Don accompanied him to the back door steps.

Lorna took his arm. 'Come and see us again, Mr Aichen,' she said.

The dogs didn't bark as Clyde walked back to the car but sat indifferently in the shadow of the barn with their tongues lolling out of the corner of their mouths. He put his sunglasses on and everything assumed a brown glow.

The brown cow didn't bother to look up as he drove past.

Cursing, Clyde punched button A. The line went dead as the coins dropped.

'…ello?'

'Moira.'

'Clyde Aichen. You've rung up to invite me for a drive.'

'Yes. Next week. My car is in dry dock having a facelift.'

'Forget about it. Your mother has died.'

'Yes.'

'I'm sorry to hear it. I only met her a couple of times. Remember that time you took me to the Rest Home and I thought she was following me all the time with her eyes.'

'I remember. Look, her death wasn't that tragic. She'd been dead a long time, I realized. The actual passing away was just a formality.'

'I'm sorry all the same.'

'And while we're on contrition, I really did ring you up to arrange the drive. Saturday morning, I'll come about ten.'

'That'll be good,' she said brightly.

'How are you, anyway,' Clyde said, looking at his watch.

'I'm alright,' she said briskly. 'I'm working right now.'

'I'll let you go,' Clyde said, relieved. 'I'm meeting Stockman in a few moments.'

'Christ, I haven't seen him in ages. What's he doing with his life?'

'Making money, going broke; the usual thing. Borrowing from Peter to pay Paul. Wasn't he at your party?'

'He could've been. I've got a gap or two in my memory as far as that party goes. Give him a kiss on the cheek from me.'

'I wouldn't dream of it.'

'You're right,' her voice sounded wooden. 'He'd probably be homophobic.'

'Homowhat?'

'Phobic. From the Greek *phobos*. Fear. You must have heard of it?'

'It's a new one on me. See you Saturday.'

'Okay Clyde.'

Clyde put the phone down, threw another twenty cents into the maw of the machine and dialled another number. He felt suitably reckless.

'Hello, Madeleine?'

'Yes.'

'It's Clyde.'

A fractional pause.

'Oh. Hello.'

'How are you?'

'I'm alright.'

But she didn't sound alright. She sounded frail and distant. She sounded as if there was something suffocating her in the chest, choking off the breath to her voice. Clyde glanced at his watch.

'I just wanted to say one thing, Madeleine. Something I feel strongly. Whatever my feeling is for you, I care for you more than I want you.' As he said it he felt it must be true.

'You don't know how that makes me feel, to hear you say that,' her voice was low and shaky.

I do now, Clyde thought. He looked at his watch again. Stockman would be waiting.

'Let's meet on Friday,' he said.

'I'll look in my book.' Clyde thought she was joking but she was not. They set a time and place and she wrote it into her diary.

Stockman was unimpressed. 'I must have been waiting for all of thirty seconds. What kept you?'

'The call of nature.' Clyde slid into the car and pulled the door shut.

'Shit.' Stockman already had the car in motion. 'We can't afford calls of nature, we're losing too much money.'

'So I notice, from my royalty cheques.'

'What royalty cheques?'

'That's what I was going to ask you.'

'Ask the Receivers. Is your door shut?' Stockman slammed the car into second and gunned it forward.

'So how come they haven't pulled the rug from under you yet, Stockman?'

'They have but I'm still standing, see.' He flashed Clyde a grin.

'I mean put you out of business in a permanent kind of way.'

'Oh,' Stockman's voice was bland, 'we have a kind of minimum terms agreement.'

'What does that mean?'

'*They* know what it means.'

'But I don't.'

'It means an eye for an eye, a tooth for a tooth, concrete slippers for concrete slippers. I'm a fundamentalist at heart, you see. If I go down *they* go down.'

'That's big talk.'

'You bet! I've got everything. I'll go off like a fucking firecracker, and they know it. You see, I'm half crazy, right?'

'The fraction could be disputed.'

'Exactly, and they know that too. If the suits move in, well that's fine, that's their job, but they have to understand one thing very clearly, very fucking clearly, that is if anyone, and I mean anyone, tries to take me down the gurgler, you know, take me to court or anything like that, or do me in a back alley, or any fucking heavying, then I'll go the full hundred percent, I mean totally berko and I'll kill everyone and anyone who's in it, I don't care who they are, lawyers, company directors, two-bit managers, small time bigshots, toadies, families, pets, I'll even poison their lawns – they can get me but they will never sleep easy again. Is that a clear enough warning?' He was shouting and dots of foamy spit sprayed across the inside of the windscreen. He turned to Clyde accusingly as if Clyde were one of *them*. 'And the best part is, they can't stop me, not till it happens, and then it'll be too late for the bastards. I've given them due warning, in subtle kinds of ways.'

'You're a subtle guy.'

'Yeah. The moment they pull the plug, they're dead. I'm fully wired.' He grinned so intensely that he'd clearly forgotten where he was, namely, pulling the car in a tight curve as they wound onto the motorway heading south.

'What are you on?'

'Explosives. Nitro glycerine. I'm like that Professor in Conrad's *Secret Agent*, which is my favourite book by the way. Christ, if you could write a book like that we'd both be in clover.'

'I will. But please jog my memory. The Professor?'

'He was wired up to explode if they ever came near him or tried to arrest him. That's the way I am.' His lips went together in a tight line. 'If they leave me alone, everybody lives to tell the tale.'

Clyde had seen this side of Stockman before and knew he meant business. He decided a change of subject was in order. 'Anyway, what's the story? Why the mysterious meeting at short notice?'

'MacDonald's have expressed interest in *A Sure Bet*. I'll show you the letter. And just keep holding that door; it has a tendency to looseness on the corners. I couldn't face the insurance bills if you fell out and hit a car. A new fender can cost five hundred bucks these days.'

'MacDonald's? You mean the deep-fried people?'

'Speak for yourself, I'm talking about MacDonald's publishers. A member of the Maxwell Pergamon Publishing Corporation. The Octopus, buddy boy, the big time.' He made smacking sounds with his lips. 'Which planet are *you* living on?' He pulled a flask out from its perch by the brake. He never knew which he might need faster, the brake or the whisky.

'But why *A Sure Bet*?' A somewhat sordid story set on the racetrack in the 1950s, Clyde considered it the least of his novels. He pulled a couple of times at Stockman's flask.

'Who knows? Maybe they got fooled by the title. Maybe they think you're Dick Francis on acid.'

190

Clyde made an equestrian sound through his lips. With a malicious twist of the wheel, Stockman swung the car into another lane, throwing Clyde against his safety belt. He clung to the door as instructed.

'But seriously…'

'But seriously, it tells a story, at least. Something happens. A body turns up. A psychopath goes down. The sort of thing people can relate to.' He was scrabbling in the glove box and steering with one hand. Clyde noted how cryptically lean Stockman had become, how thin and intense his face.

'Yeah,' Stockman said, coming up with a pair of dark glasses. 'You forget you have to tell a story. Your books don't tell a fucking story. Except *Madagascar*, which follows the outline of your source story, so you were safe there, a wise decision that. And *A Sure Bet*, which I believe was told to you by somebody else.' He turned his face, complete with mirror-shades, to Clyde.

'Yeah. A drunk in a small town pub somewhere, I don't remember. It was probably Hororata or Cheviot, one of those shitfaced Canterbury towns.'

'There you go. Small town drunks. Nothing like them. Faulkner had his Yoknapatawpha County. Maybe that's your real strength, bring to life stories told to you in small town shitfaced pubs. Hold onto the fucking door.'

'Didn't I see you at Moira's party?'

'Did you?'

'I'm asking you.'

'How the hell do I know what you saw or didn't see?'

'I saw you. With Snake.'

'Did you now? Snake and Moira, the loving couple.'

'You looked like you were having fun.'

'Fun? Never touch the stuff.'

'What do you know about them?'

'Who?'

'Don't be dense.'

'As much as the next man, or woman.' He flicked the blinker toggle and switched lanes, apparently testing the suspension. Anger started to percolate up through Clyde.

'Do you always drive like this, Stockman?'

'Like what?' Stockman looked offended.

'Like this?'

'Like a maniac, you mean?' He gave a manic grin.

'That's exactly what I mean.'

'The answer is, of course. How else would I drive? Anyway, you're changing the subject. You were trying to pry into my personal life.'

'If you keep driving like this, there won't be any subject.'

'That would simplify the conversation.' He dropped a gear, shot between two big-rigs, hung a right and a moment later, after a tight turn, swung into the fast lane.

'I didn't get this far just to die in a bloody car,' Clyde said.

'You never know,' Stockman said. 'It might be your best career move.'

'Thanks for the vote of faith.'

'And, I was going to say, *my* best business move too. I'll put it to my accountant and he can put it to the Receivers. How do you feel about immolation?'

'Anyway, I don't know what you're saying. Look at *Bloodcount*. The seduction scene alone…'

'Yeah, yeah,' Stockman waved it away, '*Bloodcount* had plenty of sex, sure, but the plot went every which way. The reader didn't know whether he, she, or it, was coming or going.'

'Neither did the narrator.' Clyde took another swing at the flask. He thought about Charles Olsen, *the material determines the form*. If Stockman was going to insult him the least Clyde could do was drink his whisky.

'That's no excuse. But look, you top yourself and there's bound to be a surge of interest in your books, right? A sales wave. Look what it did for poor old Richard Brautigan. The price of a first edition Brautigan went through the roof.'

'I don't write anything like Brautigan.'

'We could pretend. Leave a mysterious unpublished manuscript behind, maybe locked in a safe like Philip K Dick. I could discover it after you're dead. Another side of Clyde Aichen, the Brautigan side.'

Stockman reached forward and turned up the radio. A sweet, sad song was playing. Or maybe I could knock something up in your style. The 'Achin-Aichen style.'

'It's a tragedy for me to see
the dream is over…'

Stockman drummed his fingers in time on the steering wheel, jiggled his knee and sang along,

'And I never will forget
the day we met…'

and without losing his timing, he shifted the car into the outer lane and put his foot down,

'…girl I'm going to miss you.'

'My books have real people in them,' Clyde said angrily. 'Autonomous beings who live and piss and fall in love and do stupid things and have even stupider things happen to them…'

'It's a matter of timing,' Stockman pulled back over into the centre lane. 'The right story at the right time. That's politics. The Tiberius connection. It says something to that effect in the *Tao Te Ching*, doesn't it, *in action, watch the timing.'*

'…in desire, heed the device,' Clyde added.

'That's good, who wrote that last bit?'

'I did,' Clyde said, staring out the window at the dozens of other little coffins made of steel and glass, hurtling through the air at seventy, eighty feet per second encasing two or three soft, pupa like human bodies. 'In a poem.' He began to sweat. The sticky glare of the road hit up at him even through the amber tint of his shades. A terrible taste came into his mouth.

'How's the novel going?'

'What novel?'

'The Great New Zealand Urban Terrorist Novel. With me as hero.'

'I'm not writing it. You get me these illegal manuals, then I'll have a look at it.'

'It's going to take me a while. What are you writing?'

'Love poems.'

Stockman let the breathe whistle out between his teeth. 'Oh yeah?' The mirror shades turned on Clyde. 'Are you in love?'

'Probably not. It's all in my mind. A stupid infatuation.'

But Stockman didn't believe him. Clyde's silly grin was a dead giveaway.

Stockman grinned too and aimed the car for the Otahuhu exit.

'Let it stay there. In your mind. You don't want to let something like that loose in the world. As far as I'm concerned, love's just a Pat Boone song, and when was he last in vogue? You have to give up yourself to find love, and who's prepared to do that? Nobody I know.'

'When your soul is at stake, you tend to take action.'

'*Souls*, is it? You do have it bad. My soul was put up with all my other assets in a mortgagee fire sale. I got a good deal. I get to be the emotional vampire. I drink, but I'm always thirsty; feed, but am never satisfied. I get to sucker on people's passions. I enjoy that. People bleed so easily.'

'This is the plot of another novel you want me to write?'

'Not this time. I'm telling you how it is to be Stockman. Once I gave up on love it was easy. And more sexy too. Women just love that being drained away feeling.'

'I'm going to have to take your word for all of this. I'm in a sensitive state, I might believe you.'

'You're in good hands. So who's your lucky lady?'

Clyde held the seat belt as they tight-cornered into a main raid. 'Just a creature of dream. Some call her Ishtar, some call her Kali. Some call her the Anima. Her name is legion.'

Stockman was not about to be thrown off the scent. 'It's not this Melina person who sent me some poems, is it? She mentioned your name.'

'Madeleine.' Clyde murmured, watching the back of a truck rush towards them. 'Madeleine Farquar.' Her name was full of mysterious syllables; and it had a music, the music of a minuet or a Renaissance song. He slugged again at the whisky trying to quiet his belly.

'Uh huh. Lady Madeleine on the prowl is she, checking out the bait pits – Oh! caught a poet, a natural bleeder! A nice little snack.' Delicately, Stockman applied the brake.

'Sounds like you know her.'

'I wouldn't quite put it in that Biblical sense, Clyde. I saw her in action one night at the Albion, reading some slinky stuff vamped up in a Cleopatra wig. What's she like now, has she screwed you yet or is she still baiting the hook?'

'For Christ's sake, Stockman. Sometimes you make me wonder about my sex.'

Clyde thought of Heinz. Heinz had become an icon. A man kneeling, limped sexed, at the feet of a prostitute, shoulders slumped in defeat. He would kneel there forever, in Clyde's mind, never to get to his feet.

'Why? Can't you find it? Have you forgotten? Look down, it's in the usual place… I assume.'

'I mean the male species in general.' Clyde heard the acerbity in his tone. 'It's enough to turn me into a lesbian.'

'Oh, all sensitive are we darling, oh dear.' Stockman put his hand up, palm outward, upon his forehead leaving the car to steer itself. 'And I suppose we're off our food and on the booze.'

Clyde suddenly felt very drunk, and ill. Stockman's lukewarm whisky and ferris wheel driving had caught up with him. When had he last eaten? A novelistic detail but of some importance. He leaned forward and punched off the radio, putting an end to the sad, sweet song that had been clinging on. He was in tears. The road became a blurred, infinite tide of concrete over which they were rushing.

'It's a question of sincerity,' Clyde said thickly, grabbing the door handle. His slurred voice made the word sound sinful and sleazy. The door swung loose and he pulled desperately at it to close it.

'Christ, you must be off your food. I always knew that if the world turned honest, writers and whores would be the first made redundant; but if writers and whores turn honest, what's to become of the rest of us poor suckers, with dust in our eyes?'

'That's clever, Stockman. Now stop the car so I can vomit.'

The mirror shades swung towards him again. A lock of dangerous looking, black hair fell over the lens. Clyde saw his own face made bulbous and troll like.

'You're not going to vomit in my fucking car, Aichen.'

'Then pull over, Paddy. Unless you want your whisky in your lap.'

'Is my conversation so revolting?' Stockman was looking for a break in the traffic.

'And the whisky is of about the same quality.'

'It's the finest quality single malt the Receivers couldn't buy. It's bloody Glenfiddich, I stole it myself.' He was all indignant.

'Do you want spew all over your windscreen? You can vampire on that.'

Stockman pulled over fast. All the colour had drained from Clyde

Aichen's face. He felt like an ambulatory corpse. 'I've been off the booze,' the corpse said to Stockman.

'A likely story,' Stockman said. He ran the car up onto a grassy verge and hit the brake.

'It's a question of sincerity,' Stockman said as Clyde grappled with the door handle. 'Personal integrity,' he said as Clyde threw open the door and vomited onto the grass. 'Nothing crude, like a fuck.'

Clyde turned to him, vomit dribbling down the side of his mouth. 'Do you want a kiss?'

For once, Stockman had no answer.

'I'd like to make an offer,' Stockman said. He eased into a side-street.

'What kind offer. Money? Power? Virgins? Eternal Fame?'

'An interesting one I think you'll find.' Stockman was peering at the street numbers of the run-down commercial area through which they were driving. Everywhere he looked there were 'for lease' signs and blank upper stories. Every time he went into these areas Clyde was glad he didn't work there.

'I'm open to anything except another drink,' Clyde said.

'I don't believe you,' Stockman said, parking abruptly. 'I've gotta see someone,' he pushed his mirror shades deeper into his face. 'People around here usually leave at least two pit-bulls or rotties in their cars. I've only got you.'

'I'm good at heavy lidded looks.'

'I believe you,' grinned Stockman, and the mirror shades vanished. Clyde watched him cross the road, moving fast yet bringing his bare feet with a certain elasticity onto the tarseal, pulling each foot up after him as if he had adhesives attached to the soles or the tar was sticky.

Clyde waited for ten minutes during which time absolutely nothing happened in his life.

'I've had time to think over your offer and I don't think I'll take it.' Clyde said as Stockman got quickly back into the car and tossed something on the back seat. It was an antique shaving blade, the razor edge folded into the handle. He pulled the car into an abrupt U turn.

'But I haven't made any offer yet.'

'Best keep it that way.'

'Don't be too hasty now, until you've heard the details. It concerns this novel you're going to write. It needs a major character to hold the whole narrative together, the leader of the terrorists. Well, make *me* the hero and I'll publish the novel for sure. You can call it *Stockman's Dream*.'

The mirror shades swivelled. Stockman the terminator had arrived.

'You can't be serious.'

'I am. Absolutely serious.' He gunned the car towards the corner.

'Keep it slow,' Clyde ordered.

'I've always wanted to be in a book,' Stockman said reflectively. 'To be the hero. To be portrayed in print. Immortalized. I could work with you on the plot. I've lots of ideas. Go back and read Dostoevsky's *Demons*. The whole point about *Demons* is that there are no demons, just people crazed by ideology. That's your key.'

Clyde was adamant, 'I'm sorry, I'm having trouble taking this seriously. As I understand it you're offering me a bribe, a sort of bribe anyway.'

'A bribe of sorts. That's right, I am,' Stockman said sincerely. 'I want to be the hero. None of these whinging antiheroes you're so fond of, *sickled o'er with the pale cast of thought*, but somebody capable of doing something, taking action. Conrad, Hemmingway. Those big time egos.'

'Like blowing things up.'

'Might as well. Somebody's got to do it. Imagine that big petrol storage place on the harbour going up. That'd be a blast!' He thumped the steering wheel.

Clyde released some fetid air from between his lips as if he were breathing with the aid of a lung machine.

'I don't mind being a bad bastard. In fact I insist on it. This hero can't be nice.' Under the mirror shades, teeth opened up. 'I'll be a cop if you want. Remember Buckman, that cop in, *Flow My Tears, the Policeman Said*, the Philip K Dick book? Well you could portray me like that, you know, The Sensitive Fascist. It'll be great for my sex life once it gets around.'

'Stop it Stockman, you'll make me want to spew again. Or die laughing. I can't take this seriously, and too much laughing isn't good for me.'

'Look, I'll tell you what. You can put unobtainable, anorexic Madeleine in the book too. She could be a Sincere Student Radical, you know, caught up in the midst of something she doesn't understand, gets a bomb attached to her swelling...'

'And have an affair with the hero, of course?'

'He seizes his opportunity. A necessity of the plot.'

'What's got into you, Stockman? Next thing you'll be making a will.'

'We vampires don't make wills, we don't need them, Christ!' Stockman thumped the steering wheel again as he veered past a slower car. 'You've got to get your characters from somewhere. It may as well be me as someone else. I don't mind sharing the limelight with amazing Madeleine with the killer eyes. Not so bright, let's admit, so a perfect foil for Stockman's machinations, his plan to turn her into a suicide bomber. She agrees in the end 'cos it's a faster way to die than anorexia.'

'I don't.'

'Don't what? You have problems with me sharing the limelight with her?'

'No. I don't get my characters from 'somewhere'. I make them up.'

Clyde made motions akin to fitting pieces of machinery together. 'They are autonomous beings. They act for themselves, they even answer me back. They are fictional, remember? Remember Kurt Vonnnegut who reckoned that only one of his characters, a certain Kilgore Trout, was smart enough to recognise that he was a created character. He saw Vonnegut in the street one day and ran after him crying out, *make me young, make me young.*'

'Why are you lying to me, Clyde? Of course you get your characters from somewhere; you steal them from people just like Vonnegut did. You steal people's characters and put them in books. Like some kind of body snatcher.' He gave Clyde a ghoulish grin of complicity. 'Writers are soul snatchers – if they're any good.'

They were back on the motorway, Stockman was watching his driving. 'So why are you lying?'

'So that I don't have to go on discussing putting you in a book,' Clyde said aiming for the tone people use with recalcitrant children.

'Wait a minute. Let's take this a step further.' Stockman sounded uncharacteristically humble. 'These autonomous characters of yours, that don't come from anywhere, are they doomed right from the start, I mean is the plot all laid out for them, or are they capable of change?'

'Depends on who they are,' Clyde said cautiously.

Stockman gave a dissatisfied grunt. He knew when Clyde was holding out on him. Weird fuckers, writers. While he was thinking, Clyde took the opportunity to change the subject.

'Those poems of Madeleine's,' he said casually, 'what did you think of them?'

'Not bad at all. Seven or eight okay ones. I'll publish those.'

'What do you mean?' Stockman publishing them was the last thing Clyde had imagined.

'Something like a broadsheet. A foldout piece. I've even got the cover for it.' Stockman started lashing about in the back seat with one hand. A moment later he handed Clyde something. Clyde looked at it.

'She's not going to like it.'

'I wrote and told her the cover would be controversial.' Stockman sounded hurt.

'She'll think you mean a photograph of Bastion Point or something. Did you show it to her?'

'No. But she'll like it.'

It was a coloured photograph of a naked man standing facing the camera, one leg up on a chair. An enormously long, genetically freaked penis hung down below his knee.

'Apparently they can't get it up, when it's that big,' Stockman said conversationally. 'Not enough blood.'

Suddenly the rain arrived. A dirty, sweeping wave of grey that engulfed the traffic. Stockman braked. Ahead, two big rigs loomed, thundering forward together side-by-side. Their huge tires flung up a wall of spray, forming, where they met, a standing-wave between them. We're all mad, Clyde thought, looking at them. Stockman in particular.

Stockman took off his mirror glasses and gestured to the rigs. 'Did I ever tell you about being chased by a cop along this stretch on a day like this, back in my biker days?' he asked. Clyde was surprised to see how tired his eyes looked. 'I believe he wanted to *apprehend*,' he made the word sound as cumbersome as a cop on the beat, 'me for something or other, maybe not wearing a helmet, anyway I saw two big rigs like these, throwing up that spray, and I thought, here's a go, so I just aimed the bike and opened her out.'

'You went between the trucks?'

'Yup. I got wet. Couldn't see a fucking thing. Amazing! I should be a lot deader than I am. And twice as evil.'

'He didn't follow you?'

'No, funny that.'

'...the hard line of the story, my character arc, which is from pretty evil to very evil,' Stockman said, depositing him by the Downtown Square. 'See you Saturday, 10 a.m.'

A fine drizzle and chill wind came down the canyon of Queen Street.

Clyde headed for the Central Post Office, feeling in his pocket for twenty cent pieces, praying that Madeleine would be there when he rang. Strangely, the booths were empty and he walked straight into one, pulling two twenty cent pieces out of his pocket.

The steel box in front of him had no slots to place the coins. With growing fear he banged the coin against the casing where the slot should be, as if the steel would magically open, like a metal mouth in a nightmare. To quell the fear he examined the box rationally. It was a normal steel box, a phone perched securely to one side. But it was not normal. It had no slots in the top, no buttons A or B, nothing but a single, horizontal slot at the bottom into which no coin would fit. Something was written under the slot. There was a logo, a circle with a rainbow or something, and the word *Card phone*.

Card phone? Like the pokies creeping into bars, here was another sign of the alien influence of the eighties. Why hadn't he heard about this? He listened to the radio, he watched the newspapers. He kept abreast of things, or so he thought. And now somebody had replaced public telephones with space invaders.

He propelled himself back out of the booth and joined several small knots of people he hadn't noticed before, milling bewildered as he in front of the empty booths.

'I've got to ring my wife,' a small, bald man said anxiously. 'I just have to.' Clyde thought of Madeleine and Stockman's photograph of the genetic freak with the hose-pipe penis. I wonder why Stockman wants to humiliate her, he thought. What did she do to him, maybe that night at the Albion when she read her poems? What had Stockman and Madeleine done together? No, that way madness lay. A vampire! Ha!

Whatever the truth, he still had to warn Madeleine about the gross photograph. Stockman would use it, part of some game he was playing.

He walked up the ostentatious steps of the old CPO to where he knew Telecom had an office.

'I need to ring up,' he said, 'and I don't have a card, where can I get one?'

In a shitty voice, the woman behind the counter said, 'At the Print and Poster shop,' gesturing across the square.

'That's very logical,' Clyde said approvingly. 'Very logical indeed. Efficient too.'

The woman looked the other way. She'd had enough fuck-wits and smart-arses that day to last her a lifetime. If there were any other jobs for an old retread like herself she'd sure as hell throw this one in; no one in their right minds would have any dealing with the *public*.

I'm not going to let them beat me, Clyde thought as he walked over to the poster shop. A sign outside said, Phone cards $20. Looked like phone calls had just gone from twenty cents to twenty dollars. Clyde walked inside. There were posters everywhere. A huge Jimmy Hendrix smashing up his guitar. Now that was an era!

A friendly person showed him the cards. Ranging from $5 to $20, they had a slick, hypermodern, science fictional feel to them. Holding one in your hand, you had the feeling that you and your little country had really entered the space age.

There was only one minor problem.

'We had two dollar introductory cards,' the friendly person said, but we've sold out of them.

'Of course,' Clyde nodded understandingly. 'When did they change the phones?'

'Last night. They did them all in the middle of the night.'

'It's the pod people,' Clyde told her.

He walked back across the Square to the CPO, back up the steps to the Telecom office. The opening lines of Rilke's "Fifth Elegy" came into his mind.

'But tell me who are these travelling men
even more fugitive than we ourselves,
compelled from birth, oh for whose, whose sake
wrung by some never satiate will?

The shitty voiced woman had been replaced, perhaps by a wise superior, with a young woman with a pretty face and a happy smile.

'I need to make a call,' Clyde said 'and I don't have enough money to buy a card, how can I make a call?'

'Two of the phones have not been changed, one at this end, one at the other end of the row, by the phone for handicapped people.'

'That's me.'

Heartened by this pleasant interchange, Clyde returned to the scene of his former defeat, twenty cents at the ready. If she's not home I'll resign from the day, he thought. Again his twenty cent piece encountered the resistance of steel. He felt deeply betrayed. He took several paces backwards. He knew what they looked like now – the evil little slot where the card fitted in, the space-groove logo, the compact phone unit in Blade Runner steel. Virtually vandal proof, he thought. A little super-glue in the slot might do the trick. Fuck up the pod people. Perhaps he would write this novel for Stockman after all, make Stockman the hero. He could tart him up a bit, give him a sadomasochistic twist, if he needed one. It could start just like this, with thoughts of superglue, and end with mayhem and carnage in Aotea Square.

With less hope, he started for the other end of the line of booths. There was a cluster of people, a ragged line, outside the last phone. The little bald man was there. A man was in the booth, facing outward, the receiver to his ear, a deeply depressed look on his face.

'Is the phone working?' Clyde asked.

'It was,' somebody said. 'Now this guy can only get 111.'

'I don't know how I'm going to get in touch with my wife,' the bald man said in a desperate voice, looking up a Clyde as if Clyde might have some solution on offer.

Clyde walked away. He knew where he was going. There was a phone booth, a red, wooden, traditional phone booth into the bargain, at the bus station by the seedy bus station café. It was home turf. He was wrong. From a distance he could see the dilapidated red phone box had been replaced by a grey steel-framed cubical no one would ever get to call dilapidated, with the ubiquitous card phone logo embossed. They've come in the night, he thought, teams working feverishly to change our reality. Phil Dick's Adjustment Team had been at work.

He still had a phone call to make, a call which loomed in his mind larger than ever. He remembered the phone booths in the Downtown shopping complex and decided that they would have fallen, as would those in the Airport Bus Terminal. His hope lay in the two booths opposite the Jean Batten Post Office, now a branch of PostBank, itself a branch of some other bank.

Perhaps the rot has not spread that far, he thought.

But it had.

Out of reflex he continued to walk until he came to Queen Street, where Clyde found his way blocked by a cluster of people, office workers standing around with white shirts and rolled up sleeves. Ordinary pedestrians milled about as a flurry of unexpected rain swept across the street. Peering through the crowd, Clyde saw that two blocks of Queen Street had been evacuated. A police car and fire engine were parked in the middle of the road. As he watched, a cloud of smoke burst out of one of the buildings.

'It's the ANZ,' someone near Clyde said. At that moment, the rain closed over again and an Indian hawker appeared, half a dozen umbrellas hooked over his arm. 'Only ten dollar, only ten dollar,' he shouted. People looked at him and looked away. 'Only ten dollar, you stay nice and dry.'

'Bugger off,' someone said to him.

A heavy, acrid smell filled the air.

Clyde set off up Fort Street and turned into High Street. Soon he came to Vulcan Lane where he slumped into one of the steel chairs outside the Yoghurt Nook and watched the freshly released crowds surge up Queen Street. He suddenly realized he was only fifteen metres from a phone.

Bars were fugitive places, the Adjustment Team would have missed them, probably had no interest or jurisdiction over them. But he stayed, slumped where he was, unmoving. It occurred to him, now a phone was within reach, that his behaviour over the last hour was grossly out of kilter. He could have been home in an hour and rung her from there, from his hideaway, at his leisure, a beer in his hand, his feet propped up in a literary way upon the table. Stockman would move fast, but not that fast. Stockman had other things on his mind.

Clyde got up and ambled into the pub. A roar of alcoholic voices hit him at the door. The phone was there, unchanged. He'd used it before. It had a bad line that made the person's voice sound a thousand miles away. There was somebody talking into it now, shouting at the top of his voice, 'There were cops everywhere I said, The bomb squad. They blew up a briefcase full of sandwiches. That's what I said. Some silly bugger left his lunch in the bank.'

When the man had gone, the phone sat in its cradle, the receiver still warm. Clyde stood and fondled it, but made no move to punch the numbers he already knew by heart.

Clyde needed a drink. A real drink, and beer was the only language the fridge knew. Beer! He'd seen enough of it. He got off his bed, went to the fridge and emptied all the beer out, endless cans falling forward, rolling over the floor. It was the Sorcerer's Apprentice all over again. He rolled the cans right out the door and down the path, six-packs leaping and jumping. Some of them burst open and hung out their metal tongues, sending the fizzy froth into the concrete.

He knew that young dolphins got their heads snagged in the plastic can-rings, slowly strangling themselves as they grew. And what was beer? Piss-water! Gas-water! Shit-fizz! Soda-vomit! He helped the cans along with his boot. Toxic-garbage! Chemical-whiz! Bloat-blood!

He went back to a fridge that looked as shining and empty as a freshly cleaned tooth.

A bottle of Glenfiddich would be more like it. Something with a little bite-back. That's what he hated about beer, its vacuous, empty clutch, insta-fizz vanishing trick. Its bloated pomp and circumstance. A good single malt whisky lingered in the mouth, oily and insinuating, for several minutes. A fine cognac was no mouth wash.

He pulled up the blind and saw that it was morning, a morning that had been waiting behind the blind for him all night. He walked out on the deck and checked the cabbage tree. Was it dying? He was no expert. Was it flowering itself to death? If it died he would hold a little funeral, a mad, symbolic little rite for the death of all cabbage trees. At least the flax was immune; the tui would have the flax and vice versa. They'd build it back up out of nothing if they had to. They'd go from the raw rock up. My god, they'd bring the firmament down upon the land and the wasters would be wasted and the fuckers would be fucked.

He hadn't collected yesterday's mail, but he put off the short walk to the letterbox. He wanted to look at the familiar, sloping line of the opposite hill, to look up into the spindly mamaku and see if any thrush or tui were evident this morning. He wanted to do things like that. To hum a little tune, dance a little, act with that odd intimacy he shared with himself when he was alone. He even thought of retrieving one of the beers that had rolled under the deck from his grand clear out.

Finally, however, he succumbed to the demands of the world, and attended his letterbox. There were three items. One was a brief letter from Sylvia: *Sorry and thanks for everything. Caught up with Jeannette. I had to tell her what happened and she laughed (she's really got things together now, detoxed last year) and said it sounded like you hadn't changed a bit. Affectionately Sylv.*

One was an official looking envelope from Wellington. He put that to one side. He knew what the other item was as soon as he saw the large envelope.

Before he could open it and confirm his guess, the telephone, which had been playing far too big a part in his life lately, began to ring.

'Clyde, this is Sue Hyde.'

'How are things at Greenpeace?'

'Complicated. Watch for the backlash.'

'What do you mean?'

'For some people the world ends at the bottom line. When that old bottom line is at stake, environmental concerns go out the window, green goes out of fashion faster than hair oil.' Her voice was caustic. Clyde could hear her parrot squawking away behind her. 'There's one hell of a lot of people *out there* who still don't realize that ecological integrity is the bottom line. The bottom line on which all our arses are resting. But that's not what I rang you about.'

'The article.'

'It's brilliant, Clyde, it's a whiz, but we can't use it.'

'Is that because the Bealters wouldn't give their real names, or allow photographs?'

'Not really. It's all this shit about Monsanto. They could tie us up in litigation for years. Costly litigation. And the whole thing's got a real emotional slant. Then there's the bit about that funny kid you never explain. And, I'm sorry, I've changed my mind about the doctors. The way you've presented it, we could get some unpleasant reactions from these doctors.'

'You want to use false names for the doctors?'

'That part would have to be rewritten in general terms.'

'Christ.' He idly flicked at the package with his pen. His article would be gutted, all the truth drained out of it. All that sharp, implicating, human particularity. 'But I'm quoting from legal depositions and other documents.'

'Yes, but you've put them together to imply, you even state openly, that Roundup has dioxin in it. We don't have a shred of evidence for that. Just suppositions.'

'I'm not quite saying that, I'm saying that given the Company's history, it wouldn't come as any surprise if there were dioxin in the Roundup. Christ, their kitchen cleanser, used to clean kids toys, was contaminated.'

'And that's libellous. But look I think something can be salvaged out of this.'

'Salvaged? Jesus. A horse always stands with its arse into the wind.'

'What the hell does that mean?

'I dunno but it sounds good.'

'Get real, Clyde.' Her voice was sharp. 'We're happy to name companies and products, but not this way. This is going to get right up somebody's nose.'

'That's where I aim to be. I can't see any point in writing it otherwise.'

'That's either very heroic or very childish, but it's counterproductive as far as getting a review of the Toxic Board's functions is concerned. I mean look, you paint the whole thing in pretty lurid colours, you know. The poor Bealters. Mrs with dark rings under her eyes, and a *haunted* look, you say. Then there's the *Monstrum Horrendum*, you even call it that, the evil Company run by a bunch of crooks that make the mafia look like a Play Centre committee, eager to contaminate the world for a few cents on the bottom line...'

'But that's true.'

'Of course it's true, but no one will believe it the way you've written it because... well... it almost looks like you hammed it up. You loaded the dice too heavily. Played it for the drama. Drama won't get us a legislative review.'

'You're getting too deep for me, Sue. I'm only a writer, remember?'

'You've exaggerated too much. Overplayed your hand.'

'I didn't exaggerate at all.' He banged the desk with his fist. The telephone jumped. 'This whole thing makes me want to spew.'

'Go ahead, I'm at a safe distance, just don't gum up the receiver.'

'Stuff it! All the truth gets eaten out of it. You want to rip the guts out of the whole thing. First the Bealters, now you. They wanted to change names to protect the innocent; you want to change names to protect the guilty. You remind me of Stockman.'

'Who's he?'

Sneering into the receiver, Clyde said, 'Let's veil the whole fucking thing. We'll call Monsanto "Sanmonto" and Roundup "Laramie" or "Rawhide" or something. And we can't be too *emotional* and see a *haunted* look in somebody's eyes, even if it's there. That's a no-no. That's exaggeration. That's loading the dice. And we can't present it in the full grotesquery of how it really is because some bureaucrat with his arse on the bottom line of a plush chair won't like it. That's exaggeration. We're still bowing and scraping to the bastard because we believe, in our stupidity, that one day they're all going to pull finger and say, hey you're right, gee-whiz we've poisoned the earth, thanks for being so patient, guys. You know that's never going to happen. You told me yourself; they'll stick with the bottom line until the fucking bottom line itself goes down the gurgler taking us all with it. That's exaggeration! As you try to squeeze it all down into their double-dealing discourse, real language is vanquished, and that vanquished language becomes the only true tongue. If shit started raining out of the sky, how long would you hang around outside with your mouth open watching it? Fuck it, Sue. It stinks. It fucking stinks from arsehole to breakfast time...' There was spittle, hot and wet, on the inside of the receiver.

'Have you quite finished, humble servant of truth?'

'I sure as fuck have.'

He put the down the receiver and turned his back on it. If it rang again he'd chuck it through the fucking window. He picked up his large envelope and looked at the handwriting.

It was his own.

Throwing the large envelope aside, he opted for the official looking letter. It was from the Ministry of Agriculture and Fisheries. For a moment it didn't make any sense to him, for he'd forgotten he'd written to them on the question of dioxin contamination in Roundup. It had taken them long enough, and now they were just a few minutes too late; he'd had a gutsful. Without great interest he ripped open the envelope and glanced at the contents:

OFFICIAL INFORMATION

'I refer to your letter dated... in which you have sought information in respect of the registered pesticides 'Roundup', 'Nufarm Glyphosate 360', and 'Network'. In respect of your first question I would advise that POEA is present in each of the glyphosate formulations you have specified. The presence of this surfactant in glyphosate formulations has been widely reported and you can take our advice as official notification of the presence of this formulant in the respective products.

With regard to your second question, I would confirm that the 1,4-Dioxane contaminant is present, by virtue of the POEA component, in the three formulations...'

Clyde threw the letter down. To begin with, if POEA is known to kill fish and damage red blood cells why the fuck was the Ministry calmly confirming its existence as if it were of little consequence? That was for

208

starters. Next there was the question diox… he peered hard at the page. This was not dioxin they had confirmed, but *dioxane*. He remembered how quickly he'd written that letter, keen to rid his mind of the whole mess. Had he misspelt dioxin, so conjuring a chemical into a real, official existence from some stumble of the fingers? There was probably a logical explanation.

And what was 1,4-Dioxane? The next garden path.

He thought of ringing Sue Hyde and having another go, but he knew enough now to keep his hand away from the phone. This story would never end.

He threw the letter into his files.

'I don't believe this, Clyde. It can't really be happening.' Moira shut the door and settled down into the seat, clicking her safety belt securely home.

'You'd better believe it,' Clyde said. 'The age of chivalry is dead but its arts flicker on here and there, in outlandish places.'

'Chivalry huh?' Moira lit a cigarette. 'That's when the woman stays on the pedestal and just lifts her skirts occasionally, to reveal an exquisitely shaped… ankle.'

'While the poet sings of unrequited love,' Clyde said. 'Upon his harp.'

'Oh how he does harp!'

Clyde laughed, wondering if he was going to enjoy this outing. Moira's voice had edges, cliffs of fall. He tried to take off in the violently confident way Stockman might, but the old Toyota was too gutless, too shagged in the rings, to make the effort. He hated to think what his exhaust might be doing to the last chance decade's worth of clean air. It is a psychological thing, about a car exhaust, he decided; when you are driving you are going one way and the exhaust is going the other.

'And I have two or three little surprises I'm not about to reveal in advance but will entice you with the prospects of, if that makes any grammatical sense.'

'I'm intrigued.'

'That's the whole idea.' He aimed the car towards the western hills. 'Let's get out of this great arsehole.'

'That sounds gross enough to be a literary reference.'

'It is. Auckland, you great arsehole!'

'Baxter.'

'Baxter,' Clyde agreed, opting to drive around the Western bays, knowing what he was looking for. 'Let's get out of this gross literary reference.'

'Baxter had a great reputation as a womanizer, didn't he,' Moira said in a neutral voice.

'It's said he idealised women immensely.'

'The pedestal, again. Put them on a pedestal, fuck them behind the garage. Isn't that what he used to do? With other men's wives? Apparently they felt sorry for him.'

'Don't look at me,' Clyde thumped the steering wheel, 'I'm not Baxter.'

'You're not trying to tell me that he was an isolated case, are you? Anyway, I'm going to enjoy getting out of the great Arsehole. I don't do it enough. I've got friends in Coro, I should visit them more often.'

'Is all not toasty in wimmin-space?'

'Don't get dangerous, Clyde, please, it doesn't suit you. You're better off a wimp.'

'Sorry to hit a nerve so soon in the day.'

'Don't kid yourself.'

'I thought I was kidding you.'

He could get into it, this lethal repartee he always played with her. At first he'd had no stomach for it, but she had trained him to like it; now it was their *modus operandi*. The sharp barb. The quick cut. It was her 1940's tough-guy stuff. And he was doing it too, playing her Bogart lines back to her. Why couldn't something new happen?

He pulled over to the kerb and wound the window up tight. He grabbed Moira's arm and pointed.

'Look, what do you see along there?'

'Have you gone mad, Clyde?'

'What do you see, quick tell me.'

She shrugged helplessly, 'Nothing special. A street, cars, houses…'

210

'Yes!'

'Some people walking along, and a truck and…'

'Yes, what about the truck?'

'It's a council truck or something. Maintenance. For Christ's sake, Clyde, what's this all about? You're acting like a loony tune.'

'The truck! What do you see?'

'Alright. I'll play along. It had better be worth it. There're some guys on the back doing something, the truck's driving slowly, there's a dog running along watching them.'

'What are they doing? The men?'

She squinted, 'Ah, they're spraying. Clyde please. What's the punch line?'

'Are the men wearing any kind of protective gear, anything like that, goggles, masks?'

'They've got overalls.'

'Jesus!' Clyde had not seen how close the truck had got. The nozzle was near the ground but the spray blew back up in a high misty veil.

In a moment the car would be covered in it.

He started up, slammed into first and gunned out onto the road, belatedly glancing back to see what was coming behind.

'You're going to kill us.'

'Not yet.'

He bluffed it out with a car that was coming from behind, pushing the Toyota to its limit through the gears. In the rear mirror he saw the men on the back of the truck laughing and joking.

'Would you mind telling me what that was all about?'

'Forget it.'

'Forget it? Just like that?'

'That's right.'

'I mean what's so special about a bunch of guys spraying.'

'Nothing, nothing special at all. It happens every day. Without protective gear.'

'So why the drama?'

'Just testing.'

'Testing what, for fuck's sake? Clyde, you're going to have to explain.'

So he did.

'That's bloody creepy,' she said. But she didn't care that much, he sensed. Not as much as she cared about her own wounded heart.

He'd found the spot he'd been looking for and the subject was left behind as they nosed gently down a boat ramp onto a short strip of hard, flat, shelly sand that in turn gave way to a mudflat that stretched out towards the distant low water mark. Beyond the low water there was a fair view of the expanse of the harbour and the land to the north. He turned off the motor. The silence settled in around them.

'I've seen some fantastic sunsets from around these bays,' Moira said. 'Squalls over the Manukau. It is not so much a question of colour but *quality* of light.'

Clyde reached over the back and produced the first of his surprises. A picnic basket, one of the old-fashioned woven ones with a stiff, high handle, packed with food. Sandwiches Clyde had made himself. A cake he had baked. Pieces of steaming hot chicken wrapped in tinfoil. A packet of 'natural' potato chips. A variety of cheeses. A cream cheese dip with chives and garlic. A tin of Greek olives. Fresh, slender raw carrots. Diced cucumber and two bottles of Chardonnay... A civilized feast.

Moira picked up one of the bottles and looked approvingly at the label. 'Doing yourself proud again, Clyde, trying to buy *me* off.'

'Every girl has her price. But actually I'm trying to buy me off.' He clicked himself out of his seat belt and pulled the cork on one of the bottles. 'A little celebration,' he said in a mysterious voice. 'All will be revealed in the fullness of time.'

'How exciting!'

Clyde produced two crystal wine glasses and they drank with solemn mockery to each other's health, draining the first glass. As Clyde refilled, he sensed they'd crossed a boundary ritualized by the toast. As if some pact had been sealed, some deal made.

'I can't believe you organized all this, Clyde Aichen. And made the cake yourself! You must have had a dizzy spell.'

'I did.' Clyde rubbed his chest. 'I'm no stranger to dizzy spells. And dreams.'

'Mmmmmm.' She made it sound as if dreams were some sort of after dinner mint.

'I keep dreaming about Rilke, you know, the German poet. He argues with me about language and coins aphorisms. The other day he told me that prisoners dream in the language of children. And the night before he told me that poets must learn the language of angels.'

'Amazing.'

'I dreamed about him after mum died. I had to go down to the land of the dead and talk to the spirits. Rilke was there, dressed as a little girl. I asked him what it was like to be dead. He quoted himself, from the Duino Elegies,

it is tiresome to be dead
and full of retrieving, so that one must sense
traces of eternity by degrees...'

'He might be your spirit guide,' she said, holding out her glass for a refill.

Clyde winced. Talk of spirit guides had that effect on him. 'Then my spirit guide is dead. Last time I saw him he was lying on a bed just like my mother, cold as clay. There was an exhalation of mist hanging above his body, like a breath that never went away.'

Moira shuddered. 'That's serious. It could be very serious if your spirit guide dies. I've never heard of that before. A spirit is not supposed to die.'

'What would happen?' Clyde picked up some chicken and tore some meat off the leg. He hadn't told her this was no quick fried, sad eyed battery layer but a plump, free ranging bird he'd roasted himself, and he was an expert in stuffing, the childhood stuffing he remembered from Christmas's ago, rich with herbs and spice. Memories discharged into his head along with saliva into his mouth. In the days before the Silence, his mother had carved the lean meat hard when the weekend roast was on the table, but chicken was pulled away delicately, a wing, a leg at a time, as if not to disturb a still sleeping fowl in its bed of roast potatoes.

'You'd lose all direction in your life, probably. We need our guides the way a pigeon needs its homing sense, and maybe for similar reasons. Without your spirit guide you would lose the ability to orient yourself in reality.'

Clyde grinned wickedly, 'Is that a fact?' In some manner he did not understand, however, she'd got through to him. Rilke as a spirit guide. From the Order of Angels, no doubt. Rilke, the man who once cried out in lamentation to the Angelic Hierarchies had now, in death, joined them. He quaffed at his wine, ripped more meat off the bone, and chewed it. Now Rilke also, in his ghostly afterlife, had entered the great Silence. He thought of the poet on the cold marble of the sheet. Vapourish breath hanging in the air. 'Go ahead and have some,' he said, gesturing at the food. 'You know the old saying, if you can't eat you can't shit and if you can't shit you die.'

Moira put an olive in her mouth, chewed and washed it down with a liberal draught of wine. 'Christ that wine's good, Clyde.'

'Have something to eat.'

'Sure, sure,' she sipped at the wine. 'You know, Clyde…' she sipped again, 'You know, maybe the trouble with us is that we never had any children?' She coloured. 'I don't mean together, I mean…'

'I know what you mean.'

'You see older people who've never had children, you know, always going nutty over a dog or cat or budgie or something.'

Clyde drank moodily. 'Jeannette and I…' he stopped. The ocean spread out before him, the deep-sea swells calmed by the surrounding land. The noonday sun stood hard on the resultant flat surface, fragmenting it to a primary pattern of glittering Brownian motion. Out of that, the world was rebuilt into hills and sky. He bit his lower lip. If he'd had children, not with Jeannette, his mind shied away from that, but with someone else, a good person who loved him, and two or three children calling him poppa or daddy, would he now know this apparently hopeless ache. Would there be a Madeleine Farquar in his life looking for a father for her children?

'What about you and Jeannette?'

'We… she had two abortions. Then a miscarriage. The time was never right. There was never enough money.'

'The time's never fucking right,' Moira said violently. 'There never is enough fucking money. What boring shit!'

Clyde realized she must be getting drunk; the first bottle was already history. 'Have something to eat,' he urged. 'That chicken will melt in your mouth.'

Moira held out her glass for a refill. She took a potato chip and scooped some dip onto it. 'We're going to be boring, lonely old farts,' she said, 'crying into our cups with a head full of pleasant memories of abortions, miscarriages and divorces.' She nibbled at the potato chip. 'I'd like to adopt a little girl. I think we both need the nurturing part of ourselves developed.'

'But it's not likely to happen.'

She was silent, nibbling at the potato chip.

'You'd better tell me what's happened.'

'You'd better give me another drink.'

'You'd better eat.' He demonstrated with a piece of wholemeal bread with chicken and olive on top.

'Why should I fucking eat? Don't be so boring, Clyde! I'm not hungry, do you want me to eat when I'm not hungry?' She reached out for the bottle, cursed, and turned to unclasp her seatbelt. Clyde filled her glass and left the bottle where she could reach it. She sank back, the seat belt still clasped.

'Snake's been sleeping with someone,' Moira said soberly. 'I thought I'd found someone who loved me. I've lost both ways; friend and lover, lover and friend.' Clyde grimaced. 'Jesus, Clyde, talk about men exploiting women, these women go through women, or men, like there was no yesterday.'

'You mean it's not Snake you're in love with?'

'I never said it was.'

'You implied…'

'You assumed…'

'Now I start to see.'

'I'm glad.'

'But you and Snake… She implied…'

'You assumed and Snake played to it, took the piss she loves to do.'

'Shit.'

'With Snake I discovered the shadowy, unsocialised side of my sexuality. My bisexual side.'

'It's probably just a stage,' he said soothingly. When he thought of Stockman, his mind closed down like a clamp. He'd smash the bastards face in next time he saw him.

'Don't patronize, Clyde,' Moira said tiredly. 'Christ!' She rubbed her eyes. It goes on forever, she thought, in one form or another. There's only one thing that puts an end to it. She picked up a piece of bread and inspected it.

'I was only trying to say that this cocaine-speed promiscuity is only a phase in peoples' lives.' His pedantic tone gave way to anger. He opened his mouth to say more but was forestalled by something he saw out on the mudflat near the low water line, half sunk in the mud – an old bathtub around which a child was playing, a little girl. He saw the flash of a skipping rope in the sun.

'How all encompassingly liberal and wise of you, O Bard,' she snarled. 'If I want a lecture in Sociology, I'll know where to come.'

'I'm sorry if it's not working is all I mean,' Clyde said. He felt clumsy and rather stupid, getting a little drunk himself, perhaps. Pleasantly tipsy.

'Thanks. I'm pissed off. I'm throwing Snake out of the house. That'll get rid of Grace and Heidi in one grand slam, thank you mam. And the other bastard won't get a look in.'

'Forgive me for saying so, Moira, but… well…'

'Spit it out.' She put down the bread.

'Your lesbianism seemed, to me anyway,' he said hastily, 'to be a matter of conviction rather than inclination. You're angry with men and…'

'Clyde, if you carry on along this line I'll either smash up the car,' she picked up the bottle, 'or go to sleep. Whichever would piss you off the most.'

'You don't have to say anything if you don't want to,' Clyde said, his voice going cold. 'I didn't bring the subject up. And don't eat, starve if you want to. Die if you want to.'

Moira picked up a leg of chicken and held it in front of her eyes. 'Alas, poor fowl,' she said, 'I knew her well.' She sniffed at the chicken. 'Sugar and spice and all things nice,' she said in a little girl voice, putting the chicken down.

Involuntarily, Clyde glanced over to the bathtub where the little girl was playing. He noted that the tide had turned, a finger of water had crept up behind the tub from his angle of vision, suggesting lower ground behind being filled up first. The little girl was standing on top of the tub, waving her hands in the air.

'Anyway,' Moira said sniffing, 'it's par for the course, par for the

216

fucking course.' She was not looking at Clyde but out the window to the north. Clyde realized she was talking to herself about herself. 'Anyway,' she repeated, 'you have more surprises up your sleeve, remember, you promised.' She turned appealingly to him. He caught her Ophelia smile. It only came out to play when she was drunk.

'Sure I did,' Clyde said warmly, splashing the last of the second bottle into both their glasses. He cut himself a slice of Brie and placed an olive on top. 'But that comes after the feast, the food and the wine.'

'It's after the food and wine now,' Moira said peevishly, throwing back the wine. 'And now the booze is cut.' She looked sceptically down at the food and up towards the ocean. She saw the girl and the bathtub and went very still.

'She's pretending it's a boat,' she said. Clyde noticed the wisps of finer, dark hair that curled behind Moira's ears. 'The tide's coming in and it makes her feel like she's moving.'

Clyde brushed the crumbs off his hands. 'Now is the time for the second surprise, with a third to follow soon after.'

'Oh! Clydie-Clyde.' She clapped fervently. 'Oh pleeeeeaaase! Clydie-Clyde.'

'I have some misgivings about this,' Clyde murmured, glancing at the two empty wine bottles on the floor, reaching into his bag and pulling out a 40 oz bottle of Glenfiddich whisky. Better sense might counsel against it, but Clyde Aichen wanted a drink. He needed a drink before what was coming up.

'Clydiiiieeeeee!' Moira squealed, a child at Christmas. She kissed him on the cheek. 'You go straight to my alcoholic heart.' Her voice dropped out of child-mode. 'But you're not planning to *drive* are you? Let's get that clear, first.' There was a blurred hysteria in her tone. She spoke as if they were agreeing on some vast undertaking.

'I was planning on parking on the road and taking a taxi,' he said, nodding, conveying in his manner an air of responsibility, even rectitude.

'That's very fucking wise,' Moira took the bottle out of his hands. The colour drained from her face. 'Jesus, Clyde, I have to tell you this. I've been thinking about death lately, *death, death, death.* Every pot I throw is an urn.'

For the ashes of angels, Clyde thought.

She turned the bottle in her hands. 'That's why I drink, Clyde.' Her voice had a whining note of appeal in it, as if he were her final judge and arbiter. 'When I drink I don't think about death any more. Except right now.'

'We carry our deaths around with us like a secret knowledge.' Clyde screwed his face up in mock effort as he twisted the cap off the whisky. 'It's a medieval notion.' He wanted to avoid, if he could, further insincere confidences of the bottle.

'I don't want a lecture, Clyde, I want a drink.'

Clyde obliged, wiping out the wine glasses with a paper napkin and half filling them with the amber liquid. Almost the colour of Madeleine's hair, he thought.

'I have this weightless sensation in my gut. I can't describe it, Clyde.' She took the glass and gave him a crooked grin. 'Like the kind of tight, expectant gut you get before an exhibition, or meeting a lover, maybe. It destroys the appetite, it destroys everything. And I feel that any passing wind could just blow me away.' Her voice died on the last syllable. They both drank. 'My hands,' she continued, holding them out in front of her, shaking them. 'I put them into the wet clay and they freeze, as if they're already fossilized. The only way I can make them move is from here,' she banged her forehead. 'By commanding the fingers and making the wrists turn this way and that, I can make things. Not new things but fair imitations of things I've done before, as if I were engaged in an act of forgery.' She spat out the last word with contempt.

She wedged her glass between her knees and turned her hands over before her. 'My hands have gone dumb. They weren't attached to any part of me except up here,' banging her forehead with the same, violent motion. 'I'm standing there trying to work, trying to make something, and I find I'm breathing really hard, as if someone else is breathing through my chest. It's a horrible feeling. I lie in bed at night and feel myself getting bigger and bigger, like a sausage doll. I spoke to an acupuncturist about it. She said I'd gone into defensive mode, as if I were under attack, so my spirit comes out of my body to form a defence, so I feel that displacement. I feel sucked right out. Nothing but a husk.'

'And you don't feel it when you drink?'

'You don't feel any fucking thing when you drink,' she said

contemptuously. 'Nobody home.' Tears began to pour down her cheeks. She made no effort to stop them or wipe her eyes but stared out through those watery prisms towards the girl playing around the bathtub, seemingly surrounded by a shining sheet of water. Blinking the tears away, she saw that the effect was not entirely an illusion, since the tide had come in rapidly and was lapping around the front of the tub. The little girl stood on the front of it as if she were about to dive into the shining surface. Mechanically, Moira lifted the glass up to her lips.

Clyde wondered if he should just take her home right now and forget about it. Let her sleep it off before she did any more damage. Skip the next part of the entertainment, which wasn't going to be all that amusing anyway.

'You didn't buy this bottle just to turn me maudlin, Clyde Aichen.' Moira gulped breaths. 'Not that I don't appreciate it. Thinking of your old lush friend, Moira. Or is this a leg opener?'

'I've got a letter to read you, but not until after at least one more of these,' he gestured to the glass half empty in his hand.

'One of *those*, shit.' Moira clicked her tongue sympathetically. 'You're not going to lay a bummer on us, are you Clydie-Clyde?' Her voice retreated to that of a six or seven year old. 'You wouldn't do that, would you Clyde, darling Clyde.'

'Moira...'

Drunkenly she said, 'Alright alright, I'm allowed to express my fucken affection if I fucken want to. You don't have to get so fucken uptight.'

'I'm not uptight,' he said mildly, 'in fact I'm quite relaxed.'

'Bullshit! You're on a rim of fire. And you're lying to me, which is a bad sign. Let's hear this fucken letter or I won't be able to be able to get a sensible word out of you.' She laughed, 'A sensible word!'

Clive prevaricated. He finished his drink and poured himself another.

'Is it a letter from Madeleine?'

Clyde waved his arms as if to ward off evil spirits. 'No, no!'

'It's nothing to do with your chemical nasties, is it?'

'No, no,' his hands were shaking. He put the glass down and took the letter out of his pocket. It's from the College Press. It goes like this,' he smoothed out the paper, took a sip from his fresh glass and read: 'Dear Clyde, Thank you for submitting your collection of poems. They've been seen by two different readers who have considered them carefully. I'm afraid, however, that we do not think we can accept any of the poems for publication. Our readers were not in favour of the collection. Both felt that too much work was presented; but they also thought that a lot of it was thin and lacking impact, although pleasant enough to read. They were looking for a linguistic and rhythmical variety, a vigorous engagement with language, which just wasn't present. We're sorry to have to disappoint you and hope you succeed in placing the poems elsewhere. Blah-de-blah.'

'What kind of surprise is this, Clyde?'

'A nasty one.'

'It's a bastard of a surprise, but Clyde, you've been writing nearly twenty years, haven't you? You must have had dozens of rejections, especially for poetry. You must have developed a professional attitude towards this sort of thing.'

'Absolutely.' He spoke with conviction. 'Professional to the core.'

'So why go on a fucken bender just because the College Press gives you the cold, snobby shoulder?'

Clyde concentrated on the scene outside. The mudflat had become a shining silver shield. The bathtub was surrounded by water; the little girl had gone. Misty clouds had started to collect again in the sky. A rain belt was coming towards them from across the north-western coast. He thought of Chinese landscape paintings, its use of gaps and spaces to suggest misty rain and inaccessibly. They just used blank spaces, he thought, and yet it is enough, it fools the eye into seeing a lake or the line of a hill. *It fools the eye.* Just like a poem.

'What kind of poems are these Clyde?' Moira looked hard at him, hanging her eyeballs on his face. One eyelid was beginning to descend, giving her face a lopsided look. Clyde wondered, idly, just how fast the tide would come in. Sooner or later he'd have to back out up the ramp, or his shagged old Toyota would suffer the same fate as the bathtub was now facing.

'Love poems,' he said in a short voice.

'Ah!' Moira nodded ponderously. 'I'm beginning t'see.'

So was Clyde. There was something opening up, something even less pleasant than the letter. Left to his own devices, he might be able to avoid it, but Moira wouldn't let him escape. No matter how drunk she was she'd ferret it out. The drunker she got the harder she'd ferret. He looked back at his own drink. When he looked up the sun had gone and half the bay was obscured by rain, a dark tide of drizzle racing towards them.

'And how is the little romance progressing?'

'It's not.'

'You mean it's all over now, baby blue?'

'Not exactly. It never got started.'

Moira opened her mouth and closed it again. The rain hit the tub and a moment later spattered on the windscreen.

'Give me another fucken drink,' she commanded, 'and I'll tell you exactly what happened. I'll clear up any mystery. I'll debrief you. I'll take the myth out of the maggot. I'm very astute when it comes to these things, you know.'

The rain slammed against the roof of the car. Clyde watched it spring back off the bonnet. He took hold of the steering wheel, as if he were about to drive off into the rain. As he thought about it, he almost did it. How far into the mud would he get? No more than a few metres more likely. The gesture would hardly be worth it.

Moira's voice was steady, but Clyde was not fooled by that. 'Here's how I see it.' She raised one finger. 'First, you have fallen into a world of counterfeit emotions, which is the world of the unrequited lover.' A second finger joined the first. 'You strive to make the counterfeit real in your work, thus real in your life – but cannot.' A third finger joined the other two. 'Once you fully comprehend, beyond all doubt, that she doesn't and won't love you, then Rilke will come alive again in your dreams and you will find your feet in the world.' Her voice was becoming stiff and oracular. A fourth and final finger joined the other three. 'If you don't see it, and take action soon, she will. She will play the Ice Queen because you will become tiresome to her. Petitioners are always tiresome, whatever form they come in. She's got other fish to fry.' She stopped and drank deeply, apparently exhausted by the effort of divination. 'You see, Clyde,' she said in a wan voice, 'you were away with the fairies. Not an encouraging sign, at your age. Or mine.'

Clyde wasn't able to shrug her words off in the normal fashion, even though he knew she had reached that stage of drunkenness in which every word spoken was an inside tip from God. A drunk may say anything, even the truth. He had seen Madeleine the day before, and it had not been a pleasant experience. Like a bronze mirror, she had reflected everything back upon him. When he spoke of his feelings, or tried to, she had cut him off briskly, making it very clear that it was *his* material, that she was not a part of it, that she was essentially incidental to his internal process. She played the Ice Queen so well. She had around her a shining wall. When he tried to reach across it his own energy was lashed back at him, striking him across the heart. She was as cool and remote as on the day she first approached him.

Moira was watching him, her right lid having descended half way across her eye.

'*You remember Dante,*' Clyde had said to Madeleine. '*According to legend, he only had to see Beatrice once, in a church. His vision of her inspired the whole Divine Comedy.*'

'*Pah,*' she said contemptuously. '*That must be projection. How can it have anything to do with the real woman, who doesn't really count.*'

'*How do you know that's what happened? Dante had a beatific vision. His meeting her was a divine coincidence. He saw her soul shining out from her face. In such instances the universe is changed. How can you be so sure what happens when people meet? Conversation too is a form of intercourse. If you saw a divine being standing in front of you, naked to the light, what would happen to you?*' Fervently, he had hoped it would happen to her one day.

'You poor sap,' Moira said. She had to shout it over the thunder of the rain on the roof. 'We're a couple of fuck-ups, but at least I know it.'

In an agony of doubt, he thought of the poems. Did they really achieve that fragility, that translucence, that bone-china fidelity he'd hoped for?

If Moira was correct and he'd strayed into a false world, a deluded world – what had she called it? A world of counterfeit emotions – then it was hard to see how the words themselves could do other than reflect that state.

From counterfeit feeling to a counterfeit word. He was chilled at the thought beyond the reach of the whisky. Idly, he rolled the steering wheel as if turning a corner. If all this was so, then there was a fatal flaw in the poem, a flaw that ran through every line. When you reached forth your hand, there was no flesh or bone; Madeleine, the occasion for them, had no real existence in them. There was no two way response, merely the ghostly coupling of mind and word with no 'vigorous engagement with language'. He was worse off than the emperor with no clothes; not only did he have no clothes but no body to hang them upon.

The squall passed over, leaving a washed, yellowy light behind. The sea was dark and muddy, almost black, much closer now, streaming in towards the car with silvery fingers. The bathtub had vanished among the jostling anonymity of the waves. He gripped the steering wheel, imagining that he was driving into a timeless primeval landscape of mud and sky.

Morosely, he drank and Moira drank with him, echoing the bending of his own elbow. Something was coming to an end in him. He didn't know what it was, he couldn't see it clearly, but he could feel it coming to an end. It was ancient, much older than he was, more powerful and perhaps more foolish.

'So.' Moira said. 'Let's drink to the fairies.' They banged their glasses together and sat in silence again. He thought of moving the car but couldn't be bothered. His arms and legs were caught in a golden lethargy. There was plenty of time.

Slowly he said, 'All that remains, therefore, is a counterfeit staring at its own demise. In my dreams Madeleine appears as the Angel of Death, her radiant face set on top of very bony shoulders, a skeleton body. In one dream this skeleton led me past crates of beer, stacked up on either side, to a pile of rotting, filthy old sacks, and gestured for me to lie with her on them.'

'What happened?'

'The dream ended.'

'That was death, Clyde,' Moira said in a hushed voice, 'Inviting you to step in, to die. For just a moment, death crooked her finger at you.' She turned her face towards him. Her right eye was almost closed. A thin fissure of light showed between the lids. 'Death has to be invited, Clyde, like the old stories of the vampire, you remember those fucken movies, his Nibs cannot enter the house unless invited in. When we take Death as a lover, there can be only one consummation, Clyde, only one end. The vampire only ever wants one thing.'

She spoke with such conviction Clyde had to agree with her.

They both nodded their heads and had another drink. The bottle was approaching the halfway mark. How come it went so fast? The tide must be lapping around the front wheels of the car. There seemed to be some mysterious connection between the state of the tide and the level of the bottle. He knew that the tide had only just started to turn, and that it would have come in very fast over the mudflat, burying the bathtub. It had the height of the ramp behind them to rise yet to get to full tide, almost twice the height of the car. Already he could see a great level sheet of water spreading out in front of him like a vast empty highway.

'We'll drive straight across to Awhitu,' he said. 'Toyota will become amphibian.' Moira laughed hoarsely, as if at some crude joke.

'Listen, Clyde.' Her voice had changed. It was not a little girl voice, nor her drunken adult voice, but a tone that hovered between the two like a seesaw, shifting one way or the other from word to word without completely overbalancing into either. It was a terrified, vulnerable, last-ditch voice. As she spoke her hands fiddled with the long neglected food, making shapes with it. 'Clyde, I've got a proposition to put to you, a proposal more like it. We know each other, Clyde, better than we know anyone else, fuck, we know each other inside out. I know we're not kind of passionate towards one another, but why can't we get together and bring up a couple of kids, Clydie-Clyde. You need to learn to nurture more, your dreams prove that. I'm talking about a practical arrangement, not a romantic one, I mean, I'm not under any fucken illusions about...' She picked up a chicken bone Clyde had half eaten and stripped the remaining meat off it, lying the pieces in a row.

Clyde laughed, 'Are you proposing marriage to me, Moira?' He held up the bottle, 'Catching me at a weak moment?'

'Don't poke fun at me, you bastard,' she said in a trembling voice. 'I am serious.' She stopped fiddling with the food, where some sort of structure was forming around the strips of meat and bone, and grabbed his arm. 'Kids would earth us, Clyde, they'd bring us back to the planet again. We could regenerate. Put some life back into the spirit. People need kids to remind them.'

'To remind them of what? Dirty nappies?' Clyde was not about to become sentimental about kids, or to wallow in some emotional panegyric, no matter how drunk he was, and he was not yet that drunk.

224

He doubted he ever would be.

'Of their own fucken humanity,' Moira said in a terribly stretched voice. 'Of where they come from.' She was staring down at her hands as they moved. Two well picked chicken legs, the fat ends wedged in sturdy squares of wholemeal bread, were placed together to form an arch.

'...of what it feels like to get up in the middle of the night to a screaming mouth, of what it feels like to be back in the shit and piss of life. Great!'

'I would expect you, Mr Poet, to have soiled your hands with the shit and piss of life.' Thick slabs of cheese were erected at the head of each strip of chicken, one favoured with a larger, sturdier piece. 'Moira, are you proposing that we live in a loveless relationship, maybe not even sleep together, and bring up a child? A relationship of convenience, sort of?'

Her hands ceased to move. She had a toothpick in one hand, an olive and a piece of cucumber in the other. Her face swam up towards his. Her right eye was completely closed; she looked like a different person with only one eye. 'Not loveless, Clyyyyyyde,' she said, drawing out his name in one long appeal, 'Not entirely. Christ.' The olive and the cucumber slipped between her fingers. 'Maybe we could find a little love. Just a smidgeon, and make it grow.'

In a bleak, sober voice he said, 'You're saying, in effect, let's settle for second best because that's all we're good for, let's cop out because we're losers and we probably can't find anything better now anyway, so we deserve each other, we'll focus our love on some poor kid in compensation and get drunk together.'

She tried to laugh but only one half of her face moved; he shivered when he felt the dark shadow that had fallen onto the other half. Past her, through her side window, there was a shining lake of light. The sun had moved, apparently abruptly, into an afternoon quarter heading towards the western coasts they were facing, angling a shifting, watery light back across the harbour. The car appeared to float on a silver plate. He picked up his glass, filled it and knocked one back, draining it in one gulp and tentatively fingered the keys in the transmission.

Moira grabbed his arm. 'What if I am saying that?' she shouted. 'What if I fucken am? Is there any shame in it? If you think you're fucken second best, go ahead, I'm not, I'm no second fucken best to any prick, I'll cut their throats.' The sharp vegetable knife appeared between her fingers.

Clyde looked at it with amusement. His voice was not gentle, 'Not second-best but just a little bit second-hand, eh Moira? And just how will this happy little arrangement work? You're a bisexual now, remember? You want to slot Snake in two nights a week? Or this other bloke, or both. Whadda we say to one another over the breakfast table?' Her fingers went white on the knife. *'Have a happy night dear? Was Snake in good form? Did you notice our cabbage tree was dying, dear? Would you like another shot of cognac in your coffee?'* He gave her a huge, boozy grin. She dropped the knife and one half of her face tried to grin ruefully, the other half regarded him with a blank intensity.

'You'll never make a writer with dialogue like that, no matter how many fucken books you right.'

'I wouldn't even attempt such a scene.'

Her hands returned to her food sculpture. Groping, she found the toothpick, olive and cucumber. Trying not to disturb its shape too much, she took the stone out of the olive, speared the olive and the cucumber. Then she stuck the toothpick into the biggest slab of cheese. After attaching pieces of parsley to two slim carrots, she placed these behind the cheese slab with the olive and cucumber hat. Then she picked up her whisky and drank with a deliberate gesture. 'We had our moment though, Clyde,' she tried to say softly, her voice emerging more as a broken croak, 'when it wasn't a case of second best, isn't that true, Clyde.'

'It is true,' he said, matching her tone, but there was a relentless on pushing rhythm in his words. 'Maybe that's the way it is with people. There's a moment, a window of opportunity, we could call it.' He laughed, as if to unseen guests, 'It's like a door between people,' his voice became tender. 'For a short while the door is open…'

'Yes, Clyde.' She nodded violently.

'…and them it closes,' he said, observing her closely.

She kept nodding. 'That's right,' she said. Her hands hovered over her food creation like the wings of an animating spirit. For a moment she seemed to have forgotten him. Then she pointed to the chicken bone arch. 'This is the entrance to the cemetery.' Her finger moved to the strips of flesh, 'These are the graves and the cheeses are the gravestones. This big gravestone here is Rilke's tomb, dedicated to eternal silence. On top you see the headpiece, his angel with the black olive head. Behind, disguised as pieces of carrot, are two cypresses.'

'Is that strip of chicken supposed to be Rilke?'

She giggled. 'This composition is called, The Lament of Rilke's Angel, for, since the poet died, his angelic voice is also entombed.'

'Very amusing. I have my own interpretation.' He picked up the piece of chicken and ate it. Ingesting Rilke. 'But if we don't get this car moving soon, we won't be moving anywhere.' He flourished the keys.

'Can you drive?'

'I can back up and park.' He was drunk, he felt, but not formidably so. The food he had eaten was holding well. Perhaps he should raid Moira's composition for another sandwich.

'Give me a drink first,' she said. The bottle lay between them, as easy for her to reach as for him.

'I'll tell you how I feel, Clyde,' her lips moved thickly, deliberately annunciating. 'I am numb. Numbness is the flesh of whores, but all women know it. When Snake first wanted to fuck me I laughed. She said it would make up for years of being screwed around by men. And she was right, Clyde, she was fucken right. Then she screwed me around. Then another man had a go. He came in for the kill. I went numb. It started on the night you stole that fucken vase. That was when he made his play for Snake. It's a strange numbness, Clyde, as if it didn't belong to me and somehow came from the outside. Look!' She pulled open her jumper and ripped open her blouse. She took hold of her nipples and pinched them. 'No sensation, no feeling. So I didn't care. It's the fuck-me-so-I'll-know-I-can't-feel-anything syndrome. Shaft me so I know I've been shafted. And they obliged.'

'They?'

'Him and Snake.'

'Together?'

'Taking turns. I was too pissed to do anything but roll over. Do you want the gory details?'

'It's Stockman, isn't it? I saw him. I thought it was just a bad trip. The vampire brigade were there. And you were in there, sucking and fucking, only you got sucked right out. They creamed you and left you with nothing.'

Moira went for his face, not with the knife, but her fingers. Clawing his eyes out would be a good start. As they wrestled Clyde saw over her shoulder to the expanse of water around the car. He threw her back against her seat and turned to the wheel. His hands fumbled the ignition and the keys fell to the floor. When he bent over to retrieve them, Moira pummelled his back with her bare fists, screaming and shouting. The noise seemed to wake him up as he fumbled around on the floor. There was something wrong with the floor but he couldn't work out what it was. He pulled the keys up and they were dripping. The floor was wet.

The Toyota wasn't going anywhere.

He looked around in time to see Moira quickly throwing back a shot. 'There's water on the floor,' he said in a strangled voice.

'I know,' she said, indicating her stocking feet. She gave him a brilliant, triumphant smile.

'I'll kill you,' Clyde said, his mind racing. Moira laughed.

It was possible, just possible, that the water had not yet reached the engine. It was probably creeping up through the floor somewhere, through rust spots. Of course, if it was up the exhaust he was fucked. His hands tightened on the keys. Then the car shifted. Not much, just a little adjustment, a settling down. Water slopped over his shoes. Bugger it, he loved this shagged old Toyota, he realized. He'd only paid fifteen hundred dollars for it, because of the rust, but it was all he had; a constant in his life.

Moira laughed again and something in her tone caught his attention. He turned to find her grinning at him wickedly, her remaining eye bright with malice. She had not done up her blouse and her breasts, wantonly hanging forward, also seemed to be laughing at him. They were breasts he had to describe as pert, even cheeky. Now they shook, and swung somewhat drunkenly, as she laughed. He reached over and touched them lightly with the back of his hand, feeling their smooth texture against the roughness of his knuckles, remembering her small, dark, supple body, and how it had quickened to his. Her grin grew more wicked, her one eye almost merry.

'You want to be in on the shafting too, Clydie-Clyde? You're disappointed that you missed out at the party? Well, go ahead...' She drew her legs up onto the seat and moved accommodatingly towards him. He felt the car move again, settling in the way a sleeper settles into a mattress; the cold slopped up against his ankles.

For the first time in two years his desire for Moira Andrews returned. This was alcohol's illusory alliance with sexuality. The talk of shafting was turning him on. It was her inertia that was drawing him, her atrophied senses, her drunken slushiness.

This was an errant, ill-timed desire.

'It's the bottle talking,' Clyde said hoarsely, taking a gulp from his glass. He could visualize what was happening outside. The tide had come in fast across the mudflat and was now backing up against the ramp and the stone water-break, slopping back as it began to rise, nudging the car towards the open water. He could feel it, rocking them gently the way a smooth open road and a cruising speed would. He took hold of the wheel and spun it.

'Just the bottle, Clydie-Clyde,' she said in an empty, mechanical voice. 'That's right. That's all it ever is. Do it so I know I don't feel anything. Numb in. Numb out. You know Clydie-Clyde I heard something…'

'Yes, my sweet toffee apple.' He stroked her nipple. Fuck it! He'd walk home. The Toyota wouldn't be worth salvaging. Besides, he didn't have the courage to turn the key.

'…I heard a liddle story, something that really got to me. I know some of the women, you know, who work at the massage parlours downtown. They told me something really strange…'

'Yes, my triple-treat.' He sloshed his feet in the water, soaking himself to the knees.

'They said that a lot of men do not come in so much for sex but to be abused. They want the girls to abuse them; clothes-pegs on their nipples, that kind of thing.' Reflexively she touched her own nipples, covering them softly with her fingers. 'And I've figured out why.'

'Why, my soft-centre?'

'Because those men are like me. They have lost all sensation. Dead to the flesh. Pain is the only signal they are still alive.' As she spoke the last words she took her nipples and twisted them violently, leaving them in a red, shocked condition. Clive leaned forward and put his lips, gently, on each one.

'Such a gentleman, Clyde! Or is your passion overcoming you?'

He smiled ambiguously and remained sprawled across the seat, across the ruins of Moira's Lament for Rilke's Angel, his cheek against her breast. She gently rubbed his scalp.

'Do you know what I think, Clydie-Clyde?'

'What, O my caramel tart?' He was gently rocking on an amniotic sea.

'That you are a closet necrophiliac. All men are. You want to know why you're hot for me now, when you haven't been for so long?'

'It's the bottle, it all comes out of the bottle,' he said sleepily, licking the slope of her breast.

'No, Clyde. It's because I'm dead in the flesh. A piece of meat. When I was a warm, responsive, complicated, loving human being you didn't want me. Now I'm a piece of meat you'll take it, you'll stuff it in your mouth, you'll suck on it to see how sweet it is.'

'Thaz right,' Clyde said, taking her nipple into his mouth with a surer purpose, imagining it ripe with milk. An ocean of milk.

She grinned ferociously as she raked her fingernails across his cheek, drawing blood. He shrieked and flung himself back, bashing his head against the steering wheel. In a daze, he saw that the water was slopping up against the seat.

'So a woman must be murdered,' she said in a thick voice. 'Murder is the final act of possession, the final violation. Only a corpse is properly fucked, wouldn't you say? Only death can put an end to our virginity, only death can rupture that hymen. Put your bony into my bone.'

Out the window the world had changed. The sun was a cold, pale disk in the afternoon sky and messy, watery squalls passed over the western coasts. The car appeared to be nose-diving into the sea, like a submarine about to sound. Grey wavelets, gentle but utterly persistent, lapped at the bonnet.

'So that's the way it is,' he said, rubbing his cheek. He groped for the bottle, noting that they were on the final quarter. He wondered if he should hit her, slap her around a little, sober her up; he was drunk enough to do it and the anger would do him good.

'And I want it,' she said in a shaky voice. 'My body wants it, my flesh wants it. I tried the other day, I didn't tell anyone. I'm telling you now because it doesn't matter anymore.'

'What in the fuck are you talking about?' Clyde sounded very drunk. He tried to focus on her. There was a sudden surge of water that washed across the seats, slushing around their waists, finally deconstructing the food sculpture, lifting Moira's yellow dress as in a gentle wind. It had a muddy, tepid warmth, bringing the smell of sea things into the car. He thought of mussels, oysters, pipis and scallops.

'Death, Clydie-Clyde, Death!' she called, her face suffused with joy as the water poured around her. 'I tried to take a bunch of tablets but I had a brandy to finish off and vomited the whole lot up. I was still nauseous from the night before. Saved by a hangover!'

Clyde attempted a laugh. 'We'd better get out,' he said, trying to think of what he should salvage. What was left? In the backwash from the surge he felt the car settle again, more perceptibly this time. The wind, coming in from the northwest, was quickening with approaching evening, flicking the surface of the bay into action.

'I want to make love to the sea and die,' she said in a faraway voice, the lift in it matching the undulation of her yellow dress in the water. 'To have it possess me completely, enter me everywhere. She pulled her legs out from under her and in a swift but awkward movement pulled off her knickers, turned to the front, her feet on the floor rocking to the motion of the waves, her legs spread toward the open bay. Clyde realized that she had fastened her safety belt.

'Let's get out of here, Moira,' he said. A sea sickness was rising up through his body, just as it had done in the car when he was bending corners with Stockman, and with it came a weakness that was awakening terror. The sea odours were thick in his nostrils, faintly stale, yet rich, like the smell of an ovulating woman. Life and the world flickered at him between the waves.

'No Clyde,' Moira tore at his arm without turning towards him. She was in a state beyond drunkenness, the slur was gone from her voice which was quick and sharp. 'No, Clyde, you're not going to stop this, not now. This is what you brought me here for, you're not pulling out now.' The water lapped up against her breasts and fell back, her chest heaved with the impact. Her fingers tightened on her arm. 'I'm not afraid,' she said.

A faint line of foam had settled across her breasts, above the nipples, like a lacy bridal garment. The water heaved again, welling up from below, lifting her breasts again as if they were the softest of sea creatures. The diaphanous line of foam had crept up to her throat. She gave him a radiant smile.

'I'm pulling out,' he said, fumbling in the glove box for his wallet. This was not the place to blackout. The empty whisky and wine bottles clattered around in the back, along with the rest of the picnic. He couldn't remember finishing the whisky, what else couldn't he remember? Her fingers climbed down his arm to meet his hand.

'I want to just sit here, Clyde, and let it happen. It's the easiest way. You're a genius, Clyde.'

'Oh come with me, my sugar plum.' He sang, remembering the little girl on the bathtub, trying out his little boy voice on her. 'Moirey wouldn't want nasty old Death getting his bony hands on her, would she? Nasty old Death will strip her bones just the way she stripped the chicken bones to make Rilke's graaaaave,' a note of childlike bitchiness and petulance entered his voice, 'except it wasn't Rilke's grave it was her own.' Then, speaking as if they were two children playing by the sea, he said, 'Hey, we've had lots of fun, eh? But it's home time now.'

'Don't be stupid,' Moira said in a cold, uninflected voice, bitterly sober, 'don't try to backtrack now. You've done your work.'

'What do you mean?' Already he could hear the breath of the sea in her voice.

'Let's not play pretends anymore,' she said, her voice thin and ragged. 'This is what you brought me here for.'

The wavelets crowded up around her breasts like suitors, kneading and licking, while the occasional surge sloped up around her shoulders, pouring in the backwash around her throat. The tide was lapping up the windscreen. Clyde looked straight across a horizontal surface of water at the sun, rich with late afternoon heaviness. Although the water was warmish, slopping up around his chest, Clyde began to shiver. His wallet was not in the glove box. He had to get out, get out now or not at all.

'Leave me now, Clyde,' she said in a quiet voice, staring transfixed ahead of her.

'I can't leave you here to die,' he said, feeling he'd heard the line somewhere before. Some nineteen forties movie. At least it sounded very stupid in his mouth.

'Of course you can. You knew what you were doing when you drove down here.'

'It's gone beyond the joke.'

'It never was a joke. Don't fool yourself.'

His first taste of salt water woke Clyde Aichen up properly. It had a sour, oily taste. 'Go ahead and drown then,' he shouted, grabbing the door handle and shoving hard against the inertia of the sea and the flow of the tide.

'I'll come soon, my friend,' she said. A moment later he was standing up to his ribcage in water, swearing and cursing. The tide had crept halfway up the ramp and he was a mere ten to fifteen metres from shore. He began to wade the distance, looking out behind him for Moira's appearance. It was slower going than he had anticipated.

His feet had hardly touched the bottom of the ramp before he turned, cursing and swearing again, back to the car.

She had not emerged, the silly bitch, she was playing this to the very end. He set off to the car, for her side, realizing he could probably swim it faster than he could walk it. He pulled off his trousers, jacket and shirt and swam in his briefs. Half the length of a swimming pool, a few swift strokes should have done it, but Clyde had no short swift strokes left in him, and the car, three-quarters submerged, seemed to be moving away down the corridors of the ocean. He was sobbing for breath by the time he reached her door. He rattled at the handle and cursed again to find it locked.

'Moira!' he screamed, hammering on the window. 'For Christ's sake.' He opened the back door and fumbled for her front lock. A picnic blanket slopped out to meet him like a great slobby tongue. Holding it back with his elbow he found her lock and snipped it up. A moment later he was at her door, pulling it open. Moira lay back on the seat in a relaxed position, her head thrown back against the head rest, her hair streaming out towards the back seat. The surface of the water was good three or four inches above her head except during a sharp backwash when the waves fell away from her face sucking her hair after them. Her head rolled indolently to their movements and he saw, in the water around her, the stain of her vomit and the detritus of food.

He took her arm and shoulder and pulled hard, puzzled at what was holding her in her seat. Then, remembering, he took a deep breath and threw himself across her body, reaching for the safety belt. But her body slumped away from him across the driver's seat as if protecting the belt from his searching fingers. His breath exploded in front of his face and he had to come up for air, smashing his head against the roof of the car. Moira's body swelled up beneath him and he had to fight against her to pull himself free of the car, pushing hard against her pliant body to compel himself backwards. Her arms floated up and out as if following him as the next surge washed across the roof. Her head lolled around towards him and her one eye gave him a final, corroded stare.

When he was standing again, neck high in water, sucking in oxygen, he saw how close he'd just come to being drowned, and how impossible it would be to make a second attempt to rescue Moira.

Besides, Moira was dead.

He set off for shore again but he immediately sank. When he opened his eyes he saw there was a huge rainforest under the sea, stretching off beyond his range of vision. The treetops swung soundlessly to the currents. Lazily he thought, ten years, down here they have time to spare. After all, ten years was nothing; you could wake up after a hangover and find ten years gone.

He came up and went down a second time, the water probing at his throat. He coughed and came up again, noticing that he'd drifted quite a distance along the beach. He could see a little of the roof of the Toyota and the quivering radio aerial. Deathly tired, he set out again for the shore, carrying himself forward mechanically. There was a figure on the rock escarpment looking out towards him. Stupidly, he thought it was Moira who must have arrived on the shore before him. One of her legs had turned into a piece of driftwood. A little girl was beside her, playing on the rocks, skipping with a skipping rope. As he got closer he saw it was not a little girl but a man.

By the time he reached the shore he'd drifted to the east end, where the water nibbled quietly at a few yards of beach. He sat in the shallow water, trying to recover his breath as the man approached across the *rocks*. He was drawing breath in shuddering gasps, crying. Moira was dead, and the world was a smaller, meaner place. Grief took hold of him like a fever. And in the mirage of that fever he saw himself, Clyde Aichen, murderer, his caring hands rinsed in blood.

Stockman came up. Clyde got to his feet and sat down again. As Stockman approached him Clyde leaned forward and vomited between his feet. There were bits of bread, olive, chicken and the pervasive smell of whisky. Stockman stepped daintily back.

'Are you always doing this or is it just for my benefit?'

Clyde was too busy trying to vomit, breathe and stay upright to talk.

Stockman gestured across the water, 'Is that your car, out there I can see, taking a final dive?'

Clyde moved his head up and down in rhythm to the ocean pounding in his blood, breaking along the shores of his labouring heart. Moira. The enormity of the loss and his part in it kept breaking over him, dumping him again and again into a territory of nightmarish clarity where Moira would always roll with the tide, one eye shut, her hair streaming. Why couldn't he black out?

'There are city ordinances against this sort of thing, you know.'

Clyde pointed out towards the car, his mouth working.

'Nearly drowned, did we?' Stockman said with interest. 'You were supposed to come and see me this morning. Where did you hide your clothes?'

'Moira,' Clyde croaked, pointing across the water to where only the top of the aerial was still visible, poking the slenderest of reeds out of the water.

'I don't see her,' Stockman said casually.

'Still in the car,' Clyde vomited again. It felt as if he would never stop vomiting.

'Fuck me dead,' Stockman said softly, and to himself. 'This is one story we'll only ever hear half of.'

Clyde looked back along the beach toward the ramp, now mostly covered. He'd lost his sense of colour and the scene had an eerie bleakness; a black-and-white Bergmanesque shot of desolate beach and drowned car. Stockman in his leather biker's jacket was in the foreground, watching him, the wind pulling at his lank black hair, his expression unreadable.

'What are doing here, Stockman?'

'Rescuing you, apparently.'

'I mean,' Clyde tried to stand upright but a pain in his gut, like a blow to the solar plexus, bent him over into vomiting position again, 'why are you here?'

'I have to be here,' Stockman said with a touch of impatience. 'It's all part of the *deal*.'

'What deal?'

'We had a *deal*, remember.' Stockman showed his teeth. 'I've gotta be in at the end, at the dénouement. How I got here is immaterial, at this point, killer.'

Clyde lurched forward, knowing where he wanted to land his blow, but when he came to deliver it his fist shot out in some wild, unpredicted direction, punching nothing but thin air.

'Careful mate, don't overreach yourself.' Stockman's voice was full of hot metal. 'And don't try to *feel* too much; it's not good for you. Do your bleeding on paper. Only this time show some fucking style.'

Clyde took two steps forward, ready to swing again, and slipped, falling through the air as if it were the softest space, onto the stones. The hardest stones. He could feel their chill roughness against his calves.

'I slipped,' he said helplessly.

'Let that be your last,' Stockman said.

CPSIA information can be obtained
at www.ICGtesting.com
Printed in the USA
BVHW032210100319
542297BV00001B/34/P